D1351338

INSPECTOR SINGH INVESTIGATES: A BALI CONSPIRACY MOST FOUL

Inspector Singh is back – this time on secondment to Bali. A bomb has exploded and Singh has been sent to help with anti-terrorism efforts, but there's a slight problem – he knows squat about hunting terrorists. He's much better suited to solving murder! So when a body is discovered in the wreckage, killed by a bullet before the bomb went off, Singh should be the one to find the answers – especially with the help of a wily Australian copper by his side – but simple murders are never as simple as they seem, and this one has far-reaching global consequences...

Inspector Singh Investigates:

A Bali Conspiracy

Most Foul
by

Shamini Flint

Magna Large Print Books
Long Preston, North Yorkshire,
BD23 4ND, England.

British Library Cataloguing in Publication Data.

Flint, Shamini
    Inspector Singh investigates:
    A Bali conspiracy most foul.

    A catalogue record of this book is
    available from the British Library

    ISBN   978-0-7505-3155-9

First published in Great Britain in 2009 by Piatkus

Copyright © 2009 by Shamini Flint

Cover illustration © John Gray

The moral right of the author has been asserted

Published in Large Print 2010 by arrangement with
Little, Brown Book Group Limited

Magna Large Print is an imprint of Library Magna Books Ltd.

Printed and bound in Great Britain by
T.J. (International) Ltd., Cornwall, PL28 8RW

For the Major

Acknowledgements

For the Strong Women in my life:
Emma, who keeps my nose to the
grindstone; Socks, who draws the lines I
dare not cross; Trudy, who runs circles
around me; Kristine, who picks up the
pieces; Sharon, who does not flinch;
Watanan, who (tries to) help me keep on
schedule; Rhonda, who coaches me subtly;
and my Mum, who spells out the
consequences!

'The blood-dimmed tide is loosed, and
    everywhere
The ceremony of innocence is drowned;
The best lack all conviction, while the worst
Are full of passionate intensity.'

– W.B. Yeats

Prologue

Jimi's hands were clammy. There were damp handprints on the fake leather of the steering wheel.

The engine of the white mini-van spluttered. Jimi looked at the gauges. He had been told to leave the engine running. None of the others trusted him to be able to restart the vehicle. He didn't even have a driving licence. Jimi had pointed this out; he wanted to do his part, but perhaps one of the others, Amrozi or Idris, should drive the van?

The team had assured him that his role was uncomplicated. He could practise a bit beforehand. They would line him up towards his target so that he didn't have to turn any corners or stop and start. One short ride into the history books.

He knew his instructions by heart – he was to wait for one of them to ring him and then take his foot off the brakes. That had been drummed into him over and over again. They were concerned he might jump the gun. But Jimi understood. He was to wait and do what he was told. He had spent his whole short lifetime doing just that – waiting and doing what he was told, whether by his father, his older brothers or the *imam* at the mosque.

Jimi was so tense his thigh muscle was cramping. He pressed down on the brake, determined not to let the white Mitsubishi van roll forward. It was not yet time.

He had no doubts about what he was about to do. The others had assured him he was doing the right thing. It was *jihad*, the ultimate and only war.

He knew it would be quick. But would it hurt? He had seen how much of the explosive had been packed into the back. Jimi acknowledged that he was uncomfortable with the idea that there would be no body to return to his parents. Could that be right? Moslems were supposed to be buried facing Mecca. But if there was no body, nothing to bury, would he be committing a sin? Jimi supposed doubtfully that his martyrdom would trump the minor breaches.

Jimi could see the Sari Club ahead of him. The others had walked him past it a couple of times in the last few days. He had not had a good look within. But there had been enough to fill the hearts of his brothers-in-arms with outrage; girls in skimpy clothing and young men dancing and drinking. Jimi wished he had seen the girls – had they really been in skimpy clothing? Still, he would soon get his reward: seventy-two virgins in heaven. Hopefully they wouldn't

14

all be wearing *burqas*.

His phone rang. He didn't pick it up. Jimi took his foot off the brake and held the steering wheel firmly, his hands at the ten o'clock and two o'clock position as Amrozi had taught him.

The vehicle rolled forward slowly.

One

Inspector Singh could hear the heavy groans of frogs and the harsh chirping of crickets. The sounds of Bali were so different from the din of construction sites and car engines that he was used to in Singapore. The policeman scratched his salt-and-pepper beard thoughtfully. The night-time cacophony did have a certain familiarity. He realised that the racket reminded him of his wife's cross tones on those regular occasions when he arrived late for a family dinner or had a few beers too many at the Chinese coffee shop around the corner from his home.

Singh took a deep breath. He smelt the spicy warm scent of *ikan bakar*, fish wrapped in banana leaf, on the hotel barbecue. His nostril hairs quivered appreciatively. Wherever he was, the smell of cooking food was always enticing. Singh grimaced – even by his own standards it seemed callous to be longing for dinner at such a time. His ample stomach immediately protested his conclusion, rumbling like a distant storm. The policeman shrugged and ordered a cold Bintang beer and a *nasi goreng*. After all, one had to eat. He wouldn't be helping anyone

16

by eschewing food. Not, he thought ruefully, that he was helping anyone anyway.

Singh watched the luminescent white foaming tops lapping the distant shore. The beach was deserted and so was the beach-front dining room. Those few tourists who remained had ordered room service, he guessed. No one wanted to gather together in groups, not even to eat. The Bali bomb-ings had turned gregarious visitors into reclusive loners, glancing sidelong at strangers in suspicion and fear.

His *nasi goreng* arrived, a neat hemisphere of fried rice topped with a fried egg, its soft yellow yolk trickling down the sides like lava from a newly awakened volcano. A chicken drumstick, six sticks of *satay, achar* or pickled vegetables and a couple of cucumber slices, were neatly arranged around the circum-ference of the plate. He ate every last bit with gusto, including the small bowl of sliced green *chilli padi* floating in light soya sauce.

Singh tried to avoid thinking of the oily food coalescing around his arteries. His doctor had been hinting of dire conse-quences if he did not improve his diet and fitness. The policeman had listened with half an ear, nodded to show that he was taking the advice seriously, pointed out that his trademark white sneakers showed he was ready for exercise and then stopped at Komala Villas, his favourite restaurant on

17

Serangoon Road, the main drag of Singapore's Little India, for a cup of hot sweet tea and some *ladoo*, a sugar-filled Indian snack. Talking about exercise was hungry work.

Remembering the *ladoo* made him yearn for dessert. He beckoned a waiter, requested a menu and scanned it carefully. He sighed. The problem with these fancy Bali hotels was that their menus catered entirely for Western tourists. Instead of having a genuine selection of tasty meals and desserts, there was standard European fare like spaghetti Bolognese and fish and chips. The Asian food was a tepid imitation of the original – to give tourists a flavour of the East without sending them running for the toilets.

The dessert menu didn't have Asian options either. It was either a slice of chocolate cake or crème brûlée.

Singh ordered another beer.

There was not much light in the outdoor dining area. He moved the floating candle closer. The white frangipani flower perched decoratively on the rim fell into the flame and curled and blackened, its rich fragrance giving way to the rancid smell of burning organic matter.

His contemplation of the fragility of nature was rudely interrupted.

'There you are! I've been looking all over for you. I might have guessed you'd be in the restaurant.'

A mousy-haired woman wearing khaki trousers and a men's shirt lumbered towards him.

Inspector Singh gulped some beer, feeling the gas bubbles tickle his throat. A layer of foam enhanced his moustache.

She said, 'Every time I see you, you're clutching a Bintang like a favourite teddy bear.'

Singh wiped his mouth with the back of his hand. His pink full lower lip pouted slightly, the only outward sign of his discomfiture. This woman was as tiresome as a roomful of his Sikh relatives – whining about his bad habits to each other and to him. But Bronwyn Taylor was a member of the Australian Federal Police. AFP members had been sent down to Bali to assist with security and counter-terrorism measures after the Bali bombings. Inspector Singh of the Singapore police force had been despatched to Bali with the same task. Falling out with the Australians would not endear him to his bosses. He knew very well that looking for an excuse to turf him out of the police force occupied many of the leisure hours of his superiors. He didn't intend to make it easy for them.

Bronwyn, part of the AFP's public liaison team, collapsed onto the seat across from him. 'So, what's the plan for tomorrow? How do we keep the world safe for democracy?'

Singh had already deduced that the Australian's flippant manner disguised a preternaturally sensitive nature. He ignored her question and asked, 'Have there been any developments in the investigation?'

She nodded. 'A small breakthrough. They've identified bomb residue on an abandoned motorbike – it was used by someone involved in the attack.'

'What are they going to do next? Trace the owner?'

She nodded, unruly strands of hair falling over her forehead. She pushed them away with an impatient hand.

Singh noticed that Bronwyn's features were all gathered together in the middle of her face leaving swathes of flesh around the perimeter. Small gold earrings were lost on her large ear lobes.

She continued, 'The motorbike must have been stolen. The bombers can't have been as thick as to buy one here in Bali.'

'Never,' retorted Singh, pleased to have the last word for once, 'underestimate the shortcomings of the criminal mind.'

'Has there been any sign of him?'

Sarah Crouch shook her head. Her fine blonde hair, usually gleaming under the Bali sun, had lost its lustre. She sat on a polished teak folding chair, perched on the edge like a nervous schoolgirl. Her pale hands shredded a white paper serviette into tiny pieces.

The two couples, her companions around the table, stared at her with varying degrees of sympathy and concern.

One of the women, Karri Yardley, said, 'I can't believe he's disappeared like that. Do you think ... you know, there might be another woman? That's the usual reason, isn't it?'

Her husband glared at her. Karri was sunburnt. Her hair was a deep black this week. A fake tattoo of a bird of paradise adorned one wiry brown arm. Tim Yardley said gruffly, closing his hand over Sarah's, 'There's no reason to suspect that.'

Karri was in an argumentative mood. She said, oblivious to the angry looks from the others, 'Sarah's been saying that things haven't been going well. Richard wasn't communicative. He was going out on his own a lot. Sounds like an affair to me.'

'You would know, I suppose,' sneered her husband, smoothing the sparse hair over his scalp carefully with one hand, the other still clutching Sarah's limp fingers in a tight grip.

Sarah drew her hand away. She didn't want to get involved in one of the never-ending spats between the Australian couple. She noticed that Tim was trying to catch her eye but she looked away.

Julian Greenwood asked, his voice low and consoling, 'Are you *certain* he wasn't at the

Sari Club?'

Karri barked with sudden loud laughter and then put a hand with red-painted talons over her mouth. 'Sorry,' she said. 'I know it's no laughing matter – but the idea of Richard at a nightclub...'

Julian glared at her. He said, 'He might have been in the area ... passing by or something like that!'

Sarah remained silent. The others turned to her, except for Emily, Julian's wife. She was absorbed in her glass of wine, sipping it with small nervous jerks, staring into the ruby liquid as if it were a magic mirror.

'I've been down to have a look in the morgue, of course.' Sarah shuddered. 'It was awful. Bodies everywhere. The stench. I couldn't find him. I told them that Richard was missing ... gave them a photo. They asked for his dental records from the UK. I haven't heard anything since.'

Julian's accent reverted to its native Cockney from the carefully modulated tones he normally adopted. 'They've released most of the bodies for burial ... maybe you don't have to worry about that scenario any more.'

Emily Greenwood glanced up at this, her face beaming and her grey eyes slightly glazed as she struggled to focus. 'I passed a funeral on the way here this morning. It was really charming. Lots of fruit and flowers and everyone dressed so well.'

Julian said roughly, 'You're drunk!'

Emily giggled. 'Maybe a bit tipsy, love.'

Tim stood up, the table shaking as his belly knocked against it in his haste to get to his feet. He said rapidly, 'Bloody hell, Emily. Don't you think you could show Sarah some respect by staying sober just for once? After all, she's lost her husband.'

'Lucky thing,' whispered Emily, winking at her own husband and leaning forward so that her full bosom rested against his arm.

Sarah noted absent-mindedly that Julian's jaw was clenched tight and his knuckles showed white around his beer glass. He would shatter it if he was not careful. But he did not move his arm away. She would have felt sorry for him if he wasn't such a pathetic creature with his drooping moustache, bony nose and almost lipless mouth.

Karri intervened, staring intently at Sarah. She asked, 'What are you going to do now?'

Sarah closed her eyes, lines of weariness fanning out from the corners. She said, 'Keep looking, I guess. I don't know what else to do...'

His wife was taller than him. She walked away from the restaurant with a loose-limbed, masculine stride. Tim Yardley hurried to keep up, panting from the effort, his thighs chafing against each other in their baggy linen shorts. He wiped his forehead with his sleeve and glared at his wife. He was furious at her, dismayed by her casual cruelty, although he had been on the receiving end of it for so many years.

'How could you laugh at a moment like that?' he demanded angrily.

Karri stopped in front of a shop window to peruse her reflection and rearrange her hair. She tossed the black locks like a salad with her long thin fingers. 'It *was* a bit of a hoot – the idea of Richard Crouch dancing the night away at the Sari Club.'

'That's not my point and you know it. It's Sarah I'm worried about – and you should be too. She's our *friend*.'

His wife adjusted a few strands carefully on her forehead and glanced at her husband in the same smudged reflection. 'You're doing enough worrying for both of us, don't you think? Besides, I don't give a damn that Richard might be lying dead in a ditch somewhere. I couldn't stand the bastard and his self-righteous airs.'

Karri twisted around to look at her portly husband. 'At least he kept himself trim.'

Tim pulled his shirt ends together and tucked them into his shorts, trying to obscure the parts of his belly that were showing through the gaps. The freckles on his arms looked like a fine spray of mud.

'There's no need to be unkind,' he said. A rivulet of sweat ran down his nose, hovered on the end like a teardrop and fell to the ground. 'I can't help being a bit overweight.'

'You just need to eat less and drink less.'

Tim turned to walk away, his shoulders hunched against further verbal abuse.

Karri snapped, 'What are you going to do now? Run back and hold Sarah's hand again?'

Tim turned around slowly. He didn't know why he was arguing with his wife. He had been on the losing end of every single verbal spat between them since marrying Karri fifteen years earlier. He had discovered very early on in their marriage that being in the right did not prevent his wife lacerating him with her tongue – it did not prevent him walking away from their encounters feeling as bruised and battered as if he had been set upon by thugs in an alley.

He said quietly, groping for some dignity like a man in a dark room looking for the light switch, 'I don't know why you have it in for Sarah ... she's a good, kind woman who needs our help – and sympathy. I am just trying to be supportive, that's *all!*'

'You're pathetic, chasing after that dried-up stick of a woman.'

'I am not!' His face was scarlet.

'I'm not losing any sleep,' said his wife snidely. 'She wouldn't touch you with a Balinese flag pole.'

Tim sucked in his breath, pulling in his

stomach as far as it would go and puffing out his chest. He said, 'I wouldn't be so sure of that.'

Karri laughed.

Nuri set out for Denpasar.

To stay idle in the small apartment that had been her home for the last month was too difficult. She had been fidgety and nervous, picking at a loose thread on her blouse, moving the grimy curtains to peer out of the cracked window panes.

Nuri had told her brothers, Abu Bakr and Ramzi, she was shopping for dinner and to please tell Ghani where she was when he came in. Her husband was out, still looking for a suitable location for the religious school they intended to set up in Bali. Nuri wondered why he was determined to press ahead with his plans. Surely, a religious school focused on strict Islamic teachings was doomed to failure in Bali in the wake of the bombs? She had tentatively raised her doubts with Ghani. He had smiled at her and explained that Allah was merely testing their resolve and he would not stumble at the first hurdle placed in his path. Nuri had lowered her eyes and nodded her acquiescence. It was so easy, she thought, to play the dutiful wife – to fall back into the routine of subservience to her husband – the role she had performed unquestioningly from the day of her marriage a year ago to the grizzled older man.

The trip to Bali was the first time Nuri had ever left Sulawesi, the large island shaped like a headless man that was a sparsely populated part of the Indonesian Archipelago. She had taken the crowded dilapidated ferry with her husband and brothers to Java. After a brief visit to the *pesanteren* in Solo, the boarding school that Ghani had attended as a boy, to consult with the spiritual leaders there, they had made their way to Bali.

The island was an eye-opener to the young village girl. She had never seen so much alcohol and drugs and contact between men and women. She had been disgusted and embarrassed, averting her eyes from public displays of affection and hurrying past nightclubs and massage parlours with her eyes fixed on the ground. She had reprimanded her younger brother, Ramzi, when he had been unable to drag his eyes away from the scantily-clad tourists.

Nuri was beautiful with clear skin and widely spaced, almond-shaped eyes that gave her a questioning, naïve expression. She had glossy black hair but it was pinned up and hidden under a scarf. She had abandoned her *hijab*, the head-to-toe black coveralls that included a veil for her face, for the duration of their stay in Bali. Ghani had

27

insisted it would draw too much attention; Bali was an uncomfortable place for Moslems after the bombings. Nuri had agreed, as long as she was allowed to wear a scarf. But even with a length of cloth around her hair, she felt shamefully exposed – as if she was one of the Western women she had seen lying on the beaches in bikinis, their tanned bodies revealed for any passing stranger to see. Nuri shook her head at the memory and a lock of hair escaped from her scarf and fell over her forehead. She tucked it away carefully. She had worn the strict Islamic dress since puberty. Her father, back on Sulawesi, insisted that women play a secondary role in society to their menfolk. Nuri had accepted her father's strictures as being the natural order of things. The only girl in a family of thirteen children by her father's four wives, she knew how rowdy and difficult boys were. Nuri felt more comfortable when she did not offer herself as an object of attraction to men. It was her father's training as well as her own choice.

Her meandering footsteps took her to a small wooden shack with a corrugated tin roof that sold foodstuff to Indonesian labourers. Nuri bought a jar of chilli paste. It would convince her husband and her brothers that she had indeed been shopping for dinner.

All the talk between the other customers

was of the bombings and the investigation but she did not pay much attention. Nuri was not sure how she felt about the blasts. Ghani had said to her that the Balinese had turned their island home into a whore-house. But she also knew, had learnt to her cost in Bali, that however strict one's religious upbringing, and however much one knew the difference between right and wrong, an unruly heart was difficult to control.

Two

Inspector Singh had argued with his superiors long and hard when they told him that their latest effort to get him out of their hair was to send him to Bali to advise on counter-terrorism methods.

'But I have no experience in the field,' he had protested, folding his arms across his large stomach to indicate the firmness of his resolve not to be sent to Bali.

'Nonsense! A terrorist attack is just murder on a grand scale. And *murder* is your speciality.'

The senior policeman made it sound as if he had uncovered a dirty little secret that the inspector was trying to keep under wraps. Singh was not surprised. In the Singapore police force, respectable policing was cracking drug syndicates. Praise and promotions were for apprehending white-collar criminals in smart suits. The crime of murder was raw and unglamorous. It involved real people driven by greed or love or revenge to take the life of another. The gritty reality of a body in the morgue was too much for these policemen with their computer skills and profound ignorance of human nature.

Inspector Singh was a throwback to the old school – hardworking, hard-drinking, chain-smoking. His ability to cut through the thicket of lies and deception surrounding a murder and painstakingly expose the killer was viewed with the same combination of admiration and disdain by the senior echelons, he thought, as a performing dog. It was a good trick, his superiors implied, but why do it?

He asked again, a little plaintively this time, 'But why me?'

It provoked a moment of honesty from his boss. 'We need our terrorism *experts* right here to protect Singapore. But we have to look keen to help out an important neighbour like Indonesia. You have a reputation for always getting your man. *They'll* think we sent our best to Bali.'

Inspector Singh was distracted from his depressed reminiscing by the Balinese hotel staff. The doorman, smartly dressed in his cream uniform, queried politely, 'Limousine, sir?' His tone suggested that he asked more in hope than expectation. To Singh's dismay, Bronwyn Taylor had refused from the early days of their acquaintance to use a hotel car. Bronwyn insisted that there was no need to pay hotel prices when there was so much alternative transport available. Singh was of the view that trusting his ample form to an unknown young man in wrap-around sunglasses, driving a vehicle whose maintenance history was a closely guarded secret, was not the way to begin the day. He had tried to insist that there was no need to be so frugal when the Singapore government was paying expenses.

Bronwyn had been adamant. 'It doesn't matter whose money it is, we shouldn't waste it. Besides,' she had continued, 'how can we possibly find out anything about Bali if we stick to hotel transport? We need to talk to ordinary Balinese people. Find out what they're thinking.'

'They're wondering how they've gone from playground of the wealthy to deserted island. I don't need to ride around in a deathtrap to work that out.'

Singh could see the Australian woman now, hurrying across the foyer, greeting hotel staff individually by name. He shook his head despondently. If he ordered a limo, she would just cancel it. He could insist, of course – but he had a suspicion that she would harp on the subject until he regretted his impulse to put his foot down. His wife achieved her ends using exactly the same tactics – perhaps women had a special nagging gene that allowed for repetition without respite.

Across the road from the hotel, dozens of scruffy young men squatted along the kerbs under the patchy shade of *dedap* trees, fallen velvety red flowers a carpet under their feet. Each of them was equipped with a Kijang, a large utility vehicle, to ferry tourists around Bali for a few dollars. Singh cast a suspicious eye over the waiting drivers and beckoned to one who seemed less sinister than the others. Immediately the driver's face was wreathed in smiles. He stubbed out his *kretek,* the ubiquitous Indonesian clove cigarette, and hurried over.

He asked, 'You need driver?'

Singh nodded.

'So, where you from?'

The inspector from Singapore was sick and tired of the insatiable curiosity of the Balinese.

Bronwyn, panting slightly from the heat, answered for both of them. 'He's from Singapore and I'm Australian.'

'Good, good – very happy you come to Bali.'

Meeting with silence, he continued, 'Where to, boss?'

Singh looked inquiringly at the Australian.

'Bali police HQ Denpasar!' she said briskly.

'OK, *Ibu.*'

He revved the engine and reversed out onto the street, narrowly avoiding an entire Balinese family riding precariously on a small motorbike. He waved an apology and they tooted back an acknowledgement.

Singh shook his big head. He had never realised how Singaporean he was in his habits, accustomed to wide streets, orderly traffic and an almost complete absence of these horrid little motorbikes that were the main Balinese family transport.

The Kijang raced down a busy street, hooting intermittently. The mildest of apologetic toots warned motorbikes to move out of the way. Slightly more irritable honks were reserved for fellow Kijang drivers muscling in on road position and puffing clouds of grey-white smoke out of their rattling exhaust pipes. A loud blast scared a mangy dog crossing the road.

The car came to an abrupt halt. Singh craned his neck to see what had obstructed their way.

The driver said, 'Sorry, boss. Have to wait now. There is funeral ahead.'

Singh opened the door and stepped out to watch the slow procession of people; women balancing baskets of fruit and other offerings precariously on their heads, men lugging tall white tasseled umbrellas, all of them dressed in their ceremonial best. He wondered if the funeral was for a victim of the Bali bombs. The inspector felt a wave of sadness. A vicious attack had taken lives and destroyed livelihoods. Although it was the foreign tourists killed who had garnered the lion's share of the news cycles, many Balinese had been murdered as well.

Singh climbed back into the vehicle with difficulty.

Bronwyn tucked a strand of hair behind her ear as if it was an escaping errant thought. She asked in a sombre voice, 'Do you think the tourists will ever come back to Bali?'

Singh gazed out of the tinted window of the Kijang.

'No,' he said, 'I think this place is finished.'

Nuri wandered down Jalan Legian until she reached the police barriers. She had not intended to come this way but her reluctant footsteps had been drawn towards the Sari Club, epicentre of the attacks. Although she could not imagine a circumstance in which a devout Moslem like Abdullah might have been caught up in the nightclub bombings, the fact remained that her desperate forays around Bali had produced no sign of him.

Nuri was awestruck by the sheer scale of the destruction. Buildings were blackened shells, with burnt-out cars strewn in front of them. Sombre policemen stood at regular intervals. Too late to prevent the carnage – their job was limited to keeping the curious and the desperate from contaminating the crime scene.

Nuri's attention was drawn to a middle-aged woman sobbing quietly. She was Indonesian, probably native Balinese. Nuri shuffled further away to give her some privacy. The woman looked up at this and, perhaps appreciating the younger woman's tact, asked, 'You are looking for your family also?'

Nuri was determined not to give voice to the possibility that Abdullah might have been a victim of the bombings. She had a superstitious concern that her words might have the power to turn her deepest fears into reality. She said abruptly, 'No, I just came to see.' And then embarrassed at sounding like a voyeur she stared down at her feet, modestly sheathed in black socks to avoid prying masculine eyes.

The older woman continued, despair making her garrulous, 'My brother, we cannot find him. We have hunted in the hospitals and the morgue in Sanglah...'

Nuri noticed her accent. 'You are from Java?'

She nodded, smiling through her tears. 'Yes, we came here to work. Our family in Jakarta is poor. My brother was a dishwasher at Sari Club. I do the massage at one of the hotels.' Her voice cracked as she tried to continue. 'But now see what has happened ... we cannot find him.'

She stared down the street but Nuri could see that she was blinded by tears.

She said awkwardly, 'I hope you find your brother.'

'I know he is dead. I feel it in my heart.' She continued bitterly, 'They say it is Moslems who did this. Terrorists! I cannot believe it. Why would they kill innocents, fellow Moslems, young people who have done nothing to harm them?'

Nuri felt a wave of compassion for this stranger. Like her, she was looking for a lost loved one. But this woman was facing the reality that her brother had been a victim of the bombings. She, Nuri, still had the comfort of ignorance. There was nothing to prevent her believing that Abdullah was in Bali somewhere, waiting for the right moment to return to her and fulfil the promises he had made as he grasped her two hands firmly in his and said his hurried goodbyes.

Nuri put a thin brown arm around the other woman's shoulders. She stared at the devastation wrought on the narrow street ahead of her. Windows hundreds of yards from the blast site had been blown out. The smell of soot and smoke was pungent, it made her eyes water.

The weeping woman followed Nuri's gaze and put her hands together in a gesture of supplication. She said, 'I just can't believe anyone would do this in Allah's name.'

Singh looked inquiringly at one of the policemen. 'What's happening?'

The Balinese policeman shook his head. His brown, unlined face was childlike in its despair. 'We are at a dead end,' he said. 'We have examined everything twenty times, thirty times. We have the Australians here, the CIA – everyone is trying to help us.' He added politely, 'Including you also.'

Singh nodded an acknowledgement of this remark, wishing for the thousandth time that he actually had skills that might be useful to the investigation.

He asked, 'What about the motorbike?'

'We have traced it – it is strange that they bought it new from a Bali shop. The dealer remembers them well – three of them – because they did not argue over the price.' He managed a half smile. 'That is very unusual in Bali.'

'Can he identify them?'

'Yes, if we catch them first! The Australians are flying in some photo-fit experts.'

Singh was sceptical. He had never had much faith in these sketches of suspects. The memories of witnesses always seemed to involve unkempt men with wild eyes. In Singh's experience, the more serious the crime, the more two-dimensionally wicked the portraits became. A motorcycle dealer asked to describe the Bali bombers? He'd be amazed if they weren't given horns and a tail.

Singh scratched the rim between his turban and forehead with a stubby finger. 'What about the van – the vehicle bomb?'

'We have gone over every inch of what was left of that vehicle. All the serial numbers have been filed off or changed – they do not match any records.' The Balinese beckoned to Singh. 'Come with me, I will show you.'

He led the way to a separate building, waved his ID at a guard and ushered the policeman from Singapore inside. A wave of cool air from the aggressive air-conditioning turned the drops of perspiration on Singh's forehead into a soothing cold compress.

The Balinese policeman said, 'You see!'

Singh did see. There were heaps of twisted, blackened metal organised in neat rows on trestle tables. Every part was labelled. Policemen and forensic experts explored fragments under microscopes.

The Balinese policeman said, 'This is every piece of that van we could find. But there is nothing there. General Pastika is so frustrated that he has gone to the temples to pray for a breakthrough. It is our last hope!'

Singh raised his tufty eyebrows in consternation but managed to hold his tongue on the subject of policemen who abandoned the rational pursuit of evidence to hang around temples praying for divine guidance. After all, his own contribution to the investigation so far had amounted to distracting

Balinese policemen from getting about their duties. He could hardly have achieved less if he too had spent his time hollering demands at a Balinese deity.

The inspector's attention was caught by a man staring dejectedly at a pile of twisted chassis rails. As he watched, the man's expression changed from one of frustration to sudden interest. He said, 'It's been welded!' He carried the hunk of metal to a work table and prised apart the pieces using a hammer and cold chisel.

Singh leaned forward curiously, impressed by the dexterity and diligence of the man.

Protected from the blast by the now removed welded piece and etched into the metal underneath was a stamped serial number. The investigator said, his voice shaking with emotion, 'We have something. Thank God, we have something! General Pastika's prayers have been answered!'

Sarah Crouch tucked the small sum of money she had withdrawn from the ATM into her handbag and walked quickly towards a waiting minicab. She climbed into the back seat, catching a glimpse of red-rimmed eyes in the rearview mirror. The driver looked at her curiously, her drawn, pallid face curbing his natural instinct to embark on conversation. She told him where to go in curt tones that did not invite comment and then leaned back against the grimy cushions. Sarah closed her eyes. She had not been able to sleep of late. She lay in bed every night on the too-soft mattress staring at the ceiling for long hours, listening to the small brown geckos make their strange clicking noises as they pursued flies and mosquitoes across the walls of her room.

She wished Richard had been willing to grant her a divorce. She was sure he would have been delighted to walk away from the mirage that was their marriage to seek a firmer grip on happiness somewhere else. She too had longed to be free of the ties that bound them together, hastily constructed and quickly regretted. She grimaced. It was Richard, with his over-developed sense of responsibility, who had been reluctant to give up on their relationship without a last attempt to save it. He was the one who had suggested this Bali sojourn to try and repair the cracks, or at least paper over them with holiday snapshots.

She sighed. The attempt had been doomed from the start. A marriage could only be saved where affection remained. She had long since learnt to despise her husband and crave a more fulfilling relationship. He had taken to spending most of his time with the friends he had found on the island. She had formed a coterie of expatriates, including the Yardleys and the Greenwoods. On the rare occasion she had dragged Richard out for dinner with them, he had maintained a sullen disapproving silence, his contempt for her friends visible on his slim face. He had never shown any interest in introducing her to *his* companions. Sarah scowled. The expression aged her. It revealed the discontent that was usually masked by her regular features and the light make-up she used to smooth over the fine lines.

The driver said quietly, 'We are here, *Ibu.*'

Sarah carefully counted out the exact fare. She was not going to give the man a tip. He had done his job – nothing more. There was no need to be wasteful of her diminishing hoard of *rupiah*. Money was becoming very tight. She needed to find some solution to her immediate troubles. She wondered if she dared confront Tim Yardley. How would he react? Sarah clenched her thin hands into angry fists. She had no idea what to do next.

Bronwyn appeared at the door and beckoned to Singh. As he approached, his footsteps muffled in his white sneakers, she said, 'I just got a call from the Sanglah morgue in Denpasar. They want us there.'

'Who does?' asked Singh, puzzled.

She shook her head. 'Not sure. AFP? Bali police?'

Singh sighed. 'Well, I have nothing better to do.'

There was a car waiting for them outside with a police driver. He saluted smartly as the Sikh inspector trudged towards him. Singh's eyebrows shot up for the second time that morning. He slid in the back next to Bronwyn and pondered this sudden elevation in status from political window dressing to important personage. An urgent summons. A car and driver. Something was up and he had no idea what it could be.

Bronwyn's broad forehead had puzzlement etched on it. She echoed his thoughts. 'What's going on?'

He said, 'Not a clue!'

The inspector from Singapore sat back and gazed out of the window. The sky was cloudless and a piercing, eye-watering blue. It was a hot day and the huffing and puffing of the noisy air-conditioning was not helping. Singh wiped his forehead with a big white handkerchief. He ran a forefinger under the rim of his turban, trying to let some cool air drift towards his scalp. His head itched in hot weather. He wished someone would invent a lightweight version of the six yards of cotton cloth he had twined expertly around his big head that morning. He could just dispense with the turban, of course. Many of his fellow Sikhs had long since abandoned the traditional headwear, giving in to the pressures of hot weather and modern dress norms. He himself did not wear the iron bangle – it gave him a rash around his wrist – that was yet another requirement of Sikhism. But Singh knew he would feel exposed and defenceless without his turban. He had worn it for too many years. It was his security blanket.

He glanced at Bronwyn. Her face was reddened with heat. Tendrils of hair adhered to her forehead. Every single pore on her small nose was as distinct and visible as the craters on the moon. The moisture above her upper lip looked like a translucent moustache. The Bali climate was certainly not kind to pale-skinned Australians. But at least she wasn't wearing a turban. She noticed him looking at her and smiled – the dimple carved into one cheek gave the smile an infectious quality. Singh had to work hard to avoid grinning back. He didn't want any accidental overtures of friendship. It was already hard enough keeping this pain-fully chummy woman at arm's length.

It did not take long to reach the Sanglah hospital mortuary. Singh got out of the car with some reluctance. He was familiar with bodies. He had seen them stabbed, shot, drowned and strangled. But he had never been exposed to mass killing on the scale of the Bali bombings.

There was a tall thin man with overgrown sandy hair lapping the collar of his white coat waiting for them at the entrance. He demanded in a staccato voice, 'You're Singh?'

The inspector nodded. He decided to overlook the man's gruff tone. From his bloodshot eyes to the vein pumping in his forehead, this was a man at the end of his tether.

'I'm Dr Alex Barton. I'm in charge of the collection of burnt-out body parts we have here.'

'Lucky you!' muttered Singh as he shook hands with the man, noticing that the skin on his palm was dry and rough. He still had no idea why he was at the morgue. He hoped there wasn't something that needed doing for which he had no expertise – God only knew what his superiors had told the Balinese about his skill set. He wouldn't have put it past his Singapore bosses to assure them that he was a forensics expert.

The doctor looked like he wanted to say something but was not sure how to proceed. He slipped his hands into the pockets of his white coat, glanced at Singh, changed his mind and stared down at the policeman's white plimsolls, a perplexed expression on his face. He said abruptly, 'Why don't you come with me.'

Intrigued by this air of mystery, Singh trotted after the doctor, taking two steps for every one of the other man. Bronwyn had no trouble keeping pace in her soft-soled shoes that were worn down around the heels. She was almost as tall as the pathologist. Bronwyn was being reticent by her standards. Singh wondered about it for a moment. Did she know something she was not telling him? He abandoned the mental task of second-guessing Bronwyn in favour of the physical task of keeping up with the others.

Alex Barton did not stop until he reached a large steel freezer. He opened the door and gestured for them to look inside. Singh peered in reluctantly. His disinclination was vindicated by the sight of small piles of charred limbs and other human remains.

He looked inquiringly at the Australian doctor. 'Having trouble identifying these victims?' he asked.

'Yes. But it's early days yet. We're still waiting for DNA samples, dental records, information on identifying marks, you know, scars, tattoos, that sort of thing.'

'Tough job,' said Bronwyn sympathetically.

'It wasn't helped by the cock-ups after the bombs,' complained the doctor bitterly.

Inspector Singh asked in his gravelly voice, 'What do you mean?'

'There wasn't enough space here – at the morgue, I mean. The freezer was only designed for ten bodies. We had over two hundred. The remains were left in bags in

46

the garden. They were so burnt, decomposition was faster than normal. I've been in war zones that weren't as bad. But the worst part' – he shook his head in disbelief – 'anyone and everyone was allowed to wander in looking for missing relatives. People claimed bodies based on visual identification – hopeless in the circumstances.'

Bronwyn asked in horrified tones, 'Do you mean families claimed the wrong bodies?'

'That's not the least of it,' said the doctor, sighing. 'Some of the volunteers who came in to help – they didn't have any training – they mixed remains. There's a lot of cross-contamination of DNA samples.'

'But that means there are victims who might never be identified!' exclaimed Bronwyn.

The doctor nodded, his face crumpled with lines of worry and fatigue.

There was silence.

Singh broke it. He asked, 'But what do you want me for?' He continued, 'I'm afraid I don't have any expertise on the forensics side.'

Before Dr Barton could continue, they were joined by another man. Short, squat and with a big square head, he looked like a Caucasian version of Inspector Singh – except without the turban. The newcomer shook hands with Barton, turned to the policeman and asked, 'You're Singh?'

Singh was getting a little tired of dealing with brusque Australians. He said, not bothering to keep the note of irritation out of his voice, 'Yes, who's asking?'

'I'm Chief Atkinson – AFP.'

'What do you want with me?'

The Australian turned to the doctor and snapped, 'You haven't told him?'

'No. I was about to when you showed up.'

'All right.'

Atkinson gazed at the Sikh policeman appraisingly. Singh supposed he was not a figure to inspire confidence. He was short and fat with an excessive number of pens in the breast pocket of his shirt. His snowy white sneakers were in contrast to the large blue turban on his head. He had a thin upper lip, a pink, moist protruding lower lip and a neatly trimmed beard and moustache, both flecked with white.

Atkinson asked, 'You *Moslem?*'

Singh was really annoyed now. He said, 'Not that it's any of your business, but no.'

'Then why've you got that hanky around your head?'

'Because I'm a Sikh and our people have been turbaned for longer than you've had ancestors out of prison.'

Atkinson barked with sudden laughter. 'You might be right about that, mate.'

Singh maintained a stony silence, his lips pursed to indicate displeasure.

The Australian continued, 'I don't give a damn whether you're Sikh or Christian or a bloody Moslem for that matter – but as it was a bunch of towel-heads behind the Bali bombs, I thought it was worth asking.'

Bronwyn demonstrated the talent for insubordination that was keeping her at the periphery of the investigation. She said in a determined voice, 'I don't think the question was justified under any circumstances, sir.'

The doctor, surprised by the developing antagonism, interrupted them, 'Look, I've got upwards of twenty people in deep freeze waiting for me to turn them from charred remains into human beings. Are you going to get on with it? Because, if not, I've got work to do and you guys are just wasting my time – and your own.'

Atkinson said in a conciliatory tone, gesturing to the doctor, 'Show him.'

Barton raised a sandy, sparse eyebrow and then nodded in agreement. He opened the freezer door again and a blast of cold air, laced with just a hint of decaying flesh, washed over them. The doctor brought out a small black plastic carrier.

Singh decided it looked like a smaller version of the bag he used to put out the garbage every evening.

Barton took it to a gleaming waist-high steel table on castors and shook out the contents carefully. A few blackened pieces fell out.

The inspector was certain that he would not have been able to tell the difference between these human remains and the charred pieces of vehicle chassis he had been shown earlier in the day.

The doctor slipped on a pair of thin rubber gloves and rummaged through the pile.

Singh felt squeamish. The large breakfast of bacon and eggs followed by fried noodles and washed down with three cups of strong locally grown black coffee was churning in his belly. He decided his stomach felt like a washing machine in a spin cycle. He wondered at his own queasiness. It was not like him at all. Rookies in the Singapore police force spoke admiringly of his cast-iron stomach during autopsies. It was part of his larger-than-life reputation. Why was he more affected by these victims of a suicide bomber than he had ever been when confronted with a corpse in the course of a murder investigation? Singh pondered the question as he watched the doctor. Was it that, in all the murders he had ever dealt with, there was always a personal nexus between killer and victim? Whether it was a crime of passion, of greed or of anger – the two chief participants in the crime had some sort of connection. Quite often the murder was intended to sever that bond but

50

it often had the opposite effect, tying the criminal once and for all to his victim. But here, there was no connection between murderer and victims. All those killed had merely been in the wrong place at the wrong time – selected not by the murderer but by the random hand of fate.

Barton found what he was looking for. He walked over to them holding something in the palm of his hand.

It was a flat piece of bone, singed around the edges.

Singh asked, 'Part of a skull?'

Dr Barton nodded. 'Yes, I think so.' He tapped himself on the forehead. 'Frontal plate.'

'Why is it important?' The Sikh policeman was mystified. 'Presumably you've got frontal plates and occipital plates and every other bone in that macabre collection of yours!'

Barton held up the piece so they could see it clearly. The others peered at it. The doctor slipped his index finger through a perfectly round hole in the centre of the cranial plate.

Inspector Singh sighed.

Bronwyn looked at him questioningly. She asked, 'What is it?'

'A bullet hole,' said the inspector from Singapore.

Three

'I don't understand!' exclaimed Bronwyn, clutching her thin hair with both hands. 'Was this one of the bomb victims?'

Dr Barton nodded. 'Yes, in the sense that the remains were recovered from the Sari Club. No, in that he was already dead when the bomb went off.'

'But how is that possible? Surely the body would have been spotted? It was a crowded nightclub!' Singh made his doubts clear.

Atkinson said, 'It *is* almost impossible to understand. But the Sari Club was completely destroyed. There's no way of knowing for sure if there were any store rooms or corners where a body might have been stashed.'

'How certain are you it's a bullet hole? Couldn't it have been caused by shrapnel or nails or something like that?' Singh's tone was belligerent, instinctively treating the doctor like a witness whose story had to be tested under pressure.

Dr Barton remained composed. 'It's a good theory, but the Sari Club bomb was not laced with the normal cocktail of metal objects. *And* – it's not conclusive – but I tested the carbonated remains around the bullet hole' – he held up his bizarre trophy – 'and, although one burnt-out piece of bone looks very much like another, there was gunpowder residue around this hole.'

Singh exhaled, blowing out his cheeks. He said, 'So what you're saying is that in the midst of carnage, there's also been murder?'

'Well, it's all murder,' retorted Barton.

Singh scowled at him, thick eyebrows almost meeting above his large nose. 'You know what I mean – there was an individual murder in the midst of mass murder.'

'The question is – does it matter?' Atkinson posed the question like an academic in an ivory tower.

'What do you mean?' asked Bronwyn in a subdued voice.

'We're dealing with an international investigation into a terrorist attack. Do we have the time and resources to look into a murder?'

'Are you suggesting we *ignore* this?' Singh was angry.

'I'm suggesting that maybe we *should* look away. Relative to the suicide bombings – this is a minor matter!' Atkinson, recognising that he was in a minority of one, was aggressive, his head thrust forward on his thick neck.

'Why did you show this to us if you want to pretend it didn't happen?' asked Bronwyn.

Singh nodded his head to second the question. Bronwyn had the natural perspicuity that he always attributed to women. Atkinson's behaviour and opinion were not consistent.

'It's my fault,' said Dr Barton. 'I don't think we should disregard this poor bastard.'

'That's why you're here,' said Atkinson, looking at the Sikh policeman and grinning suddenly, exposing a row of small, sharp teeth.

Singh had a suspicion he was not going to like what was coming next.

'We heard that your government sent us a security expert without any expertise.'

Singh shrugged his fleshy shoulders. There was no point denying it.

'So,' continued Atkinson, 'we thought you could make yourself useful chasing down the murderer.'

Singh scratched his beard. 'It's impossible. I'm out of my jurisdiction. I don't have a team.'

Atkinson said rudely, pointing a finger at the Australian policewoman, 'You can have *her.*'

Bronwyn appeared startled but did not speak.

Singh was aghast. 'I wouldn't know where to begin,' he said, almost pleadingly. 'I mean, what do we have to go on – a piece of a skull with a hole in it? We don't even know who the victim is!'

Barton said in a smug tone, 'Oh! Did I forget to mention? I've identified the body.' He held up his favourite prop, spinning the piece of skull around a finger stuck through the bullet hole. 'Let me introduce you to Richard Crouch, resident of Bali these last six months.'

Atkinson said, 'Good work!'

Barton turned to Singh and Bronwyn. 'Look, I know this is going to be an almost impossible crime to solve. But I persuaded Atkinson that we owe it to this guy to have a go. It's not right that his killer is let off the hook because we happen to be busy.'

Atkinson added, 'I'm not wasting the manpower I need for the terrorist investigation. Neither are the Balinese. But, I thought, as we have a top cop from Singapore who has a reputation for always getting his man but knows squat about terrorism, why not get him on board? Unless, that is, you're just here for quality time on the beach?'

Singh didn't bother to respond to the blatant provocation. He was thinking hard, chewing on his plump lower lip with vigour. The bottom line was that he was not going back to Singapore any time soon. His superiors were determined that their contribution to the cause of Balinese security should stay on Bali. But he was sick and tired of being a fifth wheel on the investigative bandwagon, skulking behind his Australian babysitter, hoping – unsuccessfully as it turned out – that no one would notice that he didn't have a clue what he was doing. But murder was his expertise. And here was a murder that was at least as challenging as anything he had ever confronted before. No policeman worth his white sneakers could turn down such an offer.

Besides, the doctor was right. This Richard Crouch, whoever he was, deserved more – he deserved justice. And the pursuit of justice was Singh's favourite form of exercise.

He said gruffly, 'I'll do it.'

'We should go, love.'

Emily Greenwood ignored her husband. She wiped a trickle of wine off her chin with a well-manicured finger. The nail was painted a delicate shade of cherry. Her pink tongue darted out and licked the tip. She waved imperiously to a hovering waiter. He rushed over and poured more of the rich ruby liquid into her empty glass.

'You've had enough, darling. Let's go home now.' Julian despised himself for the pleading note that crept into his nasal voice.

Emily sipped the wine and smiled at her husband, two large grey eyes looking at him

56

with bleary amusement, unruly highlighted blonde tendrils escaping from her chignon. 'Just one more for the road, love.'

Even in her drunken state, her tone had the rich plumminess and authority of someone born to privilege. Julian, knowing how hard he worked to maintain a similar accent, doing his best to disguise his ordinary London roots, felt a stab of intense jealousy.

Why had this woman been born with a silver spoon in her mouth? More like a silver bloody ladle, he thought crossly.

He had met Emily in Bali six months before, wooed her and married her, convinced it was his ticket to the good life. He had been disappointed in his expectations. Despite her intensely hedonistic lifestyle, devoted to the pleasures that Bali offered to pamper the wealthy, she had remained in firm control of the purse strings.

Julian stared at the small hand gripping the stem of her wine glass and wondered how he was going to prise some funds from that grasp.

The situation was urgent.

He had even asked that goody-two-shoes, Richard Crouch, for a loan. It was no use asking Tim Yardley, he was always skint. He remembered how Richard had looked at him sympathetically and explained that he did not feel able to help Julian with his debts. 'I don't approve of gambling, you see,' he explained in his low, quiet voice. 'Perhaps you should get some help with your addiction?'

Julian had felt like screaming at him, standing there, looking at him with an expression of gentle sympathy. He didn't have an addiction. He just enjoyed hanging out with the locals at the regular cockfighting contests. He had been unlucky with a few wagers. He didn't need therapy. He needed to find a way to avoid having his legs broken – or worse.

The tip of Julian's long patrician nose was red with aggravation. He wondered whether he should come clean with his wife. Did he dare? Would she help him or leave him?

Julian looked at Emily, trying to recollect if he had ever felt any real affection for her. He had married her for her money, of course. But he had done so willingly. She was a small attractive woman with an exaggerated hourglass figure. In the early days of their relationship, her casual largesse had come in very useful. He had admired her effortless class – he had always been attracted to women who were further up the social ladder than him. He, with his thin long limbs and lean bony face, looked the part of an aristocrat. He enjoyed playing the role when he had enough ready cash to dry-clean his cream linen suit and dress like a tropical gentleman. But he had none of the natural self-esteem that only money could buy. Emily had drifted into his life and presented him with an opportunity to turn his act into reality. He had grabbed it with both hands.

He had known that Emily drank when he married her but not thought that much about it. Most of the expatriates in Bali enjoyed their drink. After all, what else was there to do on an island paradise where all the daily chores were carried out by willing Balinese minions?

Julian recalled that he had even decided to abandon his beloved cockfighting until he was more certain of his bond with Emily and her affection for him. But he had been unable to withstand the temptation to have a flutter and now he was in desperate need of funds. He gazed across the table. A waft of expensive perfume tickled his nose. Emily rested her head against the pillow of two folded arms. She began to snore gently.

Dr Barton stood behind the ornate carved teak desk, inappropriate in both size and design for the tiny, cramped space. The other two tried to find a place to stand that did not involve leaving muddy footprints on the piles of papers on the floor. Books propped each other up drunkenly on a large bookshelf. Singh noted that the titles were all work-related. Although the air-conditioning was running, the large window behind the desk was wide open. The policeman could feel a hot evening breeze wafting in. At the same time, the air-conditioning blew gusts of cold air onto the back of his neck. He sneezed. Barton scowled at him as he blew his nose on a large white handkerchief that he pulled neatly folded from his trouser pocket.

Singh edged forward but found himself too close to Bronwyn. She was at least six inches taller than him even in flat shoes, he thought irritably. At least she wasn't the sort to wear heels – he didn't need his lack of stature emphasised any further.

'How did you identify the body?' asked Bronwyn as the inspector from Singapore continued to belie his reputation as a canny investigator by shuffling about the room looking uncomfortable.

'Dental records,' said Barton. 'Fortunately, the jaw was mostly intact – the rest are just fragments.'

Singh asked sharply, his interest caught, 'Was it a conclusive identification?'

Barton adopted his most professional tone. 'Well, considering the fragmentation, incineration and co-mingling, I would go as far as to say we have a positive identification. The ante-mortem and post-mortem data match in sufficient detail, there are no unexplainable discrepancies, the dental work was not extensive but it was idiosyncratic. Considering some of the stuff we're relying on, this is good. Off the record – I'm pretty sure we have one Richard Crouch, Caucasian male, late thirties.'

Singh was not convinced. He asked, 'But how can you be sure the skull and jaw are from the same body? You said yourself that there was a lot of confusion after the bombs.'

Barton nodded. 'You're right. But the DNA from the teeth and that piece of skull I showed you are a match.'

Singh was impressed by the bad-tempered doctor. His casual way with bones masked both integrity and an attention to detail which was remarkable in the circumstances.

He asked, 'Dental records? That means there are next of kin?'

'Yes. There's a wife. I should be clear that the other characteristics, age and race, I've based on a picture she provided. She came to the morgue looking for her husband after the bombs and seemed to think a photo might help with identification.'

'Poor woman,' said Bronwyn.

Singh nodded in agreement. It was slightly comic, and very tragic, that the wife had thought there might be enough left of her husband for a visual identification from a photograph.

Singh asked, 'You couldn't confirm race from skull shape?'

'There isn't a single piece big enough to determine racial identity,' explained Barton impatiently. 'Besides, the wife should know if her husband was white!'

Singh said carefully, 'We have to take everything she says with a good dose of scepticism.'

'Why?' demanded Bronwyn, offended on behalf of the unknown woman.

'Because she's the only suspect we have right now.'

Met with silence, he asked, 'Have you told her?'

Barton shook his head. 'I've told the family nothing. I found the bullet hole some time back – so I've known there was a murder mixed up in this mess for a while. But we just discovered the dental match – and it took a while after that to make sure the DNA samples from the teeth matched the skull. The widow doesn't even know that we've identified the body, let alone that her husband was shot in the head before being blown to smithereens.'

He paused for a moment. 'I guess it's just as well a person can only die once.' Barton grabbed a folder from the top of his desk and held it up. He asked, 'So, you're going to take the case?'

'I really think I am,' said Singh.

He held out a grubby hand and the doctor handed the file over.

Singh remarked, 'This murderer almost got away.'

'What do you mean?' asked Bronwyn.

'Well, if the doctor hadn't found that skull fragment with the bullet hole – he'd have got away with murder. It's not every day that terrorists conspire to get a killer off the hook.'

Bronwyn asked, 'There is no way of knowing, I suppose, when Crouch was killed?' She looked at the doctor inquiringly and he shook his head.

'There's not enough left of him for any fancy analysis of time of death. I didn't find any trace of decomposition in what was left but I'm not sure what that proves. He probably wasn't dead a huge amount of time before the bombings. But that's just my best guess – could be that any signs of decomposition were incinerated.'

Bronwyn continued, 'I suppose that means it's conceivable that the perpetrator died in the bombings too?'

'Shot the guy and then was blown up? It's possible, I guess.'

Singh was disappointed. His jowls drooped. He wanted to find a murderer, not identify another corpse.

Bronwyn noticed this and said cheerfully, the dimple putting in a fresh appearance,

'Probably the killer is lying under a beach umbrella, watching the sunset, sipping a pina colada and thinking how lucky he – or she – is.'

Singh's face brightened. He said, 'I certainly hope so!'

Tim Yardley sat under a thatched umbrella, leaning back against its sturdy wooden trunk. He was shirtless and a stiff breeze ruffled the hair that blanketed his belly. His breasts drooped over his stomach.

A low full moon, hanging like a paper lantern in the sky, provided the only light. The sea waters were ebony against a midnight-blue sky. Only the frothy wave tops reflected the moonlight, each strand racing the others to shore, occasionally colliding in a wheeling eddy. It was peaceful.

Tim did his best to forget the hurtful things his wife had said to him. Karri was becoming more unpleasant by the day, playing with his emotions with the capriciousness of a young child pulling the wings off a butterfly. Indeed, she had used her spiteful tongue with good effect throughout the course of their marriage, mocking his weaknesses, insisting her maliciousness was just humour – that he was being too sensitive in taking it all to heart.

They had been married almost fifteen years now. He had met her in a Bali hotel, the sort that catered to Taiwanese package tours and low-budget corporate retreats. She had spotted him balanced precariously on a bar stool, sipping a Bintang and waiting for his colleagues from the engineers' conference to put in an appearance. With her usual self-confidence, she had sidled over and begun a conversation. He remembered being bowled over by the energetic skinny woman with the exotic hairstyle.

Half an hour later, he had abandoned his fellow engineers to perch on the back of Karri's rented scooter, holding on to her flat stomach gingerly. She took him on a tour of rowdy bars and strobe-lit nightclubs where he sipped a beer and watched her dance, proud that he was there as her escort. They had ended up in his hotel room, the first time he had had sex with a woman he had not paid for upfront.

Tim remembered how certain he was that he could not let this vibrant creature out of his life. He had been terrified of being left to his old sedate existence and regular job in Canberra, no one to come home to except his old mother who relied on him and despised him at the same time.

In desperation, he had blurted out a proposal of marriage and then cringed at the thought of her horrified response. Karri had rolled oven, her hair tousled. She had gripped his naked belly, already starting to protrude, in a firm hand. He had felt ashamed of his physique, flabby and untoned, compared to her brown wiry muscularity.

To his amazement, she had burst into loud laughter and said, 'Why not?'

Tim had immediately faxed his resignation to the Canberra head office from his hotel, his hands tremulous with anticipation as he gave the scribbled letter to the desk clerk. He was a new man, embarking on a new life. He had married Karri wearing the suit he had brought for the conference but was determined to burn it right after the ceremony – a symbolic rejection of the regimentation and tedium of his previous life. He would dress in cotton vests and comfortable surfer shorts, knock himself into shape jogging on the beach and get a tan. Tim remembered how he had peered into a mirror just before the ceremony, looking at his high forehead and wondering whether there was a Balinese potion that would magically restore his hairline. For a short while, he had truly believed in miracles.

When he arrived at the registry office, he found Karri waiting for him. She was dressed in Bali's famous white Uluwatu lace. He thought she looked beautiful. The best man was a co-worker from the office who was also at the conference. Tim had roped him in at the last moment. He was determined to provide his bride, a woman who disdained the formalities and mocked the conventions, with the accoutrements of a traditional wedding.

A week later, he had found his new wife and the best man in bed together.

He remembered how his bowels had loosened with shock when he had happened upon them. His broader despair had been subsumed into a small narrow panic that he would soil his brand new beach shorts.

Karri had seemed genuinely surprised that he expected her to be faithful. He shook his head. Even now, the memory of her words was like a knife twisting in his gut. She had said, as his colleague hurriedly left the room wrapped in bedclothes, grabbing his pants on the way out as if he were a character in some sort of staged bedroom farce, 'Tim, I might have married you – but you don't own me and you can't tell me how to live my life.'

Four

The following morning, Inspector Singh gazed out to sea. The blue-green surface sparkled as the sunlight caught the tops of rippling waves. It seemed as if a generous deity had caused it to rain diamonds onto the ocean. It was the final touch to raise Bali from the perfect to the sublime.

It was still early and the sun was a low orb on the horizon. Although bright and determined, it had not yet succeeded in turning the fresh, cool morning into a sultry Balinese day.

Inspector Singh had sand in his shoes, between his toes and under his soles. Sand chafed his heels as well. Bali sand, at least on this particular beach, was a coarse yellow. Scratchy. Not the coral white powder he had been expecting.

At least the beach was clean. The cleanliness had mystified Singh. It was no mean feat considering that it was facing the South China Sea, rubbish dump of Asia. The previous morning, an explanation for the minor miracle had been forthcoming. Coming down to gaze over the waters earlier than usual after a sleepless night, Inspector Singh had seen a large tractor trundling up and down, scooping up the top layer of sand together with all the human detritus that the oceans had chucked up overnight. Driven by a morbid curiosity, Singh had walked forward until he was close enough to look into the tractor's square, metal jaw. Empty plastic bottles, limp condoms, broken glass, much of it the toxic green that signalled the remnants of a bottle of Bintang beer, a leather shoe covered in mould, a syringe – Singh stopped looking.

He wondered idly where the garbage was dumped. On some other beach less frequented by foreign tourists? Did they throw out the sand too? Surely the beach would soon be excavated bare? After all, it took millions of years for the rocks and stones of the coastline to be whittled down to the grains of sand getting into his shoes.

Tourists, those few hardy souls who had refused to be driven away by the Bali bombings, were starting to appear, drawn to the beach by the sun. Seasoned sunbathers had baked their skin to dark leather. Others were golden brown – looking good until the skin cancer set in, thought Singh grimly. He glanced at his own arms, covered in a starched, long-sleeved white cotton shirt, with approval.

Singh's attention was drawn to a large man, bright red all over except for his bum cheeks. These, exposed in a pair of thong swimming trunks, were a flaccid white. As he watched, the man spread a large striped bath towel on the sand and lowered himself onto it gingerly. He levered a panama hat onto his inflamed bald head and rolled over. His pristine bottom needed colour too.

A few Balinese were making their way in a leisurely fashion towards the tourists. A small nut-brown boy was assembling kites. In a few minutes he had a selection, from traditional diamond shapes to intricately painted birds of prey, tethered to a bamboo construction. The kites bobbed and danced in the sky. Singh's favourite was a kite of primary colours in the shape of a ship. Its sails billowed in the wind as it tugged insistently at its anchor, anxious to be on its way.

Two middle-aged Balinese women with wrinkled, kindly faces squatted on the beach in bright-coloured *sarongs* and *kebaya*. They beckoned to the tourists, offering cheap massages in cackling tones, their teeth rotten and stained from chewing betel nuts wrapped in the peppery leaves of the *sirih* plant. Their prices dropped as their quarry moved further away. Singh caught a whiff of jasmine and coconut oil from the tray of jars on the sand.

The inspector realised he was attracting a good deal of suspicious interest. A fully-clothed, turbaned man, standing statue-like and contemplative on a Bali beach, was not a sight to reassure. There were very few Westerners, thought Singh, who could tell a Sikh from a headgear-wearing Moslem – and in Bali, since the bombs, every Moslem was assumed to be a potential terrorist.

Singh retreated slowly up the beach. He reached the hotel and flopped down on an intricately carved wooden bench. Everything in Bali was intricately carved, he thought crossly – it made it damned uncomfortable. He rubbed his back, kicked off his shoes and, puffing slightly from bending oven, peeled the socks off his feet, exposing toes sprinkled with sand, tufts of grey hair growing between the joints.

The policeman turned his white sneakers over and dusted them out. He slapped his socks against his foot, trying to shake the sand loose. An obsequious Balinese man dressed in a white bush jacket, tan *sarong* and slippers, the uniform of the hotel staff, rushed over to offer his assistance.

'I can do it myself,' said Singh brusquely.

He noticed the square bulge in the man's pocket. Singh held up two fingers, mimicking holding a cigarette. The Balinese was delighted to be of service. He extricated the packet and tapped it expertly on his palm, offering Singh the protruding fags. Singh took one and slipped it between his thin upper lip and full pink lower lip. The man whipped out a lighter and held the flame to the cigarette. Singh inhaled deeply. He smiled. Cultural differences were papered over by their mutual addiction to tobacco.

Singh leaned forward and squinted at the file he had tucked under his arm as he walked along the beach. Ash from his cigarette fell on the cover and he brushed it away with the back of his hand. He had wasted enough time staring out to sea, trying to come to terms with his new assignment. It was time for him to knuckle down and do what he did best – hunt down a murderer.

Julian Greenwood jumped on his motor-bike. He could have taken the car with its docile Balinese chauffeur but Emily would almost certainly find out where he had gone. The staff knew very well who signed the cheques every month.

He weaved between traffic. An old Bali hand, the narrow roads and erratic driving held no fears for him. He was not wearing a helmet and his thin brown hair was swept back from his high forehead by the wind. Strands of his drooping moustache were getting into his mouth.

He stayed on the main road. Telegraph poles festooned with wires measured out his journey until he was past Seminyak with its upmarket boutiques and restaurants. He turned onto a dirt track a few miles after the Oberoi junction. He followed a path flanked by paddy fields, weaving between fetid puddles. After a few minutes, he reached his destination. A collection of motorcycles, dusty from their journey, rested beside scrubby trees. He could hear raucous shouts interspersed with whistles and cheers. He made his way to a little dip in the terrain.

Julian felt the blood pump through his veins like a high-powered hose. He squeezed between the hordes of sweating, screaming men. The scent of hundreds of clove cigarettes made him feel lightheaded. This was the Bali he loved. Not the smooth servile surface but these sudden outbursts of energy and passion that sprung through the cracks of society like bubbling geysers. A female vendor tried to sell him a snack but he shook his head impatiently. He was not there to eat.

The arena was circular and surrounded by a low woven temporary fence. Two cocks were held at separate ends of the enclosure. One was red and white and the other speckled green and black, both with long plumes for tails and flared ruffs. Their owners had tied on the *taji*, a small steel dagger about four inches long, to the legs of their respective fighting birds. They were priming the birds for the fight now, ruffling their feathers, plucking their combs and kneading their muscles. The crowd was almost hysterical, shouting out their favourites, taking side bets by gesticulating across the crowded arena and offering odds.

Julian felt in his shirt pocket and pulled out a ten thousand *rupiah* note that he had stolen from his wife's handbag. He had not dared take more in case she noticed. He took a deep breath and jumped into the fray.

The handlers released the cocks which charged at each other with single-minded fury. They attacked in a flurry of feathers and flying claws, trying hard to slash at the opposing bird with their spurs, enhanced by the vicious *taji*. In a few seconds, one of the birds was injured, the blood splashing onto the sandy pitch, its white feathers turning red. The referee blew his whistle and the handlers dashed in to separate the birds. The owner of the injured bird looked at the referee and shook his head. The cock would not fight again. He put the bird in a portable woven basket of green leaves and slung the long string handle over his shoulder. His day was over, his cock defeated in its first fight.

There was an exchange of bundles of notes from hand to hand. Small wads of cash were tossed across crowds to the winners. Julian had doubled his money and a slow smile spread across his face. Maybe his luck was turning.

A hand reached out and snatched the grimy notes from his unsuspecting fingers. He whirled around angrily but stopped short when he saw who it was.

The Balinese man, his unbuttoned shirt exposing a hairless chest, said, 'Very good, I also backed the *buik*, the green and black cock. Now you owe me two million *rupiah* less this,' and he waved Julian's winnings under his long nose.

Julian thrust out his chin, trying to look confident. He said, 'I will get you the money soon.'

The Balinese smiled, exposing the large gap between his two front teeth. 'Better you do that – you have only one more week.'

The first few pages consisted of the forensic dental investigation that had identified the deceased as Richard Crouch. Singh noted that the dental records provided were from England. That meant that the records were reliable and also that Crouch was probably English. He would confirm that with the wife later in the day.

A photograph slipped out of the file into Singh's ample lap. He picked it up and gazed at the smiling young man leaning against a car, light brown hair curling around his collar, scraggy beard a couple of shades darker. He was dressed in a white T-shirt and blue jeans frayed at the knees. His arms were crossed in front of him. There was a date in the corner. The photo had been taken almost two years ago. Singh wondered why the wife had not provided something more recent. They were in Bali. Surely they must have taken some shots?

There was not much else in the folder. DNA test results confirmed that the various remains belonged to one and the same person. Photos of the charred body parts, taken individually next to a ruler, gave a sense of their dimensions. Singh noticed the long femur – the young man had been tall.

He gazed at the pictures side by side – one of vibrant life, the other of blackened remnants – then slumped back in his chair.

Bronwyn Taylor's voice, foghorn loud, interrupted his contemplation.

She said, 'Geez. I thought you'd given up the evil weed?'

Singh sucked in a lungful of nicotine and decided he really disliked hefty women with fleshy arms and large thighs in badly cut trousers. He noted the silhouette of her overhanging tummy against the soft cotton T-shirt she was wearing. The top was at least two sizes too small. He realised shamefacedly, looking down at his own large gut, that his mental rant constituted a good description of himself. He decided he needed a good kick on his generous posterior for agreeing to have this woman on

76

his team. He preferred the people who worked for him to be timid, quiet and competent. Bronwyn's bouncy exuberance made him feel like lying down in a dark room with a wet towel over his eyes.

Singh tried to remember how he had got entangled with Taylor in the first place. When he had arrived in Bali he had reported to the joint Balinese–Australian investigative team. Once it had become apparent that he had no useful skills, he had been fobbed off on Taylor. Singh had suspected at the time that Bronwyn had annoyed her superiors. Why else would they waste manpower providing him with an escort?

He stood up and became conscious that he was in bare feet with his socks in his hands. He felt as undressed as the man in the g-string on the beach.

Bronwyn Taylor, her volume only slightly adjusted for proximity, said, 'Been for a walk on the beach, eh? I've been out too – swum for miles, lovely sea this morning. You should try it – although I can't imagine you in a pair of budgie smugglers!' She grinned. 'Or maybe I can!'

Taking Singh's horrified silence in her stride, she poked him in the stomach with a long fleshy finger, reddened around the knuckles as if she had been in a fistfight. She said, 'I'm sorry to say it doesn't look like you get much exercise, mate!'

Singh sat down and pulled on his sandy socks, his cigarette clenched between small, brown-stained teeth. He put on his white sneakers and tied the laces in a double knot.

Bronwyn Taylor asked, 'Have you finished with the file yet? I'm keen to have a look when you're done. Today, I hope!'

Singh took a deep breath. He was not surprised that her superiors had sidelined this woman from the main terrorist investigation. He slid the folder across the table.

She sat down heavily on a cushioned wicker chair and started flicking through, stopping as he had done to look at the picture of the laughing young man. Singh saw her round shoulders sag and guessed she was feeling the same pity he had felt for Richard Crouch, a vital young man reduced to fragments.

As he pondered the woman in front of him, he sensed she had ceased to concentrate on the contents of the file and was instead contemplating something unrelated. It caused her high forehead to furrow. The neat, parallel worry lines reminded him of the tractor trail he had seen that morning on the beach.

She looked up and held his gaze with her mild blue eyes. 'I have no experience,' she said.

'Experience of what?'

'Murder!'

'Well, that's a good thing.'

She gave him a small smile but her heart wasn't in it. She said, 'I have no experience of murder investigations.'

'I have plenty,' remarked Singh.

Bronwyn Taylor snapped, 'I realise that. My point is that I'm not sure I'm going to be of much use.'

'That's probably true,' Singh agreed cheerfully.

'So, if you want me off the case, I'll understand.'

'We haven't started yet and you're pulling out?'

'I'm not pulling out. I'm giving you the chance to find yourself a more able assistant.'

'Where?'

'What do you mean, where?'

'Where, in Bali, with every policeman on the island hunting terrorists, am I going to find a more able assistant?'

Bronwyn didn't say anything.

Singh asked suddenly, 'What are you doing here anyway?'

She sighed and tugged at an earlobe. 'I was supposed to help with communications. I speak Bahasa Indonesia and I volunteered to come out.'

'That doesn't explain why you were assigned to look after me...'

'One of the first questions I was asked by reporters was whether the Australian government should have done more to warn citizens to stay away.'

'And what did you say?'

'That there had been background terrorist chatter about targeting Australians ... and specific mention of Bali.'

Singh stared at the woman half in admiration, half in shock.

'Didn't you realise how politically sensitive that would be?'

'I guess not. I was told to be honest – that it would keep everyone from flying off the handle. They didn't realise I had access to some of the high-level briefing memos.'

'I'm amazed you weren't put on the first flight back!'

'They didn't want to turn it into a bigger story – you know, "brave policewoman who speaks the truth sent home in disgrace" headlines. So they gave me the job of squiring you about instead.'

'And you didn't kick up a fuss?'

'I didn't want to become part of the story – use up resources at the expense of the families.'

Singh nodded. He could understand that.

Bronwyn dimpled. 'But when this is over and I'm back in Oz – well, I might decide to talk about some of the things I saw and heard!'

'But now,' said Singh, *'we* have a murder to solve.'

'You're sure about that?'

The policeman from Singapore nodded. Anyone who was courageous or foolhardy enough to shine a bright light on secretive government activities deserved a bit of support. After all, he was from Singapore – no one knew better than him the heavy hand of the state.

Five

Bronwyn selected a taxi, negotiated the price of the trip like a housewife on a tight budget, and waved Singh over with an imperious hand. He was standing under the tenuous shade of a frangipani tree, inhaling the spicy scent of its white flowers and regretting his impulse to involve Bronwyn in the case. She was not even going to allow him the choice of transport. Her inability to knuckle down in the face of authority was going to be a real pain. At her summons, however, he lumbered docilely over, walking around exposed manholes and stepping over uncovered drains. Singh wondered for a moment whether anyone in Bali ever walked in a straight line from point to point. He narrowly avoided stepping on a small offering, a square receptacle made of coconut leaves with flowers and a biscuit perched on it – Bali streets were littered with them – and clambered into the back seat of the Kijang.

As usual, despite its appearance of superfluous size, the inside was cramped. Singh's knees were bunched up uncomfortably. Bronwyn climbed in next to him and the vehicle became claustrophobic. Singh felt around for his seatbelt, found the strap and discovered that there was no receptacle for the buckle.

He leaned forward, tapped the driver on the shoulder and said, 'No seatbelt?'

The man giggled. 'Buckle broken already!'

Singh noticed that the driver was not wearing a seatbelt either although his appeared to be fully functioning. He scowled at Bronwyn. He didn't approve of chauffeurs who did not treat personal safety and the safety of their passengers as a first priority.

He asked, 'So how long will it take to get to Ubud?'

'About one hour...'

'I don't understand why Crouch's widow had to go and park herself in the middle of bloody nowhere,' grumbled Singh.

Bronwyn said, 'You'll like Ubud.' She leaned back against the imitation leather seat, slipped on a pair of enormous black shades, rested her head against the car door and shut her eyes.

The driver revved his engine. Singh gestured with a full, flat palm for him to stop. He got out of the car, walked around and hauled himself into the front passenger seat. The seatbelt was functioning and he put it on with a pleased look.

The driver looked at him inquiringly and Singh explained, 'I want to see some of Bali.'

The driver nodded enthusiastically. His big grin emphasised the surgical scar of a repaired cleft upper lip. He said, 'My name is Nyoman. Where are you from?'

Singh ground his teeth.

Bronwyn said hurriedly, 'I'm Australian and he's from Singapore.'

Nyoman said, 'I will show you everything. You want to stop to buy presents, yes – for your beautiful wife?' He jerked his head at Bronwyn. 'You tell me, ya. Then I stop the car for you.'

Singh said heavily, 'She is *not* my wife.'

Nyoman nodded, his enthusiasm undiminished. 'Yes – OK – we buy gift for your girlfriend. Bali has lot of beautiful things.'

Singh grunted and pulled out a map.

'It doesn't look far but it takes so long to get there?' he asked.

'Yes, boss. It is very busy road. Lots of handicrafts. Many tourists – except now not so many because of the bombs.'

If it wasn't for the breakneck speed and the close shaves with chickens, dogs, children and motorbikes, Singh would have been completely absorbed in the view. Instead, his right thigh muscle began to spasm from his instinctive, imaginary braking.

Outside Denpasar, stone statues lined the roads like petrified armies. There were multi-armed Hindu deities, Balinese mythological figures with goggle-eyes and curling tongues, placid, plump Buddhas and modern statuary, including, to Singh's amazement, a life-size garden gnome.

As he stared out of the window, Nyoman said, 'This is Batubulan village. Here many people do the stone carving.'

'You don't say,' murmured Singh.

'The statues are carved from compacted volcanic ash – they call it *paras*,' said Bronwyn from the back.

'I thought you were asleep.'

'Too much hooting and tooting,' she said wryly, pushing her sunglasses back onto her hair and revealing grey roots along her hairline.

'So, the statues aren't really stone?'

'No, *paras* decays in a human lifetime. Each generation has to rebuild them in the temples and courtyards. It keeps the village carving traditions alive – some of these skills date back hundreds of years.'

Singh raised an eyebrow. 'I just saw a Mickey Mouse.'

Bronwyn grinned. 'Occasionally they cater for tasteless Westerners.'

Nyoman said, 'You want Mickey Mouse? My cousin in the village is very good carver. Can do any size that you like. I take you there, OK?'

Singh said, 'No thanks.'

The next village was a mere two miles away. The road between Batubulan and

Celuk was packed with shops selling gold and silver jewellery.

Nyoman whispered, 'You want to buy something for your girlfriend, yes? I can get you very good price in Celuk.'

'She is *not* my wife and she's *not* my girlfriend. She's a colleague,' said Singh categorically.

Nyoman's face fell. But then he brightened up again. 'Maybe you take home present for your wife?'

Singh tried to remember if he had ever taken a gift back from any of his travels. His wife would disdain silver but she would love gold. As a traditional Indian woman she viewed gold both as a decorative item and as an investment for a rainy day. She had ropes of gold squirrelled away which she trotted out from time to time to wear at weddings.

Singh smiled. If he was to stop and buy her something, she would assume he was having an affair. She would never believe that a persuasive Balinese cab driver and a charming village had convinced him to break a habit of a lifetime.

He shook his head at Nyoman. 'Drive on,' he said firmly.

The next village, Nyoman told them, was Sukawati.

'And what do they make there?' asked Singh, an edge of sarcasm to his voice.

'Not so much,' said Nyoman. 'It has many

temples. It was part of great kingdom. Many famous *dalang* are here.'

'*Dalang?*'

'The shadow puppet masters,' explained Nyoman.

Bronwyn said, 'It's quite remarkable actually. They use the puppets to cast shadows on a screen. The *dalang* tells a story, operates the puppets, sings and plays musical instruments – all at the same time. Remarkable multi-tasking for a mere man.'

'How come you know so much about Bali?'

'I was here for a holiday a few years back. I've always been interested in Indonesia. I did Indonesian studies at university and learnt the language.'

Nyoman piped up, 'The *dalang* tells a story of good and evil. Evil always loses but can never be destroyed.'

Singh thought about the case for the first time on the drive. He had consciously avoided dwelling on it. The prospect of having to tell the widow that the body of her husband had been identified was bad enough. He would also have to break it to her that her husband had been murdered by someone *other* than the terrorists while keeping an open mind about the possibility that she was responsible for his death. Even for a detective as experienced as him, it was a fine line to walk.

Singh said heavily, 'Well, let's hope life imitates art.'

'What do you mean?' asked Bronwyn.

'That good triumphs over evil.'

Nyoman, latching on to Singh's reference to art, said excitedly, 'You want art? Next village is Batuan. Very famous Balinese artists are there!'

Singh stared out of the window. Sure enough, the narrow trunk road was now lined with little glass-fronted art galleries. There was an almost infinite variety of artistic styles; black and white ink drawings, traditional paintings featuring daily life in the paddy fields as well as complex depictions from the Indian epic *Ramayana* with gods and demons battling for supremacy.

Singh's fancy was caught by a collection of lurid, hallucinogenic portrayals of Bali.

Nyoman said, 'That is the Balinese Young Artists' style – but now the young artists are old!' He guffawed loudly at his own joke.

They had been climbing steadily. Exquisite water-filled rice paddy terraces were staggered into the hills and surrounded by coconut trees. Small figures bent over their crops. Thin long flags hung vertically and fluttered in the breeze.

'To chase the birds away,' explained Nyoman. 'Or they eat the rice.'

Singh said, with genuine awe in his voice, the contrast to the highrise buildings and non-existent horizon of Singapore upper-most in his mind, 'This is a truly beautiful place.'

Nyoman said simply and with complete certainty, 'It is the Island of the Gods.'

They passed the woodcarving village of Mas with its intricate sandalwood, teak and ebony work. A row of life-sized wooden horses prancing by the side of the road did not elicit comment. The occupants of the Kijang were sated on Balinese artistry. Even Nyoman did not offer to take them to a particular shop, run by his cousin, the most famous and best woodcarver in the village, who would offer them a special price. Either discouraged by his passengers' reluctance to have a look at the shops *en route* or de-pressed by the realisation that the Gods had not protected their island playground of Bali, he was silent for the rest of the drive too.

Nyoman pulled up beside a small guest house. Chalets were scattered about its compound, tucked away from the road and protected by a large stone wall. He said, 'We are here now.' He continued hopefully, 'I will wait for you, yes?'

The two officers hesitated for a moment, glanced at each other, and then Bronwyn jumped in. 'Yes, please. One of us will tell you if we don't need you any more.'

Nyoman said, '*No worries*, boss.'

Singh smiled a little to hear such an Australian expression on the lips of the Balinese man. Nyoman had obviously chauffeured his fair share of Aussies around over the years – he sounded like Bronwyn.

Singh walked in slowly, his heels brushing the floor with each step. He regretted spending so much time staring out of the Kijang window and talking to Nyoman. Bali, as it unfolded outside the windscreen, had fascinated him and distracted him. Now it was time to speak to the widow and Singh was not sure of the best approach.

They asked the young man at the front desk if Sarah Crouch was in. He nodded at once and said, 'Yes, *Pak*. She is here.' He added in a conspiratorial whisper, 'She has not found her husband yet...'

The desk jockey was a slight fellow with pimply skin, bushy hair and wide-spaced eyes. He looked no older than fifteen. The possibility of random death did not frighten him. He was young and still believed in his own immortality, thought Singh.

He asked, 'Was Richard Crouch also staying here before the bombs?'

'Yes. They have a long-term rent – already they are here for six months.'

'I wonder why they decided to move to Bali,' pondered Bronwyn.

'I thought maybe they have second honeymoon ... but they are not together very much – you know?' The young fellow winked at Singh and Bronwyn.

Singh was interested now. He asked, 'There seemed to be trouble between them?'

'I don't know what you mean...'

'The husband and wife, they did not get along? They fight?'

'Oh! Fighting not so much. But they don't do things together. When they have breakfast, they do not talk. He reads a book, always the same one with a green cover. She ... she looks far away even if she is staring at the wall.' And he put a flat hand in front of his face to indicate the blankness of Sarah Crouch's stare.

Singh wondered whether to read anything sinister into this marital disharmony.

As if reading his thoughts, Bronwyn murmured, 'It's suggestive.'

'Actually, it sounds pretty much like breakfast at my home every morning.'

'But you haven't caught a bullet,' pointed out Bronwyn.

'Give my wife time,' said Singh.

He turned his attention back to the young man. 'What's your name?'

'Wayan, *Pak*.'

'Wayan, can you tell us anything else you noticed about the two of them?'

Wayan's young face took on a worried expression. He said, 'I am not supposed to talk about the guests, *Pak*. Already I say too much.'

Singh said, 'We're police,' and flipped out his Singapore ID.

Wayan did not query his statement.

Singh had noticed this respect for authority amongst the Balinese. He would have to ask Bronwyn, the walking encyclopedia on Bali, for an explanation. It did not seem fear-driven or oppressed, more a casual acknowledgement of a social hierarchy and the Balinese individual's own place within the structure.

Wayan guessed, his big eyes deep and curious, like an infinity pool at an expensive Balinese hotel, 'You have found the husband?'

Singh nodded.

'He is OK?'

There was no response from the police.

'He is dead?' asked Wayan.

'I'm afraid so,' said Bronwyn.

'Bali bomb?'

Singh shrugged, his stomach swaying in synchronicity with his shoulders.

Wayan seemed to take this as an affirmative. He said, 'The wife, poor thing. Are you going to tell her now?'

'After you tell me everything else I need to know,' said Singh curtly. It was time for Wayan to understand that this was not a friendly chit-chat with passing tourists.

'What do you want to know, *Pak*?'

'Would he usually go to the Sari Club without his wife?'

'I don't know where he goes. But yes, always he goes out on his own.'

'Did he have any driver he used regularly?'

Singh mentally crossed his fingers. If Crouch had used a regular driver, as people often did in Bali – once they found someone reasonably priced whose vehicle did not appear to be a deathtrap – it would be easy to trace his movements.

Wayan said, 'No, no. He has a motorbike.'

That trail went cold pretty quickly, thought Singh with disappointment.

Wayan added, 'Sometimes his friends pick him up.'

Singh's ears quivered although his voice betrayed no excitement.

'Friends?' he asked.

'Yes, some men...'

Singh noticed that Wayan was hesitating – on the verge of saying something but having second thoughts. He was about to follow up when the young man's fair skin flushed as red as his acne. He said, 'Good morning, Mrs Crouch. The police are here to see you.'

Singh and Bronwyn both turned around, Singh with curiosity and Bronwyn with sympathy.

Sarah Crouch was a slight strawberry blonde with light-blue eyes. She wore a wide floppy hat to protect her fair skin. Although she had been in Bali for six months, she was still pale, almost translucent, faint blue veins visible on her cheeks. Singh thought that she would have been pretty once. He could imagine that, young and smiling, with her small even features and blue eyes, she would have turned a few heads. But her looks had not withstood the uncertainty of wondering whether her husband was dead. Sarah was thin and worried-looking, her face covered in spidery lines that radiated out from the corners of her eyes like a fan and down the sides of her mouth. Her lips were thin, chapped and almost bloodless. Her blue eyes were faded, the whites tinged with red.

She said, 'You were looking for me?'

Singh said, 'We're the police. We'd like to talk to you about your husband.' He took out his police ID and so did Bronwyn.

Here there was no instinctive respect.

'Singapore? Australia?'

Singh said, 'We're assisting the Balinese police and have been seconded to your husband's case.'

'What's going on? Have you found him?'

Bronwyn said gently, 'Is there somewhere private we could go?'

Bronwyn had telegraphed that the news was not good. She had given the woman time to prepare. He, Singh, did not have so much tact. Forewarned was forearmed. He

94

would have preferred to break the news harshly and suddenly and then watch this widow of a murdered man for any reaction that did not seem entirely consistent with hearing about her husband's death for the first time.

Sarah said, 'The patio is normally empty at this time,' and led them through the guest house. They walked out the back door into a small walled garden with lush tropical ferns against mossy stone walls. At the far end, the highest point in the garden, there was a carved stone gargoyle with bulbous eyes, curled lips and fangs on a pedestal. The creature was draped in a black and white checked *sarong* and had a flaming red hibiscus behind one ear. It was no more appropriate, mused Singh, than if he took to wearing a flower behind his ear. Balinese men with their delicate features and wide smiles might get away with adorning blossoms. It certainly suited the women with their streaming black hair and colourful *sarongs*. But him and that gargoyle? It was like putting lipstick on a pig.

There was a large timber deck protruding into the garden with a few tables and chairs and green umbrellas for shade. Sarah led them to one, pulled out a heavy wooden chair with difficulty and sat down. She faced them squarely but there was an unblinking quality to her stare that suggested fear.

Too much fear, wondered Singh. After all, the odds were that the disappearance of a man at the same time as a major terrorist attack was not a coincidence. Surely she must be prepared for the most likely explanation for his absence.

'He's dead, isn't he?' Sarah Crouch seemed unable to bear the silence from the police officers.

Bronwyn sat down opposite her and leaned forward sympathetically. 'I'm afraid so.'

Singh watched the widow carefully. She seemed composed.

She asked, 'Was it the bombs?'

Singh nodded curtly. It was not strictly true but he wanted to observe this faded creature before showing his whole hand.

She sighed. 'I guess I knew. Richard would have contacted me if he was all right. I just thought ... hoped, he might have been one of the survivors.' She paused and glanced at them. 'But deep down I knew that he wasn't.'

'How did you know?' asked Singh, more sharply than he intended.

'I beg your pardon?'

'How did you know he was unlikely to be wandering around with amnesia or something like that?'

Singh noted Bronwyn staring at him in the periphery of his vision but he did not take his eyes off the widow.

Sarah said, 'I visited all the hospitals – they let me in to see the injured – those who had not been identified. Actually, it was such chaos that no one stopped me when I walked through the wards looking for Richard.'

Her eyes went dark. 'I'll never forget. There weren't enough doctors, medicines, anaesthetics. There were desperate family everywhere, checking the living before the dead.'

She dragged herself away from the memory of the victims. 'He wasn't there. Richard wasn't there.'

Her voice trailed off for a moment. Then she said, 'But now I guess you've found him?'

Singh relented. He said, 'Yes, the body of Richard Crouch has been identified from dental records.'

She nodded. 'They asked me to get those from the UK. Richard had quite a lot of dental work done when he was a kid. He was still afraid of the dentist. I used to laugh at him about it.' She smiled at the memory, revealing small even white teeth of her own.

Singh wondered whether it demonstrated a heartless streak – to laugh at a husband's fear of dentists. He knew he was grasping at straws, trying to find something in this woman that might demonstrate a capacity for murder.

Sarah asked, 'Will they release the body

for burial?'

Bronwyn said apologetically – Singh thought that she was the sort of woman who would always be apologising for things that were outside her control – 'There's not much left of him, I'm afraid.'

Singh added, 'The body won't be released for a while yet.'

The widow asked, 'Why? I read in the papers that bodies are being shipped back to Australia. The Balinese have held a few funerals as well!'

'There are reasons,' said Singh non-committally.

'Reasons? I've been sitting on this island for ages waiting for news.' Her voice broke and she started to sob. 'I'm running out of money!'

Singh said, apparently oblivious to the sudden breakdown, 'We'd prefer it if you didn't leave the country.'

'Me? Why?'

'Because you're a suspect in a murder investigation.'

'What? You think *I'm* a terrorist? Are you mad?'

Bronwyn broke the news. 'Richard Crouch was murdered. He didn't die in the bombings.'

Sarah looked blank.

Bronwyn said patiently, 'Your husband was killed, but not in the bombings.'

'But how can that be? You just said there was not much of him left! Where was he found?'

Singh realised how difficult the case was going to be. The coincidence of murder and mass murder was too much for the widow to take in. How was he to find the thread that led to the murderer in the tangled skein of the terrorist offence?

The policeman explained, 'He was at the Sari Club. But he was killed beforehand.'

Sarah said, 'But, but ... that's impossible.'

Singh said, 'Improbable, I grant you. But the forensic investigation was conclusive. Your husband was shot in the head with a small-calibre weapon. His body was in or around the Sari Club at the time of the bomb and was caught up in the explosion.'

When this met with no response from the widow, he continued, 'So, I'm afraid you *are* part of a murder investigation. If you don't mind, I'd like to have your passport ... and Richard's.'

'You think I might have done it?' The disbelief in her voice was convincing.

Bronwyn put out a hand in an instinctive gesture of denial and said, 'No, of course not. But I'm sure you can see that we have to investigate this very thoroughly. It would be a dereliction of our duty not to consider you a suspect ... and ask you to stay in Bali.'

Singh was tempted to smile. If that did not

lull his only suspect into a false sense of security, nothing would. Bronwyn might be quite useful after all with her overdeveloped sense of empathy and misplaced sense of pity.

'Of course,' said Sarah, 'I do understand. It's just been such a shock.'

Singh stood up. 'Right, we'll leave you your privacy and meet back here this afternoon at three o'clock.'

Bronwyn and the widow wore matching expressions of surprise.

Singh pretended not to notice. He turned sharply on his heel – his rotund shape and small feet made him look like a spinning top – and marched out.

He could hear Bronwyn thanking the woman for her time. Her footsteps beat a sharp staccato on the stone floors as she hastened to catch up with him.

Nyoman was waiting for them in front of the guest house. They clambered into the back of the vehicle.

Bronwyn said, 'I know why you did that!'

'Did what?'

'Walked out just then – you want to keep her off balance because you think you might get better information that way. Isn't that right?'

'Nonsense,' said Singh. 'It's lunch time and I'm hungry.'

Ghani walked in.

Nuri thought she had rarely seen such as unassuming creature as this man she had married. Ghani was of medium height. He wore a nondescript pair of unbranded blue jeans and a white T-shirt. His hairline was receding. What was left formed a neat semi-circle running around the back of his head from ear to ear. His most prominent feature was his florid nose. His lips were obscured by a grizzled beard and moustache. His lids were heavy. It gave him a superficially sleepy look but the pupils that gazed out were black pinpoints of engagement with the world around him.

He looked like a good-natured sort of uncle, she decided, the type who brought sweets and thought childish mischief was amusing.

Her husband took off his shoes and socks and placed them neatly by the door. He looked approvingly at the table where lunch was laid out. He said, 'This looks good, wife. Let us eat.'

Nuri nodded her thanks.

Ghani looked around and asked, an irritable note creeping into his gruff voice, 'Where is Yusuf?'

Nuri had noticed that all the men found Yusuf annoying. She often wondered why they had brought him along to Bali from their village in Sulawesi. He was not learned

101

in the scriptures like her older brother, Abu Bakr. He did not have Ramzi's ability to attract young men to their proposed school. He was just Yusuf, slight, annoying and diffident. She supposed there was always room for an odd-job man.

She hurried to the smaller of the two bedrooms and knocked on the door.

Yusuf, short hair standing on end as if he had gone to bed with it damp, emerged, blinking nervously. His round glasses reflected the light streaming in the small window overlooking the street. He tugged at his beard nervously.

She said gently, 'Lunch is ready, Yusuf.' Yusuf followed her into the room.

'Yusuf, your beard is supposed to be a fist long. You can barely grow it at all and now you are pulling it out at the roots,' Ramzi remarked cheerfully.

They all laughed. Yusuf managed a weak smile to show that he did not mind being the butt of their jokes.

The Prophet's exhortation to grow a decent-length beard was challenging to Asian Moslems who were not hairy by nature. Of the men, only Ghani had a full beard and he kept it trimmed. Ramzi was clean-shaven. Yusuf and Abu Bakr both had straggly goatees, well short of fist-length except for a few wayward hairs.

Ghani had been adamant that there was

no need to be exacting in adhering to this particular religious stricture. As he had put it, when Abu Bakr had questioned his younger brother's decision to shave, 'The police think that everyone with a long beard is a mad *mullah*. Let us not give them an excuse to look at us twice in these difficult times after the Bali bombings.'

It was going to be a fraught meal, thought Nuri. Ramzi, her younger brother, was on edge. He was picking on Yusuf and her repeatedly, using his sly humour to good effect. Yusuf was visibly agitated. He kept taking off his glasses and cleaning them with the edge of his shirt. He would stare at Ramzi while doing this. His unfocused gaze was unnerving.

Ramzi turned his attention from Yusuf to her. He was complaining loudly about the food, the lamb curry and fried vegetables with steamed rice that Nuri had painstakingly cooked on the small hob in the kitchenette.

'It is too spicy,' he said, sticking out a curling red tongue and fanning it with a curried hand.

Yusuf said stonily, 'I think it is tasty.'

'Nonsense,' said Ramzi. 'We might as well chew on raw chillies. My sister is unskilled in the art of cooking. I have no idea why we brought her along.'

Abu Bakr said, 'Her husband is not complaining. Only he has the right to chastise Nuri.'

Ramzi giggled. 'I would not dream of scolding my dear sister. As she knows, I am just doing my duty as a brother by pointing out her shortcomings – as I *always* do.'

Nuri glanced at her husband to see if he had noticed this pointed criticism of her. Ghani was still eating, shovelling the rice and lamb into his mouth at regular intervals with his right hand. He chewed slowly and methodically, his mouth opening and closing so that all of them could see the gradual process by which the food was broken down into digestible pulp. His forehead was shiny with perspiration. The food really was spicy, thought Nuri, but Ghani was too lost in thought to notice. She felt a moment of profound dislike for her spouse, a visceral disgust for the way he sat stolidly at the head of the table, oblivious to the tension in the room. She remained quiet, determined to ignore Ramzi, serving the men more food when their plates became empty.

Yusuf was staring at her with a half-worried, half-admiring expression on his face. She was tempted to sigh out loud. She had always known that Yusuf, anxious, devout and a complete failure with women, found her attractive. The time spent with her in the small Denpasar apartment had magnified his admiration until it was something very akin to love.

Nuri smiled ruefully, forgetting her annoyance at Ramzi and her husband for a moment. For the first time in her young life, she realised, she was sensitive to the signs of new love, her senses picking up signals like the antennae on the small kitchen table radio in her home in Sulawesi.

She dragged her attention back to the meal, quietly ladling more rice onto Yusuf's plate. Ramzi was still complaining about the food. She felt a sudden crashing wave of anger at her younger brother – doing his best to aggravate her, oblivious or indifferent to her suffering at the disappearance of Abdullah.

Nuri stood up suddenly and left the table. She marched to the bedroom and slammed the door, the sharp crack causing all the men at the table to stare after her in surprise.

Inside the dark dingy room lit with a single lightbulb, Nuri looked into the cracked mirror. A furtive creature, divided in two by the fractured mirror – as if the glass had the ability to reflect the truth in her heart – looked back at her.

Bronwyn stared at the inspector in disbelief. 'You don't mean that, do you?'

Singh didn't answer immediately. Instead

he said, 'Nyoman, what's good to eat around here?'

Nyoman grinned. 'Do you want to go to a *warung* which is very cheap, just a few *rupiah?* On we can go to the Amandari – everything US dollars!'

'What's a *warung?*'

It was Bronwyn who answered. 'A food stall.'

'What sort of food?'

'Maybe like *ikan bakar* or *nasi goreng*,' said Nyoman.

Singh asked Bronwyn, 'You know Bali. Don't you have somewhere to recommend?'

'Asian or Western?'

'Asian, of course,' he said.

Bronwyn said to Nyoman, 'Take us to the Dirty Duck Diner!'

Nyoman nodded enthusiastically.

Singh said suspiciously, 'Doesn't sound very Asian...'

'No worries,' said his Australian counter-part, 'it's the best place to try Ubud's signature dish – duck – first stewed in local spices and then deep fried. Served with steamed rice and Indonesian vegetables.'

Singh did not look convinced.

Bronwyn laughed. 'You look more suspi-cious now than when we met the widow! Do you always radiate such hostility to the recently bereaved?'

Singh said, 'Only when they are my only

link to a murdered man. If she decides to tell us a pack of lies about their time in Bali, we have no practical way of finding out the truth.'

Bronwyn said slowly, 'I suppose they've not been here that long. There isn't the usual network of friends, relatives and workmates to contradict or corroborate what suspects and witnesses choose to tell us...'

'Exactly,' said Singh. 'We're operating in a vacuum.'

Bronwyn was more optimistic. 'The Balinese are inquisitive and observant. More than half the island works in the tourist trade.' She corrected herself. 'Or they did before the bombs anyway. They pass the time between being obsequious to foreign tourists by gossiping about them.'

Singh nodded his great turbaned head thoughtfully. 'You may be right. That young fellow Wayan had a bit to say.' He slapped his knee hard in sudden frustration. 'In fact, do you remember he was about to say something about Crouch's friends when the widow turned up? I wonder whether she was listening somewhere...'

Bronwyn interrupted. 'The expats form cliques very quickly – even your reticent English types probably have a few mates on the island.'

'You may be right – I look forward to asking any newfound friends for the dirt on

Sarah Crouch.'

Bronwyn shook her head emphatically. 'I can tell you once and for all she had nothing to do with it.'

'On what grounds?' asked Singh.

'Women's intuition,' she replied and then burst into laughter at Singh's disgusted expression.

The Dirty Duck met with Singh's approval.

He chewed his way through the flaky duck, drank two bottles of cold Bintang beer and said, 'So where do we go from here?'

'Back to the widow, I guess,' said Bronwyn.

'And we need to bully Wayan.'

'I'll leave that to you,' replied Bronwyn.

'The Bali police should have collected all Richard Crouch's possessions by now. We'll have to go through that.'

Bronwyn was impressed. 'When did you arrange that?'

'I told them to do it last night – but I said to wait somewhere till after we'd broken the news to the widow and then follow us in. I saw two coppers walk in as we got into the car.'

'Why did you want them to wait?'

'In case she made a mad dash to destroy any incriminating evidence. That would have incriminated *her*.'

'This murder stuff is quite complicated,

isn't it?' said Bronwyn, patting her mouth with a napkin.

Singh shook his head. 'No. Actually it's the simplest of crimes. Murder is such an extreme, absolute step that there are only a very few people capable of it. And of those few, an even smaller subsection will ever find themselves in a situation where killing another person seems like the appropriate solution.'

'You really believe that? You don't think that we're all capable of murder given the right circumstances?'

The Singaporean inspector said, 'I'm talking about premeditated murder. In a fit of rage, in self-defence, to protect loved ones – we might all be able to kill a fellow human being. But to plan, to think, to decide in cold blood that murder fits the needs of a given situation best? I believe that very few people could do that.'

'Inspector Singh, I do believe you're a romantic!'

The policeman scowled at the grinning Australian. 'What do you mean?'

'You wander around with a long face hunting murderers but you're convinced of the essential goodness of human nature.'

Singh stood up, dropped a fistful of crumpled *rupiah* on the table – inflation was such that it took a lot of paper money to pay for things in Indonesia – and said curtly,

'Let's get back to the widow.'

The widow of Richard Crouch was composed. She sat primly, like an extra from a Jane Austen television drama, with her knees together and her hands folded on her lap. She had even smoothed her skirt after sitting down to make sure her knees were covered.

She asked, as if it was a social visit or – perhaps on the evidence of the cold formality – a business meeting, 'What can I do for you now?'

'Help us find your husband's murderer!'

'Of course,' she said. 'I'll do everything I can. I'm just not sure what use I can be.'

'Tell us about him,' interjected Bronwyn.

'Richard? There's not an awful lot to tell. He is ... was an only child. His parents are both dead – they died in a car crash a few years back.'

'Was he close to them?'

Sarah looked at Singh in surprise. 'I guess so. I met him for the first time about six months after the accident.'

'And you got married – when?'

'About six months after that – two and a half years ago.'

'A whirlwind romance,' remarked Singh.

She said, 'Looking back, I think maybe he was looking for a family to replace the one he lost.'

'That implies that all was not well with your relationship,' pointed out Singh.

She glared at him, a crack in the ice, swirling cold dark waters underneath. She said, 'We were fine – there were a few issues, there always are. This move to Bali was a way for us to iron out some of our difficulties – get away from it all.'

'Sounds to me like he spent most of the time – before he was killed, that is – getting away from you.'

'That's nonsense!' Her voice was uneven, but it was anger, not sadness, that Singh sensed. Sarah Crouch was trying to keep a tight lid on a resentment that ran very deep. He reminded himself that it did not make her a killer.

'What was the trouble? Another woman?'

'Of course not! Richard worked very hard, that's all. I felt that he was not spending enough time with me.'

'What did he do?' asked Singh. 'For a living, I mean.'

'He was a chemical engineer. He travelled a lot for his work – there was always a project in some far-flung part of the world.'

'It's awful when they do that, isn't it?' said Bronwyn. 'My ex-husband used to be away a lot – it makes it very difficult to sustain a relationship.'

Sarah did not respond to this attempt at solidarity.

111

Bronwyn was trying to forge a bond with the widow. Singh was not sure that, tactically, it was a good idea. Practically, it was a waste of time.

'What was your routine in Bali?' Singh did not plan to change his own approach of being unpleasant. He hoped it would provoke the woman into saying something revealing.

'The usual,' she said. 'We shopped, visited art galleries and temples, went down to the sea, met friends for meals or a drink, tried out the local cuisine.'

Singh became animated. He said, 'You should try that place – the Dirty Duck.'

Sarah said coldly, 'I don't have much of an appetite.'

Singh did not seem to realise that he had been a trifle insensitive. He asked, 'Who were these friends?'

'It's mostly Australians out here, isn't it? It took us a while to meet people...'

Singh could see that Bronwyn was about to ask her what was wrong with Australians.

He said hurriedly, 'I know exactly what you mean about Aussies. They're excruciatingly friendly.'

Sarah responded in an almost affable tone, 'And love telling you about their personal lives.'

Singh stole a glance at Bronwyn and noticed that the tips of her ears were red but that she was focused on the widow's answers. That was good. A competent police officer always knew when to set aside personal feelings to concentrate on the information provided.

Singh asked again, 'So who were these friends of yours?'

'An English couple, the Greenwoods ... and' – she smiled sheepishly – 'an Australian pair, Karri and Tim Yardley.'

Singh made a quick motion with his hand, indicating that Bronwyn should take the details down.

'Were they Richard's friends too?'

The widow hesitated. At last she said, 'Yes, but perhaps more so mine.'

'Did he have friends of his own?'

Sarah Crouch pressed her palms together. Singh noticed that her nails were colourless but well-maintained. He glanced down at his own hands. The nails were too long, the tips dark with grime that matched the fine hair between each joint. He rubbed them against his trousers.

Sarah's nostrils flared slightly, indicating her distaste at what she was going to say. 'Richard was much less particular than I was...'

'You disliked his buddies?'

The widow shrugged non-committally.

'Does that mean that he would go out on his own with them?'

113

She admitted reluctantly, 'Sometimes.'

'Do you have their details?'

'I'm afraid not.'

'But they were Australian?'

'No, that was just my particular prejudice. Richard had made some friends amongst the locals.'

'Really?'

'Yes, most of the times he went out without me, it was on his scooter with the Indonesians.'

'That's quite unusual,' said Bronwyn. 'Very few expats fraternise with the Balinese.'

Sarah said, 'Well – Richard was unusual. He spoke Bahasa Indonesia.'

'How come?'

'He spent a few years in Jakarta with his parents as a teenager. He was always very comfortable with ... with "native" types, if you know what I mean.' She curled the index and middle finger of both hands to indicate inverted commas as she said 'native'.

Singh had never actually seen anyone do that before. He decided he had reached his limit as far as Sarah Crouch's company was concerned.

He said abruptly, 'Be at the police station in Denpasar tomorrow. We will continue this interview then.'

On the way out, Singh stopped at Wayan's desk. There was a young woman manning it and he asked, 'Where's Wayan?'

'He has gone home, sir.'

Where's home?'

Her delicate Balinese features creased worriedly. She asked, 'Why do you need him? I know you are police.'

'Why do you care?' asked Singh.

'He's my brother.'

'Excellent,' remarked Singh. 'Then you can take us to him.'

'I have to work,' she pleaded. 'It is my shift.'

Singh stood his ground, his bulk making him physically intimidating. He gave the impression that he could stand around and wait indefinitely. The receptionist looked terrified.

He said with feigned sympathy, 'I'm sure the boss will understand. As you said – we are the police.'

She rode a small scooter, her long hair streaming behind her. They followed her in Nyoman's Kijang.

Singh asked curiously, 'Why are the Balinese so docile?'

'What do you mean?'

'They seem to cave in to authority immediately.'

'Maybe you frightened the poor kid?'

Singh grinned. 'You could be right – but compare and contrast Sarah Crouch and that young lady. I wouldn't put it past the widow not to turn up tomorrow. That girl' – he nodded at Wayan's sister – 'is prepared to lead the cops straight to her brother.'

'I guess most Balinese rely on some aspect of the tourist trade for a livelihood. Maybe they've learnt the hard way that disagreeing with foreigners could cost them their jobs.'

Singh rubbed his beard between thumb and forefinger thoughtfully. 'It's more than that – it's like an institutional bias in favour of authority.'

'It's a hierarchical society. Historically, the Balinese have been ruled by kings and sultans. And there's quite a strong caste system – the Brahmins dominate the priesthoods. I suppose you could say that they have respect for authority woven into the very fabric of society.'

'That's the way I like it,' said Singh comfortably.

And when Bronwyn did not respond, he added, 'You sure know a lot about Bali!'

Six

Bronwyn realised that despite her purported knowledge of Bali, she had never visited the home of an 'ordinary' Balinese. Her forays had been limited to the temples and the shops.

They were driving through a small village. The road, off the beaten tourist track, was stony and full of potholes. The Kijang rode the surface like a boat on a stormy sea. There were small piles of rubbish, the standard third world fare of plastic bags, bottles and leaves, at regular intervals. Someone had swept the detritus of village life into neat heaps but it had not yet been collected by any garbage collection agency, assuming there was such a thing.

A cowering stray dog with huge distended teats and patchy fur was frantically scratching a flea-ridden ear. Children in bare feet and outsized T-shirts happily played in the dust and sand. Their mothers hung clothes out to dry. Young men hung around in small groups smoking *kreteks*.

Wayan's home was tiny. Despite its humble size, the typical elements of Balinese architecture, red brick and grey cement walls, were visible. The garden was a square lush patch of grass with an altar built at the highest point of a stone pyramid. The small structure at the top, with its thatched straw roof and wooden pillars, reminded Bronwyn of an elaborate birdhouse. Incense was burning and Bronwyn sniffed appreciatively. It tempered the smell of fermented mangoes. A tree next to the house was so laden with golden fruit that much of it had been left to fall to the ground and rot.

Wayan's sister rode her motorbike into the midst of rapidly scattering chickens. She jumped off and ran indoors without a backward glance, scurrying in to warn her brother that she had the police in tow.

Their reception from Wayan was the height of hospitality. He ushered them in and invited them to sit down on an eclectic selection of chairs that appeared to have been pilfered from an assortment of Bali hotels. He disappeared into the kitchen and came back with whole coconuts, a hole neatly knocked in one end.

Bronwyn thanked Wayan, sipped her drink through a straw and wondered when they would turn the visit away from social courtesy to police business.

For some reason that she could not fathom – what about the fat man *did* she comprehend, she wondered – Singh seemed happy to make small talk.

Wayan's sister was perched on a small wooden stool. She rocked back and forth, distrusting the peaceful social scene before her. She had led the police back to her brother. It was unlikely that it had been for a chat about the weather or the health-giving properties of coconut water.

It was Wayan who brought up the reason for their visit. Unable to carry on in the role of unsuspecting host, he asked, 'You want to talk about Mr and Mrs Crouch, yes?'

'Why do you say that?' asked Singh.

Wayan was genuinely surprised. 'But otherwise why would you come to my house?' His raised eyebrows compressed the acne on his forehead.

Singh stopped beating around the bush. He said abruptly, 'Tell us all you know about them.'

'I told you everything already,' protested Wayan.

'You told us they were not happy. What gave you that impression?'

'I don't understand what you mean, *Pak*.'

'How did you know they were not happy?'

Wayan's face lightened. 'If you work in the hotel you always know about guests staying in the villas,' he explained. 'She read the book in the patio, he stay in the room. Or she is in the room and he go out with friends. When they eat together, they not talk. They just look at the food...' Wayan

119

trailed off.

'What is it? What else do you know?' asked Singh sharply.

Wayan looked mischievous. 'They do not sleep in the same bed.'

'How could you know that?'

'Their suite got two rooms, two beds – both are messy in the morning.'

Singh clapped his hands together and said, 'That is good work. You should be a policeman, Wayan.' He continued, glancing over at Bronwyn, 'Not much marital bliss in the Crouch household.'

She replied tartly, 'It doesn't prove that she had anything to do with his death. I just can't picture a scenario where she shot her husband and left the body at the Sari Club.'

Singh sighed. 'It's a bit far-fetched. What if Crouch had a bit on the side and she followed him? She might have done it if she saw them together at the Club?'

'Then why isn't she dead? And where would she have got the gun?'

Singh said, 'We need to get back to Kuta and have a look at the Sari Club – try and get the floor plans. She might have shot him in the bog or in the bushes and had a bit of time to get away.'

He turned to Wayan. 'Did Crouch have a girlfriend?'

Wayan said, 'I do not know, *Pak*.'

'You never saw him with another woman?'

'No, *Pak*.'

'He wouldn't have flaunted a girlfriend around the villa,' pointed out Bronwyn.

Singh rubbed his eyes tiredly. 'That's true, of course. Wayan, you mentioned Crouch had friends – who were they?'

'You mean the white people they used to meet sometimes?'

'No, those people were friendly with Mrs Crouch. She said that he had other Balinese friends that she didn't like.'

'I do not know them. But I have seen them around Ubud.'

This time even Bronwyn sensed that there was something Wayan was holding back.

Singh asked abruptly, 'What was it about Crouch's friends you didn't like, Wayan?'

He stared down at his feet. 'Why should I not like them?'

'That's what we're wondering.'

'It is nothing, *Pak*,' Wayan said reluctantly. 'Only his friends were *not* Balinese.'

'Not Balinese?' Singh was surprised. 'But I thought both you and the wife agreed that Richard Crouch didn't hang around with expats that much?'

'That's right,' agreed Wayan.

'Then what *do* you mean?' Singh was fed up.

Bronwyn suppressed a grin. The Balinese could smile and talk and appear to co-operate without actually saying anything if

121

they set their minds to it.

'His friends were Indonesian, but not Balinese. They were mostly Javanese, I think.'

Bronwyn, unlike Singh, understood immediately. She told the inspector, 'There's a lot of resentment amongst the Balinese about the influx of Moslem Indonesians from the rest of the country. The Balinese are extremely protective of their Hindu ancestry and culture.'

'Is that so, Wayan?' asked Singh. 'Do you dislike the newcomers?'

Wayan was embarrassed but defiant. 'They take jobs from Balinese, sir. They work in construction and they run *warungs*. Also, they are all Moslem and we Balinese are Hindu. It is very important that we are a Hindu island – if too many Moslems come, there will be more mosques than temples!'

There was a silence as Singh and Bronwyn digested the information.

Wayan added defensively, 'And now you see what the Moslems have done to Bali? It is they who do the bombings. Now all of Bali suffers.'

'I want a divorce.'

'What?'

'You heard me...'

Tim Yardley watched his wife carefully. She seemed genuinely shocked, her finely plucked eyebrows, redrawn with a dark pencil, were arched. The pupils of her grey-green eyes had grown large in the evening light.

'I don't believe you – you're just upset.'

Tim sighed. He had been reluctant to take this step without consulting Sarah Crouch. But it had been impossible to reach her. She was lost in an emotional maze of her own. And he could not help her, be there for her, until he was free of this woman staring at him, an expression of bemusement on her face. His gaze was drawn to the streaks of white across the orange sky, jets flying over and leaving their poisonous trail. The setting sun was behind a huge embankment of cumulus clouds but golden rays were pouring through the gaps like a benediction. Tim felt confident of his decision. He would not change his mind.

'Stop staring into the distance and tell me what this is about!'

He turned back to Karri, noting the long-suffering tone she had adopted. She was still not taking him seriously, convinced that this was some minor rebellion that would soon recede.

'I want a divorce because I can't carry on like this – you treat me like dirt, you sleep with other men. You've destroyed our marriage – almost destroyed me. I want ... I need a last chance to look for some happiness.'

He saw that he had annoyed her. The

scarlet tips of her long fingers were pressed together as she tried to keep her temper.

When she spoke, her tone was scornful. 'What is this – some sort of mid-life crisis? You don't have the courage to make it on your own. That's the only reason you've hung around making a fool of yourself – letting me make a fool of you – all these years.'

Tim was stung into a response. He said, 'Maybe I won't have to make it on my own!'

Karri laughed, a genuine guffaw of amusement at the idea that her overweight spouse with his careful comb-over would have a substitute in the wings.

Her husband came to the painful realisation that he actually hated the woman standing a couple of feet away from him on a dusty Bali street. The gulf between them was a chasm with his shattered hopes and dreams scattered across the bottom.

He said again, trying to inject firmness into his voice, make her understand that he meant what he was saying, 'I want a divorce.'

Legian Road had reopened to pedestrian traffic.

Singh and Bronwyn walked down the narrow street. It was late evening and they had just returned from Ubud. It was Bronwyn who had suggested they make a detour to the bomb site. They stared at the destruction in shock – even the usually garrulous policewoman was stunned into silence. Buildings up and down the Street had had their windows blown out. All that were left were jagged shards of glass forming the sharp teeth around square open jaws. There were burnt-out vehicle wrecks along the road.

The debris-strewn thoroughfare was lined with pieces of white cloth on which people – passers-by, relatives of the dead, Balinese mourners and tourists – had left messages. There were flowers and wreaths, some old, some freshly laid, their bright colours discordant against the blackened background. As the two approached the site, the piles of flowers grew higher until there were small mountains of blossoms commemorating the dead.

In the immediate vicinity of the bombs, there were photos of victims stuck to makeshift memorial pillars. Some had been placed there as tokens of remembrance, but many were frantic entreaties from relatives asking if anyone knew the whereabouts of the persons in the photo – they had been missing since the bombings.

As they reached the entrance of what had once been the Sari Club, opposite the road from Paddy's Bar, they could see the huge bomb crater, a few feet deep, right in front of what was left of the building – heaps of rubble, a few concrete stumps and melted, twisted metal pieces. It was impossible to guess the provenance of the metal without expert forensic help.

The policemen toting machine guns in front of the shell of the Sari Club were unimpressed with their identity cards. It was only when a senior AFP member walked past and was hailed by Bronwyn that the guards were persuaded to let them in.

'Just make sure you don't touch or take anything,' said the AFP man.

'Of course not,' said Singh. 'But haven't you finished the site examination?'

'Yes, but there's so much information to sift through – so many samples to examine. We're just concerned that we might have to scrape up more evidence with a teaspoon if they find anything odd.'

Singh nodded. Looking around at the destruction, it was impossible to know where the clues, if any, could be hiding.

'Do you know how it happened?' asked Singh, his voice subdued.

'As far as we can piece together,' the AFP officer told them, 'a suicide bomber detonated a bomb inside Paddy's Bar. As the crowds ran down the street, a van drew up in front of the Sari Club. The vehicle exploded. It killed visitors to the Club – and some of those escaping the chaos at Paddy's.'

Singh was standing at the edge of the crater, peering in.

He said, 'There wasn't much left of Richard Crouch. He must have been pretty close to the eye of the storm. Anyone around him could've been killed too.'

Bronwyn asked, raising one eyebrow, 'That means the killer was likely one of the victims?'

'It's quite possible. But we should keep sniffing around.'

'Do you know what this place was like before the blasts?' asked Singh, turning to the other policeman.

'More or less,' said the AFP man, who had been listening to their conversation with interest. 'The Sari Club was a sort of open-plan outdoor club. It had thatched-roof bars with high walls around it.'

Singh said, 'That explains why there's nothing left.'

The AFP man added, 'People who survived were towards the back or behind some sort of structure that took the brunt of the blast. The bomb was so big that the shock wave alone would have killed anyone in the vicinity.'

Singh tried to imagine the Sari Club on the night of the bombing. Crowded with backpackers, surfers and rugby players – all dancing and swigging from their bottles of Bintang – the heavy beat of the music punctuating the sounds of revelry. The lighting would have been subdued on the fringes. There would have been dark corners, areas that were in the shadows. The dance floor by contrast would have been lit with colourful, moving disco strobe lights. The noise would have drowned out conversation, perhaps even a gunshot.

All that and then the explosion. Singh had read that, for many in the Sari Club that night, the blasts were followed by a complete unnerving silence because their eardrums had been damaged by the force of the explosion. The electricity grid had failed and the lights across Kuta had gone out. For the victims, it had been a silent darkness lit only by the raging fires.

Singh asked, his voice suddenly husky with doubt, 'Do you feel that what we're doing, looking for the murderer of one man in the midst of this ... this horror, is a waste of time?'

Bronwyn shook her head reassuringly. 'Of course not. Richard Crouch deserves justice too.'

Nuri lay on her side, feigning sleep. She pulled the thin blanket over her shoulders and curled into a foetal position on the narrow sagging bed. Her eyes were squeezed shut but she could picture the bedroom. Small, with flaking white paint, faded patterned curtains and a brown damp water stain on one wall. A pipe had burst and the water was seeping through the brick and paint. Ghani complained often that the damp in the bedroom made his bones ache. It reminded her of how much older he was than her, suffering the pains of late middle age.

She had half-expected Ghani to follow her into the bedroom. She knew that many husbands would have demanded an explanation for her flash of temper that lunch time. But not Ghani. He was such an unassuming, undemanding man for a respected village elder, well known both for his piety and Islamic scholarship.

And he had picked her, Nuri, to be his wife from all the village girls. She had been so grateful and happy – although surprised to be his first wife. She would have been content to be one of the four wives he was permitted as a Moslem.

Abu Bakr had explained that Ghani had not had time to settle down previously. He had continued, 'Your marriage to Ghani will forge a bond between our families. It is important that the ties of friendship be strengthened by this marriage.' There had been pride in her older brother's voice when he said, 'You have done well, sister.'

Provoked by her younger brother, she had walked away from the dining table. It was her first act of rebellion. She wondered again whether she would get into trouble. Her entire fate was bound up with that of Ghani. He need only say 'I divorce thee' three times and she would be out in the street. She would have no means of survival. Her parents would be too ashamed to take her back. Without an education, except in the Quran, she was ill-equipped to get a job.

She listened hard. It sounded, from the clattering outside, as if someone was washing the dishes in her place. No prizes for guessing who it would be. Only Yusuf would think to protect her by doing her chores.

Nuri buried her face in the pillow, hardly noticing its rancid odour. She was determined not to cry. What in the world would Ghani think if he came in and she was in tears?

But the overwhelming sense of loss she felt was too much – tears, round and full and glistening like pearls, welled up past her tightly closed eyelids and dripped on the pillow, leaving a spreading damp patch under her cheek.

She was so terribly ashamed. She knew – who better? – her obligations to her husband. She had been taught over and over again that Allah did not look kindly on those who failed in their duties. Nuri rubbed her eyes with her knuckles like a small child.

In her heart, she knew very well that her tears were not for her failures and short-comings. She was weeping – great racking sobs now – for Abdullah, a man who had left her with all the world of promise in his eyes and then never returned.

Emily Greenwood picked up a mug of black coffee and gulped some down.

Julian had noticed that the long boozy lunches usually caught up with his wife by late evening. He would almost have felt sorry for her if concerns for his own well-being were not uppermost in his mind.

His wife placed the mug carefully on the handmade beaded coaster on the polished table. The wood was old teak, recovered from railway sleepers, its history worn into the rich smooth surface. Even in her tired state, thought Julian, she was careful of her expensive possessions, determined not to mark the wood with a burnt ring from a hot mug.

Emily was heavy-eyed, dark shadows forming crescents of contrast to her pale skin. She stayed out of the sun despite living in Bali. She said the heat made her un-comfortable. Julian was not surprised. He had seen his wife turn slick, the sun reflect-ing off her damp arms like carlights on a rain-soaked road, after the short walk from her air-conditioned chauffeur-driven car to

131

their luxury villa on the beach.

Julian took a deep breath. He leaned across and took one of Emily's hands in his. The palms were warm and moist. It reminded him of the perfumed towelettes provided on airlines.

He said, remembering to adjust his tone – Emily did not like to be reminded that she had married beneath her – 'Darling, I need a bit of help.'

Her eyes, fringed by light, almost invisible lashes – the mascara had worn off after a long day – narrowed and she pulled her hand away. A small gesture of rejection that Julian knew meant trouble.

He had no choice but to proceed. He was running out of time and excuses. He laughed a little, sounding strained even to his own ears. He reached for her hand again and she tugged against him. For a moment, they indulged in an unseemly juvenile tug of war. Julian let go.

He continued, trying to adopt a casual reassuring tone, 'Nothing too serious.'

Emily demanded, 'How much?'

Julian felt his face flush. He chewed on the end of his drooping moustache. His prominent Adam's apple bobbed merrily as he swallowed hard. He could not believe this woman. She had more money than she could spend in three lifetimes but she was as miserly as a village moneylender sitting cross-legged under a banyan tree.

He said, 'Two million *rupiah*.'

'Cockfighting?'

He nodded sullenly. 'It was a sure thing but the bird wouldn't fight. I think it might have been a fix.'

Emily started to giggle. Tears streamed down her cheeks. She said, 'It was "fowl" play!' She was shaking with laughter, her double chin dancing with delight.

Julian's nails dug into his palms. He thought he might draw blood. He knew that he had to stay calm, stay cool. He tried to laugh along with his wife but it was too difficult. He turned his attempt into a dry cough and then curved his lips in an effort to simulate good humour.

Emily stopped laughing as suddenly as she had begun. She dabbed her eyes and wiped her cheeks with a small silk handkerchief she extracted from her clutch purse.

She said, her tone unyielding, 'I won't lend you money.'

'It's such a small sum, dear. I'll pay you back. I just need it to tide me over this rough patch. It won't happen again, I promise.' He forced a chuckle. 'I think I've learnt my lesson, love.'

She looked at him. Her round, pretty face was expressionless. She said, 'I am your *wife*, not your banker of last resort.'

Seven

Richard Crouch's possessions were profoundly uninteresting, thought Singh. He was going through the plastic bags of stuff the Bali police had confiscated from the widow. There were a few pairs of dark slacks, a number of smart plain T-shirts and neatly folded boxer shorts. The policeman wondered who had kept the clothes in such pristine order. Was it Crouch or his wife? From what little he had heard about their relationship, he could not picture Sarah Crouch lovingly folding her husband's underpants.

Bronwyn looked up from where she was thumbing through the dead man's passport and said, 'I bet he was killed outside the Sari Club, maybe on the street.'

'Why do you say that?' asked Singh, refolding Crouch's underwear with careful attention to the earlier fold lines.

'He wasn't a man who knew how to have fun. I doubt he would have been at one of the hippest clubs in Kuta.'

This time Singh glanced up. His interest was caught. When Bronwyn did not embellish further, he said, 'Well, go on – how do you know he didn't know how to have fun – aside from the evidence of his choice of spouse.'

Bronwyn wrinkled her small nose. 'I don't know why you have it in for that woman.'

Singh waited for her to continue and she gestured at Richard Crouch's possessions. 'What sort of collection is that? Where are the swimmers, the surfer T-shirts, the sandals and the sunscreen? He looks like he packed for an engineers' conference in Singapore! And there isn't a single souvenir.'

Singh realised she was right. It was a pathetic effort by Crouch to equip himself for a Bali lifestyle. He stared down at the contents. There was a certain familiarity about them and he couldn't quite put his finger on it. He wondered if it was a clue he was missing. He hated investigations that were outside his natural turf in Singapore. He could never be sure if any discordant note he picked up was his nose for crime operating at its best or the unfamiliar surroundings leaving him feeling uneasy without any cause that was relevant to the investigation.

He rifled through the T-shirts. Simple, plain, cotton, of good quality but not branded. They weren't even the fake designer tops that were available at the tourist haunts in Bali.

It came to him suddenly.

Richard Crouch's belongings were familiar because the well-ordered, dull contents reminded him of his *own* suitcase back at the hotel. Bronwyn's observation that there were no swimming shorts, surfer T-shirts, sandals or sunscreen applied equally to his packing. To be fair, he had been sent out to assist the Balinese police on terrorist prevention methods. He had not arrived on the tropical island to adopt the lifestyle of the Bali expats and tourists. Also, he preferred long-sleeved shirts to T-shirts.

Singh pictured himself in a pair of floral beach Bermudas and open sandals, exposed belly hanging over the elastic waist band, turban intact and hairy chest collecting sand. He laughed out loud. He would be competing for attention with the thong-wearing tourist.

Bronwyn looked up and grinned. 'What's so funny?'

Singh shook his head. It was a mental picture best kept entirely private. Instead, he asked, 'Anything in the passport?'

It was one of those extra-thick documents that the well-travelled could request in exchange for paying an extra fee if their passport was unlikely to last until its expiry date otherwise. The gold crest on the front of the reddish-maroon book was worn out and almost invisible.

Singh flicked it open. The familiar Indonesian passport control stamp, green with the words 'Ngurah Rai', the name of the Bali airport, was marked within. He turned the pages of the passport slowly. It was a tour of Third World countries. Sarah had not been kidding when she said that Richard Crouch travelled a lot. And apparently on these trips to South America, India, Pakistan and Indonesia, he had been happy fraternising with the locals, rejecting the traditional overseas experience of living in expat ghettos and avoiding the natives except as being handy to do the cooking and gardening.

'So, what do you think?' Bronwyn stood up and stretched. The bones clicking in her shoulders were audible.

'Nothing stands out as being particularly interesting. Do chemical engineers have work-related enemies?'

'Who might hunt them all the way to Bali? Seems unlikely!'

'We need more suspects,' said Singh. 'Tomorrow, we're going to track down these so-called friends, his *and* hers. Richard Crouch lived in Bali for six months. In that time, he made an enemy who was willing to look him in the eye and shoot him in the middle of the forehead at close range. I intend to find out who that was.'

The inspector from Singapore opened the passport to the photo of Richard Crouch.

Bronwyn took it from him and gazed

down at the likeness of the dead man. She said, 'He looks like such an unassuming young man ... it's hard to imagine that anyone hated him that much.'

Agus did not expect to be spotted by his quarry. In plain clothes, he did not look like a policeman. His hair was a bit shorter than the average but the residents of Bali were a well-kempt lot. It did not mark him out too much.

He had been told by that fat policeman from Singapore to watch this woman if she left the villa, to follow her unobtrusively and see if she spoke to or met anyone. He had no idea why he was taking instructions from a foreign cop. But he was too low down the food chain to ask questions of his superiors. Besides, Agus liked the idea of tailing someone. It was the kind of work he had signed up for when he joined the police force. Instead, he had found himself directing traffic at one of the busy intersections in Kuta or Denpasar. That was a thankless task. No one paid much attention to him as he stood at junctions blowing his whistle frantically and waving his arms like windmills. Directing Balinese traffic was like herding cats.

Agus had been devastated like everyone else by the Bali bombs but a small part of him hoped that there would be a role in the investigation for him. After all, it was the worst act of terrorism in Indonesian history. Surely they would need every cop they could lay their hands on?

But he had been left on his traffic detail with additional instructions to look out for any suspicious-looking characters or vehicles, and *especially* suspicious-looking characters driving vehicles. They feared another car bomb. He had done his dogged best. He stopped closed vans and insisted he be allowed to look in the back. He randomly flagged down cars and peered into the rucksacks of men on motorcycles. Considering how little traffic there was on the road with so many of the tourists having left, he had done a good job of snarling up traffic in central Denpasar. Needless to say, it had been a futile effort. It would take a huge amount of luck to spot the right vehicle at the right moment. It did not seem to Agus that Bali was a lucky place any more.

But now he had been given a real job to do. He had no idea who this woman was or why he had been told to follow her, but he would do his job. She was white and thin, with a puckered mouth and yellow hair tossed about in swirling gusts. Agus was not one of those Balinese men who fancied Caucasian women. Many did. Female tourists with their tans, blonde hair and sense of natural

139

superiority appealed to quite a few of the young Balinese hotel employees and beach-combers. The reverse was true as well. If Balinese men found the independence and assertiveness of Western women attractive, white men were often captivated by the gentle beauty and quiet manner of Balinese women. It was not healthy, thought the policeman. It was an attraction of opposites. But neither side had any real knowledge or understanding of the culture of the other. It was a superficial appeal, good for a holiday romance, but without substance.

It would never do for him. Agus was a serious young man. His wife was from the same village as him.

His attention was drawn back to his prey. Her taxi pulled up outside a guest house. It was a run-down building about a hundred yards away from the Kuta coastline and on the opposite side of the road to the beach. It was the sort of place that surfers on a tight budget would stay at as they experimented on Kuta's gentle beach break.

The woman got out of the taxi and walked quickly to the guest house. She asked an employee a question – the policeman was too far away to hear what it was. The doorman pointed in the direction she had come and said something, a smile accompanying his words.

The policeman dropped to his knees and

tied his shoe lace as she walked past. She did not even glance down at him. He suspected she would have not bothered to look his way even if he had been standing directly in her path. She was probably one of those women who were unable to distinguish between the local Balinese. To her, they were all slight, brown men with dark hair and friendly smiles, waiting to be of service. The policeman tried to control his sudden burst of irritation at the hordes of tourists who had made Bali their holiday destination of choice without having the courtesy to acknowledge her residents. Then he remembered the bombings. He might be resentful of these foreigners, but they were the livelihood of his people.

The woman was waiting to cross the busy road that separated the guest house from the seaside. She made a dash for it, causing a motorbike to swerve dangerously. Brushing away the hair that was clinging to her forehead in the humidity, she hurried towards the beach.

The policeman sauntered after her. He watched her look up and down the coast. The person she was looking for wasn't there. Her shoulders slumped but she continued scanning the horizon.

Suddenly, she hurried to the water's edge.

A surfer was riding the waves. The swells were not huge but the young man was cruising the white tops with casual elegance, angling towards the shore. As he got closer, the woman waved her arms and shouted something. The wind snatched her words and scattered them across the beach. His trajectory took him past where she was waiting impatiently. He hopped off his colourful, fibreglass board into knee-deep water fifty yards down the coast from where she was standing.

The woman hurried towards the surfer and this time the policeman could hear her. She was shouting, 'Greg! Greg, it's me.'

At last, the surfer heard his name. Agus, that much closer, saw him grimace slightly. As she approached, he smothered the expression in a wide smile and waved in response. When they reached each other, both paused for an instant. The woman flung her arms around the man's waist and put her head against his bare chest. The surfer hesitated for an instant, made up his mind, and wrapped dripping wet golden arms around her.

She said, 'They found him, Greg. They found the body.'

'Where?'

'The Sari Club.'

'Poor bastard,' said the tall young man with easy sympathy.

The policeman noted that his blond hair was bleached almost white by the sun and

142

glowed like a halo around his head. His dark, smooth, tanned chest made a sharp contrast to the pale white face of the woman.

Sarah Crouch said, 'What's important is that *we* can be together now.'

Singh, gazing around the table, decided that he had rarely seen such a motley crew.

Individually, they were ordinary, some even good-looking. Julian Greenwood reminded him of one of those actors always asked to play the lord of the manor in period television dramas. His wife, Emily, had a self-satisfied air, like a well-fed pedigree feline.

The Yardleys were less prepossessing. Tim looked like a million other overweight middle-aged men with thinning hair and an air of quiet desperation. His wife was a strange one with burnt leather skin and a wiry strength. Karri's hair reminded Singh of a nest made by a careless bird, twigs and straw sticking out at all angles.

He would not have given any of them a second glance on a Bali street, or even on a Singapore street. They were typical of slightly dissipated expatriates. Singh imagined that they had read Kipling in school and when the opportunity arose, come out to Asia in order to enjoy the superiority of 'whiteness' – the unspoken assumption amongst most Asians that anyone white-skinned was that much more likely to be wealthy, educated and related to Hollywood stars. The inspector from Singapore was surprised to find that he resented the two men and two women sitting in a semi-circle across from him like a panel of gameshow contestants. He found their aggressive sullenness aggravating. He did not need to be a student of human nature to realise that they looked down on him as a 'native', as Sarah Crouch might have said.

Greenwood interrupted his reverie. He said bitingly, 'I thought you said you had some questions for us?'

Singh grinned at him. Julian did not know it but the Sikh policeman was grateful to be reminded that he had a job to do – this was not the time for cultural generalisations, it was the time for the investigation of individuals.

Besides, if he was in luck, one of these losers would turn out to be a murderer.

Greenwood continued, 'What's this all about anyway?'

Singh snapped, 'Richard Crouch!'

He noted that everyone stared at him with real interest – everyone that is except Tim Yardley who did not glance up at the announcement. Singh filed away his reaction, or lack thereof for later consideration.

'What about him? Have you found him?

Where is he?' The questions were coming thick and fast, from everyone except Yardley.

'Yes, we've found him...'

Greenwood leaned forward, his long nose quivering with irritation at the absence of detail. 'Well then? Tell us! Where is he?'

'I should have said we've found what's *left* of him.'

It took a moment to sink in. Singh watched as the implication of his words registered. Both women, so different in appearance, reacted the same way. They covered their mouths with shocked hands.

Tim Yardley looked up – he met Singh's eyes briefly and then dropped his gaze to the table top again. Singh noticed that his fingernails had been chewed to the quick.

It was the other man who breathed, 'Bali bombs? Sari Club?'

Singh nodded his head, his turban bobbing up and down like an exclamation mark.

'Poor bastard,' muttered Karri.

Singh realised that she both disliked Richard Crouch and felt sorry for his fate.

Emily spoke, and her unspoken assumption that her words had authority was compelling. She said calmly, 'That does not explain why you've asked us here.'

Singh did not answer the implied question. He was not in the habit of subjecting himself to cross-examination by suspects or witnesses. Truth be told, he thoroughly enjoyed annoying interviewees by ignoring their queries and revealing what he knew with all the slow cunning of a card player.

It was Tim's turn to butt in. He blustered, 'Emily's right! Why've you demanded to see us?'

Singh asked, his tone conversational, 'So how did you become friendly with Crouch?'

'Why do you want to know?' It was Emily again.

Singh said brusquely, 'I'm asking the questions.'

There was a sudden silence as the two men and two women adjusted to the change in tone.

Tim Yardley was conciliatory, immediately succumbing to the air of authority. Singh thought rather sadly that Yardley was undoubtedly one of those children who had been bullied at school. Still, it was useful in the context of a murder investigation to have someone who would always try and ingratiate himself with the strongest personality in the room.

'We met at a restaurant in Kuta ... and we became friends. Although, to be frank, we were probably more acquainted with Sarah than Richard.'

Singh was silent, inviting further confidences. They were immediately forthcoming. Yardley was garrulous – filling the threatening empty spaces with words.

'There was some dispute about the bill – the Balinese were trying to pull a fast one – you know what they're like...'

Singh sensed Bronwyn stir beside him and hoped that she would have the sense not to interrupt Yardley in defence of Balinese integrity.

'Go on!' he barked.

'Sarah was making a fuss about being overcharged. Richard didn't seem to care that much. She sort of asked us – we were having dinner at another table – whether we thought the bill was reasonable...' He trailed off.

Julian took up the tale. 'We started talking – in the end they walked out without paying. We made a plan to meet up at an Indian restaurant in Sanur that Emily and I recommended ... I guess we just started to spend time together after that.'

This time Singh was not quick enough to prevent Bronwyn leaping in. She said, her tone brittle, 'So what you're saying is that a bunch of expats ganged up to cheat some poor Balinese restaurateur – and that you were so self-satisfied with what you'd done that you became friends?'

She was being facetious but Singh sensed that there was an element of truth in her characterization. He was familiar with the same attitudes in Singapore. He had overheard expatriate wives complain of the poor service in Singapore restaurants and service stations, conveniently forgetting the surly student waiters in London or the self-service petrol stations in Sydney. It was important to a sense of belonging as an expat to be able to bitch about the locals, he realised, and friendships really *were* formed on such weak foundations.

'How often did you meet up?' he asked.

Julian said, 'About once a week...'

Singh nodded. He said, 'You knew him well then. Excellent! Perhaps one of you could tell me who killed him?'

The widow of the murdered man was in the hotel restaurant, sipping a cocktail. She had chosen one of those tropical concoctions with pineapple juice and dark rum. A small pink umbrella was stabbed through the heart of a cherry floating on the surface.

Wayan, the front desk operator, hurried over to her. He had a sheaf of notepaper in his hand. He held it out respectfully. *'Ibu,* there were a few calls for you while you were out.' She took the notes – the calls were from Tim Yardley. He was becoming a real nuisance. She regretted her interaction with him, but she had been desperate, ready to seize any opportunity, however tenuous, to win her freedom from her husband.

Sarah did not regret the death of her

148

husband. She felt sorry for him, but it was the distant pity of a stranger reading a sad tale in a newspaper or watching a tragedy unfolding on television. She felt none of the gut-wrenching immediacy of a loss of family. The discovery of the body had shocked her, but in some ways it had also come as a relief. It had, after all, never been very plausible that her husband had done a runner. Not Richard, who occupied the moral high ground as if he paid the mortgage on it.

Richard's death meant that she could spend every spare moment with Greg Howard. The thought of Greg – easygoing, lighthearted, always willing to squeeze every drop of joy out of a day – smoothed the lines on her face like an iron running over starched cotton. It was amazing to think they could be together now. She knew quite well that Greg did not feel as strongly about her as she did him. That did not bother her. Now that she had her freedom and some ready cash, she would have no trouble keeping the surfer by her side. Sarah realised with a start that she was happy. A small contented smile played about her lips. She struggled to control the expression spreading across her face like a radiant Balinese sunrise. She needed to keep her emotions in check. It would not do for word to get to the Sikh policeman from Singapore and his large Australian counterpart that she was not at all devastated by the loss of her husband. Singh was quite likely to leap to all sorts of tiresome conclusions. Her thoughts turned unerringly to Greg again. This time she could not prevent her lips curving like a plucked bow. When she looked up, Wayan was staring at her, an expression of genuine consternation on his face.

A gust of wind cast the paper napkins into the air like miniature untethered kites. Only Karri had the presence of mind to grab her serviette. The rest of them were staring at Singh with flabbergasted expressions. All, that is, except for Tim, who was still absorbed by the red tablecloth.

Like Singh earlier, Bronwyn wondered at his response. He did not appear surprised by the question. Was he forewarned? And, if so, by whom? Had there been a leak of information or was there a more sinister explanation? Try as she could, Bronwyn found it difficult to imagine circumstances where a man like Tim Yardley would be driven to kill someone.

Perhaps, she speculated idly, Richard Crouch had been having an affair with Karri and Tim had killed him in a fit of jealous rage? Bronwyn had to work hard to prevent herself from grinning at the absurdity of her hypothesis. It seemed highly unlikely that the dead man, whose suitcase had indicated a rigid, well-organised conservative disposition, should have been in a relationship with the highly-coloured woman still gripping her napkin as if it were an unwitting prey.

The silence at the table was oppressive. Bronwyn watched Singh. He was carefully picking a nail, trying with all the concentration in the world to extricate a bit of dirt. She wondered why he was not watching the men and women. Surely it was important to gauge their reactions? She supposed she just did not understand murder investigations – or, more likely, she did not understand the Sikh policeman's methods.

She would have to follow her own instincts. It was impossible to anticipate or imitate the inspector from Singapore. Bronwyn stared at the two couples. She would put money on Emily Greenwood speaking first. She seemed the most confident. Her expression, the shock having cleared her mind of the befuddlement of alcohol, was thoughtful, not frightened.

On cue, Emily asked, her matter-of-fact tone at odds with the angry words, 'What in the world are you talking about?'

'I want to know who shot Richard Crouch!' Singh's tone was cheerfully conversational.

'Shot?'

'Yes, you know' – Bronwyn was aghast to see him cock his fingers like a child imitating a gun, pointing his index finger at his own forehead and curling his middle finger to indicate a trigger being pulled – 'shot!'

If Emily was taken aback by his crudeness, she did not show it. Instead, she said, 'I thought he was at the Sari Club?'

Singh scowled, his brow wrinkling like a cheap rug.

Bronwyn guessed he was annoyed at being reminded of the unlikely physical nexus between his murder probe and the Bali bombings.

The Sikh policeman snapped, 'Shot first!'

Emily took it upon her plump freckled shoulders to speak for all of them. 'Well, it had nothing to do with us!'

Eight

'No sign of them?'

Bronwyn shook her head. She said tentatively, 'It's not even certain that Crouch's friends were Javanese.'

'What do you mean?' growled Singh.

'Wayan said they were Moslems from Java, but they could just as easily have been from Lombok or Sulawesi or Sumatra. There are hundreds of islands in Indonesia. Bali is the *only* bit which is not predominantly Moslem.'

Singh ground his tobacco-stained teeth in frustration. He was quite certain it would be impossible to piece together Richard Crouch's Bali life without these so-called friends of his. And murders were not solved when crucial witnesses went walkabout.

Wayan had been hopeless. He had not been able to give them a description that would distinguish these men from the Balinese, let alone other workers from the Indonesian archipelago.

Singh had insisted that Wayan be driven around Ubud – especially to construction sites and areas where the workers from Java and the rest of Indonesia were known to congregate. But he had been unable to spot the men. Worse, he had explained nervously, he was not sure he would recognise them even if he did see them.

'They were just men, *Pak*,' he said plaintively. 'One was quite old with a beard, one was a bit younger and quite handsome – but I did not look at them so carefully.'

Singh stared at the men smoking clove cigarettes under a rain tree at the entrance to the Monkey Forest. He could see an older man with a beard, most of the others were young and a few might have been described as handsome.

'You're going to have to do better than that, Wayan – if we are to find these people.'

Wayan said miserably, 'But maybe they went back to Java. A lot of people have gone – not just tourists.'

Singh knew it was a real possibility that the men had left Bali. There was not much work left on the island. He cracked his knuckles. 'I need to know what Crouch was up to in those days leading up to his death!'

'We've heard from the widow,' pointed out Bronwyn.

'To rely on Sarah Crouch as the only source of information is a complete waste of time,' insisted the inspector.

As the only viable suspect, everything Sarah Crouch asserted had to be treated with a degree of scepticism that suited

Singh's temperament but did not get him any closer to solving the murder.

'Besides,' he continued, 'she wasn't spending much time with the dearly departed.'

Wayan, who had been sitting on the kerb looking glum, suddenly brightened up. He said, 'There is one thing, *Pak*.'

Singh gazed at him hopefully. 'You've remembered that one of them had a third eye?'

Wayan got to his feet looking bewildered. 'No, *Pak*. I would not forget such a thing.'

Singh, regretting his attempt at sarcasm, asked, 'So what do you remember?'

'They had a motorbike!'

'I know that,' said Singh, feeling his head begin to throb.

'It was a new bike with a big engine – and it was red.'

Singh looked around at the rows of motorcycles parked along the street. They were mostly grimy and sober–coloured, black or grey, with small engines.

He clapped a beaming Wayan on the back, causing the thin young man to take two hurried steps forward to regain his balance. 'You know – that might actually be useful!'

The men were out. Abu Bakr and Yusuf had gone off together. Her husband had left shortly after.

Ramzi had revved his bike and disappeared in a cloud of Bali dust. His last words to her, as he had glanced around the messy flat in disgust, had been, 'I hope you will *finally* remember your womanly duties and clean up this mess!'

Nuri tried watching television. They had arrested one of the Bali bombers. Amrozi was in his house in Solo in Java when the Indonesian police tracked him down. He did not deny his role in the bombings. He seemed delighted to have a chance to boast about it as he was led away in handcuffs. It was reported that a policeman had found a serial number under a soldered piece of metal. The police had traced the van.

Nuri switched off the television in disgust. She had no interest in the investigation into the bombings.

She considered stripping the beds and finding a launderette for the sheets. But she was bone weary – a tiredness born not of physical activity but of the sheer weight of mental fatigue and worry.

Where was he, this man whom she had known so briefly and loved so intensely?

She tried to remember if Abdullah had said anything, hinted at anything that might explain his disappearance. She could think of nothing. They had spent so little time together. She could recall all their conversations verbatim – the courtesy, followed by warmth and then a realisation of love. It had dawned on them, if not simultaneously, then close enough in time that there had been none of that awkwardness of mismatched emotions. It had been brief and perfect.

She wondered if, sheltered her whole life, married to a man much older than her, she was reading too much into the experience. Maybe, as her parents had warned her, men were not to be trusted, they were too weak to resist temptation. That was why, they had explained, it was the duty of good Moslem women to remain covered from head to toe, to eschew make-up and to behave with circumspection and modesty so as not to tempt men into feelings of misplaced lust or desire.

There had never been much talk of love in her home. Between individuals, the language was of duty and responsibility – and piety. Nuri had absorbed the lessons well. She had never stopped to wonder if her husband loved her. She had never asked herself if she loved him. If she was honest, as she was now, in these long empty days and nights, she respected Ghani – chiefly because of his efforts on behalf of oppressed Moslems. She had some affection for him. He no doubt felt some for her – he had married her after all – and there had been a measure of choice in his decision. But love? Until this visit to Bali, she had never known what it meant to feel a heart literally jump with joy, to meet someone's eyes fleetingly and feel as if they had kissed, to feel the desperation of separation.

Yet, here she was, alone in a filthy apartment in Bali. The man she planned to live her life with had left without saying goodbye. It was too much to take in. Had she been such a fool?

Nuri felt a burst of energy. She would go looking for him again. She had wandered the streets for days on various pretexts – looking for *halal* meat, shopping for essentials, stocking up on cleaning goods – and there had been moments when she had completely forgotten why she had set out and been almost caught out by returning empty-handed.

She remembered that the day after the bombings, when it first became apparent that Abdullah was not coming back as he had promised, she had served the men chicken she had bought from a non-Moslem vendor down the road. Ghani would divorce her if he found out. Well, what he didn't know couldn't hurt him. Theirs seemed to be a vengeful God, but Nuri presumed that some element of informed consent was necessary before transgressions were punished. *She* would be the one to feel the wrath of God. Nuri realised, with some surprise, that she didn't give a damn.

She would go out and see whether she could find some sign of her man. Rationally, she knew there was no hope of suddenly coming across him wandering down the street. But there was nothing else she could do. She couldn't stay in the small, claustrophobic flat waiting for her husband and brothers to return.

Singh radiated contentment.

Bronwyn could not help smiling at him. She asked, 'So why the good cheer – do you think we're making progress?'

Singh leaned forward in his chair, elbows on the maroon *faux* satin tablecloth. He shook his head briefly at his Australian counterpart. 'We haven't made *any* progress – I don't know about you but I haven't got a clue who killed Richard Crouch.'

'Then why so happy?'

'Indian food,' explained Singh, nodding his great head towards the menu that was holding his attention like a conclusive piece of forensic evidence.

'Eh?'

'Indian food,' repeated Singh loudly, choosing to believe that she had misheard him rather than misunderstood him. 'I'm sick to death of *nasi goreng!*'

Bronwyn chuckled. 'I wondered why you thought it was necessary to visit the restaurant Julian Greenwood mentioned...'

'You're too cynical – I'm here in order to further our investigation and nothing more.' He grinned suddenly. 'I might be prepared to admit I decided to further our investigation at lunch time for personal reasons.'

Bronwyn perused the menu and realised that she was hungry. The food smells wafting out of the kitchen were tickling her nostrils and her fancy. She tried to fit a thumb into the waistband of her trousers – it was impossible. She hadn't eaten anything that wasn't fried or curried since meeting the inspector from Singapore. At this rate, she would need a new wardrobe.

Singh beckoned to a waiter and ordered a large bottle of Bintang and an assortment of dishes.

'Are we expecting anyone else?' asked Bronwyn rudely.

'I am a simple man with simple tastes – and I'm famished.'

Bronwyn glanced at the fat man but refrained from further comment.

She looked around the restaurant. It was open-fronted and faced out onto a Sanur high street. It was deserted except for a man sitting at the bar, sipping a beer moodily. As she watched, he beckoned to a waitress and indicated a stain on the floor. Bronwyn realised he was the proprietor when the waitress scurried away and returned with a stringy grey mop.

Singh had obviously reached the same conclusion. He waved to the man, who sauntered over.

'You're the owner?' he asked.

The dark Indian man with a military moustache and a head of bottle-black hair nodded.

'Food smells great.'

'Customers are all gone, though.'

Singh nodded.

'How come you're still here?'

'Police!' explained Singh.

The man's eyebrows shot up and to Bronwyn's consternation, he clicked his two false front teeth out and back again. 'Bali bombings?'

'Sort of...'

If he thought this was a peculiar response, he did not follow up. Instead he stuck out a hand, the lines on which looked like they were marked out with a black felt pen and said, 'Call me "Major".'

'"Major"?'

'Retired, Malaysian Air Force. My own name is too difficult for the expats.'

'Singh – Singapore police. And this is Bronwyn Taylor, AFP.'

The Major pulled up a chair, beckoned for his beer, clamped his teeth around an unlit cigarette and asked, 'So, why are you here?'

'Murder investigation ... one Richard Crouch.'

'Tall Englishman – skinny wife with bad attitude?'

Singh folded his arms across his belly and smiled. 'It seems we've found the right man!'

Further conversation was interrupted as the food arrived. Bronwyn was amused to see that both men felt that this was an event that merited a respectful silence. She herself was agog to hear what the restaurateur knew about Sarah Crouch's friends.

Singh ladled a generous helping of food onto his plate. He inclined his head at the Major, inviting him to join them.

The Major shook his head, chewing on the end of his cigarette instead. He patted his belly. 'This is from drinking with the guests – if I eat with them as well...'

Bronwyn noticed that his eyes strayed to Singh's tummy but he refrained from finishing the thought out loud.

The restaurateur asked, 'So what do you want to know about Richard Crouch?'

'Who killed him?'

The Major shrugged. 'Hard to imagine why anyone would. He was probably the least aggravating of that lot. They came here regularly. Two couples in addition to Crouch and his wife. Actually, Crouch didn't come in that often. He didn't drink so never really got into it...'

'What were the rest like?'

'The pretty fat woman has money. Her husband looks like ... one of those English character actors, bony face and pale eyes. The other man was a real loser – with a freakshow host for a wife.'

'So why did they hang out together?'

The Major gestured with two open palms. 'Who knows? They enjoyed the food and beer, listened to my war stories and chose to believe they had enough in common to be friends ... I've seen it often enough in Bali.'

Bronwyn interrupted. 'What about Crouch and his wife?'

He said unexpectedly, 'I've been running this restaurant for ten years – and it still amazes me, the couples that stay together when they have nothing in common, no affection left...'

'So they weren't happy?'

'Always at the opposite ends of the bar to each other... Tim Yardley was the one hanging around Sarah Crouch – like a mutt hoping for a pat.'

'Sarah Crouch did what?' exclaimed Singh.

They were back at the police station after a long lunch and Sergeant Agus was reporting his findings.

'Like I told you, sir,' said the policeman patiently. 'I followed the woman with yellow hair from her villa in Ubud –she took a taxi to Kuta beach and met a young man there.'

'Did you get his name?'

'She called him Greg. I did not hear any other name but I have identified the budget motel where he is staying – opposite Kuta beach. Usually, the surfers stay there.'

Singh settled into thoughtful silence.

It was Bronwyn's turn to ask, 'Are you sure they were having some sort of relationship?'

Agus blushed. He did not meet Bronwyn's eyes when answering, 'Yes, *Ibu*. She ... she, er, kissed him when they met on the beach ... on the mouth.'

Bronwyn too relapsed into silence.

Singh said, 'I knew the good wife was behaving a bit odd but I never suspected a boyfriend. It's a great motive.'

'It doesn't explain how her husband's body got mixed up with the bombing,' pointed out Bronwyn.

'No,' agreed Singh. 'But nothing explains that! I'm going to catch myself a murderer and then ask him or her how come they dumped the body there.'

'Actually, I have a theory about that,' said Bronwyn diffidently.

Singh looked at her expectantly, eyebrows raised into semi-circles.

'Maybe Richard Crouch's body wasn't at the Sari Club.'

Singh's eyebrows flattened into a straight line.

Bronwyn continued hurriedly, 'Not at the club or on the street – the body could have been in a car. Maybe in a boot?'

Singh opened his mouth to say something, probably something rude, thought Bronwyn, closed it again and looked at her. He bit his pink bottom lip, and said, 'Do you know – you might be right! That would explain a few things, certainly.'

'But not who killed him,' said Bronwyn flatly.

'No, not who killed him,' agreed Singh. 'But at least now we have a suspect with a tried and tested motive.'

'Even if Sarah wanted to run off with her surfer dude, why didn't she get a divorce like everybody else?'

Singh said, 'You're thinking rationally. In my experience, people who are thwarted in love can be pretty erratic in their behaviour. Crouch might have refused her a divorce. Maybe she needed money – we need to check his financial situation. Did his death benefit her greatly?'

'Or maybe,' interrupted Bronwyn, 'surfer boy got impatient and decided the quickest way to get the girl was to get rid of the competition.'

'I find it very hard to believe that anyone killed Crouch in order to get that nasty, thin-lipped, dried-up stick of a woman.'

Bronwyn scowled. 'Maybe he didn't judge

by appearances.'

Singh chuckled. 'That's not how it works in real life – especially amongst twenty-something Aussie surfers. You should know that!'

He turned to Agus, the policeman who was waiting politely, listening to the exchange between the Sikh and the woman with interest.

He asked, 'Did Greg seem as keen on her as she was on him?'

Agus's plain, square face betrayed his confusion. 'I beg your pardon, sir?'

Singh's foot, in its white sneaker, beat a silent but impatient tattoo on the ground. Bronwyn wondered whether she dared suggest tap shoes for the policeman from Singapore. She decided against it.

Singh asked, 'Who likes the other more – the girl or the man?'

The policeman's face cleared. 'The girl likes the surfer, sir.'

'But not the other way round?'

'Well – maybe he likes her a bit. But he is not very excited when she says they can be together.'

'What did I tell you?' crowed Singh. 'Surfer boy is not in it for *love*.'

Bronwyn asked the Balinese policeman, 'Did she realise he was not that interested?'

The man shook his head. 'No, *Ibu*. I could see his face. She couldn't because they were, you know' – he held out his hands in an arc – 'hugging each other.'

'Surfer boy is not in it for love but he's hiding his lack of interest from the girl. Hmm, I sense cash!' said Singh gleefully. 'Bronwyn, check the money situation – they should have found out a bit about Richard Crouch at Scotland Yard by now.'

Bronwyn said doubtfully, scratching her head with both hands, 'They weren't staying at an especially nice place in Ubud.'

'Yes, but what counts as being enough money for murder varies from person to person. For our young surfer hero, there might have been enough.'

Bronwyn got to her feet. She said over her shoulder, 'Give me a moment. I'll see if anything has come in from the UK.'

The Balinese policeman cleared his throat and said, 'Excuse me, sir.'

Singh ignored him.

Agus repeated the interjection a little louder this time and Singh stared at him in surprise.

'Do you need me for anything else, sir?'

'No.'

'Then I will report back to my station?'

Singh nodded brusquely and the police-man saluted sharply and turned to go.

Singh said to his receding back, 'We will call you if we need anything else.'

The policeman did not turn but at the

door he stopped and looked back into the room. He said, 'Thank you, sir.'

He walked down the corridor with a spring in his step and passed Bronwyn going the other way clutching a sheaf of papers. He grinned broadly. She looked at him in surprise but did not break stride. She suspected that no one on an errand for the fat policeman from Singapore stopped on the way for a friendly chat. She did not intend to be the first to test his patience by dawdling.

Bronwyn marched into the room and held out her bundle to the inspector. He took it reluctantly and said, 'What does it say?'

'I just had a quick glance,' explained Bronwyn, 'but he seems to have been reasonably well off. There's a flat in Brighton, some cash in the bank and an insurance policy for about ten thousand pounds.'

'That's enough to tempt someone to kill him,' remarked Singh.

'There's no will, so the wife gets everything as next of kin. The UK police confirmed the story that he was an only child with no brothers or sisters. His parents died in a car crash in Spain.'

Singh was leafing through a pile of papers with the Barclays logo on the top. 'His current account is interesting,' he said.

'What about it?'

'There's been money going in – US dollars.' Singh ran his finger down the column. 'Three batches of ten thousand each.'

'So? He must have been paid for this work he does – as an engineer. I guess he was a consultant or something,' said Bronwyn, revealing her blue-collar respect for the mysterious ways others made money.

'But he withdrew that same amount of money, half of it in Jakarta and the other half here in Bali.' Singh grabbed a high-lighter, marked off the transactions and handed the record to Bronwyn.

Her close-set eyes seemed to overlap in her concentration. 'The Bali withdrawal was just a day before the bomb – so at least we know he was alive then.'

Singh nodded. 'Yes, that amount of money in a single withdrawal, he couldn't have used his ATM card. He must have gone to the bank. We need to check on that. Maybe some stranger saw him leave the bank, followed him, shot him, stole the money, hid the body in some vehicle and left it on Jalan Legian.'

'Could be,' said Bronwyn absently. She was still staring hard at the statements. 'There are withdrawals of lesser amounts, a few hundred dollars each, from ATMs in Bali right up until the day of the bombing.' She turned the page. 'And beyond!'

'What do you mean?' Singh barked the question, his compressed belly elongating as

169

he sat up straighter.

'The last withdrawal is just last week – the bombs were on the twelfth of October.'

Singh dragged himself out of the chair and walked over to Bronwyn. He stared down at the paper in her hand. It was quite clear. Richard Crouch's ATM card had been used after the Bali bombs.

Bronwyn said, 'We might not be able to pinpoint the *earliest* point that he could have been killed – but we know for a fact that the last point that he might have been alive was just after eleven at night on the twelfth.'

'The dead man is like Hamlet's ghost then. He walks until he is avenged. Very well.' Singh slapped the table with both hands. 'We will have to avenge the killing of Richard Crouch.'

Bronwyn was silent. She had no idea what the Sikh policeman was talking about. Of a practical turn of mind with no literary pretensions, Bronwyn just wanted to know who had been using Crouch's ATM card.

Singh asked, 'Do you think they have CCTV?'

'What?'

'At the ATMs and banks, do you think they have CCTV?'

'I don't know,' said Bronwyn. She noticed Singh's thick eyebrows inching towards each other in exasperation and added hurriedly, 'I'll check.'

He nodded.

At the door she stopped and looked back in, her pert nose wrinkling as if she had caught a sudden whiff of a clogged Bali drain.

'What is it?' asked Singh.

'Are we any closer to finding out who done it?'

The overweight policeman sucked in his breath and chuckled. 'You've been watching too much TV,' he said. 'I'm afraid real life murder investigations are painstaking and time-consuming.'

He added, swivelling his chair and planting two large feet in their white sneakers lazily on the table, 'And require a lot of leg work...'

An off-duty policeman on his motorcycle pulled over. He debated whether he could be bothered to act on what he had seen – he was done for the day, after all. He sighed and got off his scooter, wriggling to unstick the trousers from his crotch. He had been told to look out for a red motorbike with a big engine, at least 250cc, and here was one parked on the street. He could not just carry on as if he hadn't seen it, notwithstanding that he was already late for the temple.

The bike was innocuous enough. A nice model – a red Yamaha. He was not sure why the police had been told to keep an eye out for it but he knew better than to question his instructions. He was just there to follow orders. He took out his radio and walked further along the road. He needed instructions on what he was to do next.

His radio crackled with static and he whispered his find.

His instructions were simple. He was to maintain surveillance of the bike until he was relieved by another policeman. If the owner returned, he was to follow the bike to its destination.

In half an hour, Sergeant Agus arrived, breathless but determined. He was delighted that he was being given a fresh role in the investigation. His surveillance of that woman Sarah Crouch had given Singh confidence that he, Agus, was up to the task. His chest puffed out proudly. He could have leapt in the air and kicked his heels together. Instead, he sent the off-duty policeman smartly on his way – he was in change now – and sat down under an acacia tree. He pulled a small black comb out of his back pocket, spat on it and quickly ran it through his hair. Just because he was out of uniform did not mean he should not be a credit to the force at all times. Agus lit a clove cigarette and inhaled the heady spicy fragrance. It reminded him of sandalwood and curry. He settled down to wait for the owner of the bike to return.

'They've found the red bike!' Bronwyn was red-faced with excitement.

'They've found *a* red bike,' murmured Singh.

'Nonsense,' said Bronwyn, refusing to have her enthusiasm dampened. 'We've had our eyes peeled. There's hardly a brightly-coloured big bike to be seen. If someone's spotted a red bike with a powerful engine, it's the one.'

'Well, I certainly hope you're right.'

'Why aren't you more excited? This could be a huge breakthrough. If we can trace Crouch's friends, we'll soon find out if he had any enemies, anyone who wanted him dead on this small island.'

'Other than his wife and the surfer boyfriend, you mean? Not to mention that gang of washed-up expats lurking in Sanur. It's *possible* they've found the bike. But you'll forgive a cynical old murder hack if he can't get excited about a "breakthrough" until something has come of it.'

'You're a grumpy old bastard, aren't you?' said Bronwyn affectionately.

Singh ignored both the express insult and the implied fondness. He asked instead, 'Is the wife here yet?'

Bronwyn nodded. 'In the small interview room. I thought she could wait there a while and wonder why we're anxious to see her again – and at the police station to boot.'

'Excellent!' said Singh. 'I like the way you're thinking. The best way to solve a murder is to keep the suspects off balance.'

He hauled himself to his feet using the table edge for leverage and stood very still for a moment, waiting for a bout of dizziness to pass. It appeared that it wasn't only the suspects who were off balance. He really needed to lose some weight.

The inspector continued thoughtfully, 'In fact, why don't you send someone to pick surfer boy up. We should drag him in as she's leaving – that'll give her something to think about.'

Bronwyn said, 'Sure thing.'

She hurried out of the room and the policeman wondered why anyone with such a large posterior would wear her shirts tucked in.

Singh walked slowly towards the interview room, considering his tactics. He was not sure how to deal with someone like Sarah Crouch. She seemed so cold and in control. But if she was in love with some twenty-something beach bum, there was a lot going on beneath the surface. He had not been able to crack the façade – harsh questioning was not a sufficiently powerful tool. Sarah was like a high-stakes poker player. Calm, very aware of the cards she'd been dealt, and determined to play them to her advantage.

And so far the luck was running with her. How else could one explain having her husband's death conveniently entangled in the randomness of the Bali bombings? The threads of this investigation were snarled up in the Gordian knot of a terrorist attack.

Singh knew that it would be very difficult to bring the murderer of Richard Crouch to justice. Even if he could be certain, in his own mind, that Sarah – or someone else for that matter – was the killer, he would struggle to prove the case in a court of law. There would be too much uncertainty over the forensics.

The pathologist, Dr Barton, had been convinced that the body was that of Richard Crouch and that he had been shot. Singh believed him. But any good defence lawyer would raise the possibility that, in the midst of so much bloodshed, the chain of evidence had been contaminated.

And what in the world would they have to say about the body being caught up in the blasts?

He could just imagine a judge asking in that dry, sarcastic voice they all had – it seemed to be a prerequisite for the job – 'Surely it's more likely, Mr, er, um, Singh, that Richard Crouch was killed *in* the blast and that piece of skull you've been waving about so enthusiastically was holed by accident?'

Singh heard heavy footsteps behind him and turned to wait for his Australian sidekick.

She said, 'I've asked Sergeant Agus to arrest Greg.'

Singh grunted his approval and the two walked down the corridor in silence, both deep in thought about their anticipated encounter with Sarah Crouch. Bronwyn Taylor was half a head taller than the man by her side. She had a pointy head and he had a pointy turban. They were dressed alike, dark slacks and tucked-in white shirts. From behind, there was a similarity in their gait. It was the waddle of the overweight, thighs brushing together and arms sticking out. But there was a sense of purpose to their big strides which trumped the element of comedy.

They opened the interview room door without ceremony. Sarah, lost in her own thoughts, jumped. Singh noted the slight start with approval. She was on the back foot. That was the advantage of leaving suspects to cool their heels for a while. Typically, a suspect would sit on the edge of his or her seat, all keyed up for the encounter with the police. He did not doubt that the widow had done just that. After a while, he guessed, she would have become cross at being kept waiting. She might have paced the room, stopping from time to time to stare out of the small window pane in the door to see if anyone was coming. Eventually, she would have sat back down and whiled away the time, perhaps by imagining romantic evenings on the beach with her young surfer. That was the point for the police to barge in. He and Bronwyn seemed to have timed it to perfection.

Sarah was too tense to stay silent. She asked immediately, her voice a few notes higher than usual with tension, 'Why have you asked me to come here? Have you found out anything? I don't like being treated like a criminal. I haven't done anything!'

'Treating you like a criminal, eh? You've led a sheltered life, my dear woman, if you think this is being treated like a *criminal.*'

Inspector Singh seemed much struck by her observation because he went on in a thoughtful voice, 'No, no, this is not it at all. Being treated like a criminal involves handcuffs, sometimes police sirens. What do you think, Bronwyn?'

Bronwyn opened her mouth and closed it again.

Singh ignored her inability to contribute to his discourse and continued to muse, 'And, of course, there would be thumb-prints, photographs and holding cells with the Bali criminal fraternity. No, I don't think we would class this as treating you like a criminal.'

Sarah said sullenly, 'I think you're mad.'

Singh noted Bronwyn's guilty expression. She was probably in agreement with the widow. He wished for a moment that it was his sidekick who was suspected of a crime. Her face was a mirror to her thoughts unlike the tiresomely impassive mien of Sarah Crouch.

He said, 'I mean, the thing is, the choice is ours – whether to indulge you a bit or lock you up on suspicion of theft, fraud – call it what you will. We don't even have to get to *murder* – not yet anyway.'

'What in the world are you talking about?'

'How did you and your husband pay for expenses?'

'What do you mean?'

'When you fancied a good dinner or a shopping trip to Uluwatu – how did you pay?'

Sarah was looking at him suspiciously but could not find a reason to prevaricate. 'Usually cash, they don't take credit cards here except in the big hotels. Besides, it's silly to pay by credit card in a foreign currency. The banks take you for a ride on the exchange rate and quite likely the shopkeeper will duplicate the strip and your card will be used all over Indonesia before you notice anything wrong.'

Singh nodded approvingly. 'It's nice to meet a tourist who is not entirely naïve.' He added, 'But where did you get the cash?'

'Get the cash?'

'Exactly!'

She was puzzled, thought Singh, but she answered, 'Richard brought some US dollars. When that ran out, he used his credit card to withdraw cash from the ATM a few times.'

'And you?'

'I didn't have an ATM card that worked here.'

'No,' said Singh, 'but you used *his*.'

She was silent for a few moments, considering her answer. 'No, I wouldn't do that,' she said at last.

'Probably best not to,' agreed Singh with undiminished good humour. 'But what if I was to tell you that your husband's ATM card was used in the days *after* the Bali bombings?'

She decided on surprise but it was not well executed. Her eyes widened a trifle too much. And surely no one in real life, thought Singh, raised their eyebrows to denote consternation.

Sarah asked, 'Are you sure?'

'Quite sure!'

'Well then, whoever killed him must have stolen his card.'

She was quick, thought the inspector approvingly. He liked that. It made the chase more interesting.

'That's a great theory,' he exclaimed. 'We should have thought of that!' He continued sorrowfully, 'There's only one problem...'

'What's that?'

'We found this in your bag.'

He slid an ATM card across the table to her.

'How dare you go through my things?' she shouted angrily. 'You had no right.'

'On the contrary,' pointed out Singh, 'we had every right. We suspected a crime was being committed and here's the proof.' He nodded at the card. Sarah Crouch did not touch it.

'All right, look, I'll tell you the truth.' The capitulation was sudden and complete. 'You're right – I had his ATM card. He gave it to me – so I could help myself to some pocket money. He said he could always go into the bank to get cash if he needed it. Besides, I was shopping and stuff. He wasn't doing anything much.'

Singh asked, 'And after he died?'

She was not so easily trapped. Or maybe she was innocent, conceded Singh.

Sarah said, 'I had no idea he was dead. He didn't come back that night. But there was no reason to think he'd been involved in the bombings. I mean, we were staying in Ubud. The attacks were in Kuta. I needed some cash, partly to pay for taxis to go looking for him. I withdrew a little bit more.'

'Six thousand US dollars over the weeks leading up to the bombings – and after,' said Singh.

'I hadn't realised it was so much,' said Sarah. 'But I was on my own so much.' Her voice cracked. 'I guess I spent more than I realised.'

'All right,' said Singh unexpectedly. 'That's all we wanted to know. Thank you for coming in.'

Singh got to his feet and held the door open for Sarah Crouch. He trudged after her into the corridor. Bronwyn trailed after them. The trio walked into the lobby in silence. With perfect timing, Sergeant Agus opened a side door and frog-marched Greg the surfer into the room. The young man looked confused and frightened. He had his hands cuffed behind him.

Singh nodded in the direction of the prisoner, apparently oblivious to the expression of open-mouthed horror on the face of Sarah Crouch. He said smugly, 'Now that's what we call treating someone like a criminal. You see, it's quite different.'

Nine

'What have you done? Tell me why you did it, you bastard!' The voice was a scream. The woman was middle-aged and brown-haired with a blotchy tear-streaked face. Her eyes were swollen from crying.

Singh was flabbergasted. He had been standing in the hotel lobby trying to decide whether to have dinner or return to his room and shower first, when he was accosted. He said, looking around quickly at the small audience her shouts had already attracted, 'I'm sorry, madam. But I have no idea what you're talking about.'

The woman clutched the front of his shirt with two arthritic claws. 'You killed my daughter! Why? What did she ever do to you or your people?'

Singh tried to walk away but she grabbed his arm. She clung to it like a small child who would not leave a toy shop. 'No, you're not getting away so easily. Tell me why you did it!'

The Balinese hotel staff had screwed up the courage to intervene. One of them put his arm around the hysterical woman and tried to lead her away. He said, 'Please come back to your room, *Ibu*. You are very upset. This man is a hotel guest. He has not done anything.'

'My daughter is *dead*. They told me today that there isn't enough of her left to bury. His people, these Moslems, they killed her – and all the others. Why?'

Singh said as calmly as he could, 'I am not actually Moslem. I know the turban looks similar to the headgear Moslems wear sometimes but it's quite different. I'm a Sikh.'

The woman spat. A frothy foaming gob of saliva, like the white tops of Balinese waves, landed on Singh's cheek.

There was a collective gasp of horror from the onlookers.

Singh took his big white handkerchief from a trouser pocket and wiped his face. He felt sick with disgust. He was also overcome with pity for this poor woman. He, Singh, had no children. His own parents were old. He had only a tepid affection for his wife. Singh had never felt the overwhelming biologically-mandated love of a parent for a child. It was a source of occasional regret and mild relief. But now, here in front of him, was that parental love in the form of a grief-stricken mother – who thought he was a Moslem like the Bali bombers.

Singh put his hands on the woman's shoulders. 'Listen! I'm not Moslem. I had nothing to do with the bombs. I do not support the actions of these lunatics. I think that they are cruel and bloodthirsty and I hope that they face justice.'

She said dully, 'You look like a Moslem. Some of them wear that head thing.'

'Sikhs wear turbans too,' replied Singh quietly.

The woman nodded but Singh was not sure that she had heard, understood or, for that matter, cared. He added, 'The bombings were carried out by a very small minority of people. Most Moslems were devastated by what happened.'

Singh knew he was wasting his time trying to communicate to this woman that the actions of the few should not be allowed to tarnish the many. He was not even convinced that he was right to try. Perhaps she should be allowed her anger even if it was misdirected. Her child was dead, killed randomly by bombers who smiled when they were arrested and gave the 'thumbs up' sign to waiting news crews. But if that image of triumphant terrorists was allowed to become the shorthand for all Moslems, the misunderstandings between the Western and Moslem worlds would just get worse and be punctuated by more violence. Already, he was caught in the crossfire both professionally and now, it seemed, personally.

He said again, 'It's not Moslems, just a few madmen who will be executed for what they've done.'

The woman let go of the front of his shirt and stood before him, arms limp by her sides, completely still. She said, 'They killed my little girl.'

Singh didn't reply for a moment. He folded his handkerchief and put it back in his pocket. At last, he said, 'I'm so sorry about that.'

The rush of adrenaline was over and with it the sudden rage that the sight of Singh's headgear had provoked. She whispered, 'Thank you,' and walked away, her steps slow and uncertain. A hotel employee hovered at her elbow, wishing to be helpful but not knowing how to do it in a way that would not intrude on her grief. The crowd dissipated. A few backward suspicious glances were tossed at the policeman from Singapore. They probably still believed he was a Moslem and a terrorist to boot, thought Inspector Singh of the Singapore police, wishing once again that he had not been deployed to Bali.

The front door creaked and the men turned to watch Nuri walk in.

She, lost in the maze of her own thoughts, did not appear to notice the semi-circle of men, all staring at her intently.

Ghani asked brusquely, 'Where have you been, wife? It is growing late.'

Nuri glanced at her husband briefly, her face impassive. She asked, tying her head-scarf more firmly under her chin and dropping her carry bag by the door, 'Were you worried about me?'

This was such an unexpected response, personal and provocative, that Ghani did not respond. Instead, he stared at his wife as if she had grown a second head.

Abu Bakr stepped in hastily. 'We were all concerned about your whereabouts and your safety, Nuri.'

'And there was no dinner,' pointed out Ramzi flippantly, grinning broadly at the opportunity to needle his sister.

Abu Bakr waved a hand at Ramzi, the gesture designed to silence him. He said, 'That is of no concern, sister. But it is best if you are not out in Bali so late. It is a sinful place, full of bad influences. There are many men wandering about. The Westerners are probably drunk or on drugs. They would not know how to respect the modesty of a Moslem woman.'

Nuri muttered, shooting a defiant glance at the men, 'They seemed fine to me.'

Ghani found his tongue. He said angrily, 'Wife, you should go to bed now. I do not know what ails you but your tone is not appropriate. You must remember that you are speaking to your husband...'

'And brothers!' It was Ramzi, still finding

the situation amusing.

Nuri walked up to Ramzi until they were standing toe to toe. She raised her hand and slapped him once, hard across the face. The sound, like the crack of a whip, ricocheted around the room. She said, her voice quiet but quivering with anger, a finger stabbed into Ramzi's chest, 'I may owe my husband some respect, but *not* my kid brother.'

Ramzi held his face where he had been struck. His brown eyes were wide with shock. Abu Bakr had taken an uncertain step forward when she lashed out but now he stopped and glanced at Ghani.

Nuri's husband was staring at his wife, his jaw slack and his mouth hanging open.

Bronwyn wandered into the lobby and raised an eyebrow. 'What's going on here?' she asked in her booming Australian voice.

Singh winced. Had he not already been the object of enough attention?

He said, trying to inject humour into his voice and failing, 'I think I've just been accused of being a terrorist.'

Bronwyn said matter-of-factly, 'It was bound to happen.'

He stared at her in annoyance. 'What's that supposed to mean?'

'There's plenty of ignorance to go around. I'm sure your job has taught you that. After September 11th, quite a few Sikhs were attacked in the United States.'

Singh felt obliged to defend his accuser. He said, 'It was a mother. She said her daughter was killed in the blasts ... I guess she was too upset to think clearly.'

They were both silent, contemplating the enormity of that loss.

Singh changed the subject with his usual abruptness, preferring not to dwell on the incident. 'What happened after I left the station?'

'Not much. We took surfer boy and locked him in a holding pen – we'll need to charge him soon or let him go.'

'Have someone search his luggage,' said Singh. 'There's bound to be something illegal to smoke in there. We'll be able to charge him with possession of a banned narcotic – it will give us leverage. He isn't in love with the widow. He'll sing like a canary if we give him a reason.'

'We shouldn't really be looking in his luggage to find something to incriminate him with,' pointed out Bronwyn diffidently.

'I'm not planning to lock him up forever!'

'All right, I'll arrange it,' said Bronwyn reluctantly.

Singh guessed that Bronwyn was having to bite her tongue on the subject of proper police procedure and the civil liberties of scumbags like Greg Howard. As far as he was concerned, if the rules reduced his chances of successfully solving a case, the rules would have to be re-written or the rule book jettisoned. The liberty of the subject was just leverage to Singh – something within his gift – and he was willing to forfeit it if it suited his convenience.

'Did Sarah Crouch go quietly?' Singh, assuming Bronwyn's compliance with his instructions and indifferent to her doubts, had moved on to the next topic of interest to him.

'She was in two minds. She did ask once we were out of the building what we had surfer boy in for, but I said I didn't know.'

'Did you ask her if she knew him?'

Bronwyn nodded. 'Yes – but she said not, she was just curious, nothing more.'

'What did you say?'

Bronwyn grinned. 'That I would be interested in such a fine specimen of manhood myself.'

Singh rubbed his grubby hands together, forgetting his earlier embarrassment at being accused of being a terrorist in the thrill of the chase. 'That's great. Let's see how the grieving widow reacts to a bit of pressure.'

When Bronwyn did not react, he asked, 'Well, are you going to stand there basking in my reflected glory or are you going to send Agus to rummage in Greg Howard's luggage?'

'You can't arrest me. I haven't done anything!'

The inspector did not deign to respond to this first line of defence.

Bronwyn wondered why suspects were so lacking in originality when it came to their opening statements. It was patently obvious that the fat policeman *could* arrest the young man and the young man knew it all too well.

Greg Howard's eyes suddenly lit up. He said, 'I'm an Australian citizen. I want to speak to someone at the embassy. You can't treat me like this.'

Singh burst into loud guffaws. His gut was quivering in synchronicity with his amusement.

There was a silence while the surfer and the policewoman waited for Inspector Singh to gather himself and explain the reason for the sudden laughter. The policeman sat up straight in his chair and made a show of wiping away tears with his big white handkerchief. Bronwyn was unimpressed by his theatrical antics. She decided that the inspector's stage forte would undoubtedly be pantomime.

Singh changed his tone. 'Do you really think the Australian embassy has time for a surfer boy like you? Right now, after the bombs?'

Bronwyn conceded that the policeman

was right. The Australian embassy was unlikely to be concerned about a possible miscarriage of justice involving a youth who did not appear to own a pair of shoes when they had the aftermath of the Bali bombings to deal with.

Greg seemed to recognise the truth in Singh's words because he said sullenly, 'What do you want with me? I really haven't done anything wrong.' His fear was exposed when his voice cracked like an adolescent's on the last syllable.

Singh gazed at him with the objective interest of a scientist looking at a bug under a microscope. Greg Howard squirmed in response.

'Well, there's this...' remarked Singh, slipping a small packet of white powder across the table.

Bronwyn had followed the policeman's instructions to the letter and had Greg's very limited luggage searched. Agus had reported that the young man in front of them was certainly travelling light. He had a rucksack with a few pairs of board shorts, a toothbrush, sun block ... and a packet of cocaine.

Greg stared at the small packet. Bronwyn noticed that he had gone pale beneath his tan. He asked, 'Where did you get that?'

'In your luggage...'

'You went through my things?'

'That's right,' said Bronwyn. 'Don't worry, we tidied up very neatly. No one will know we were there.'

'But you're not allowed to do that!'

'Nonsense,' said Singh briskly. 'We can and we have – and this little packet turned up. You have some explaining to do before I decide whether to have you charged with possession of a dangerous narcotic or ... trafficking.'

Ten

Bronwyn realised from his trembling hands that Greg Howard understood the distinction – possession of a banned substance might involve a slap on the wrist. Trafficking on the other hand would ensure that the surfer was a much older man before he could work on his tan again – assuming that he wasn't sentenced to death by a Balinese court.

Greg was shaking one knee so violently under the table that the surface was vibrating. He didn't seem to notice. He locked his hands together in his lap to stop the quivering and leaned forward as far as the table would allow him. 'I was not trafficking,' he whispered. 'It's just a tiny bit – for my own use.'

'The fact is,' said Singh comfortably, 'there's enough in that packet for me to put you away for a very long time.'

'But I don't understand,' said Greg plaintively. 'What do you want from me?'

'It's funny that you should ask me that,' remarked Singh. 'There is something you can do for me – and it might help me decide that you had that bag of white powder for *personal* use...'

'What is it? I'll do anything!'

Bronwyn felt sorry for the young fellow as he looked up with hope dawning in his eyes – the prison door had been left open a crack. He was not much older than her own sons, she thought. She really, really hoped that none of her boys ever found themselves in the clutches of a figure as dominant and dangerous as Inspector Singh. To have something that the inspector from Singapore wanted was to be in a very tight spot indeed. He was, for someone on the side of the angels, capable of some very dirty tactics.

Bronwyn had never believed that the ends justified the means. She was a strong believer in due process. She didn't trust results that were obtained under duress – even if it was mental and emotional pressure rather than physical intimidation. She doubted that Singh would resort to roughing up a prisoner. Despite his gross exterior, he was far too subtle for that. But a weak youth like Greg was no match for a master manipulator like Singh.

Singh had abandoned his nonchalant pose. He sat up straight in his chair, his belly straining at the buttons of his shirt. Bronwyn noted that he had actually put on weight. She was not surprised. She had watched him eat his *nasi goreng* with dessert and sweetened coffee and then cleanse his palate of the oily, rich food with cheap beer. Many of the policemen in Australia prided themselves on keeping in good physical shape. Singh, she thought, was limited to a more cerebral approach. She tried not to smile at the image that popped into her head of Singh trying to restrain someone physically. He struggled to get out of a chair sometimes.

'Tell us about Sarah Crouch.'

It was the last topic in the world that Greg Howard had expected. His mouth hung open in an expression of foolish surprise. The astonishment passed and was replaced with relief. 'Sarah Crouch? Why do you want to know about *her*?'

'I'll ask the questions,' barked Singh.

'That's fine with me. I just don't know very much about her. We met a couple of months ago, had a few drinks together – that's all really.'

Singh asked, 'So you're saying you didn't conspire with her to kill her husband?'

'What?'

Singh acted as if the young man had failed to hear him rather than disbelieved the contents of his question. He repeated it more slowly and much louder, 'Did you conspire with Sarah to murder her husband, Richard Crouch?'

'Murder? She said he was killed in the

195

bombing at the Sari Club!'

Singh said pedantically, 'Well, if he had died in the blasts at the Sari Club, it would still be murder – but *you* wouldn't be one of the suspects.'

The surfer looked confused. 'What happened to him?'

'He was shot!'

'Geez, that's just unbelievable!' His vowels flattened as his Aussie accent got stronger. He continued, 'You think I *shot* Sarah's husband? I never even met the guy.'

'But you were sleeping with his wife.' Singh made it a statement rather than a question.

Greg shuffled in his seat uncomfortably. 'Look, it was a holiday romance. It didn't mean anything.'

'Is that how Sarah felt about it?' It was Bronwyn, interjecting herself into the interview process for the first time.

Greg Howard was silent. He was visibly trying to decide the best answer.

At last he said quietly, 'She might have taken it more seriously than I did.'

'Have you told her?'

Greg glanced at Singh, a troubled expression on his face. 'No. I wasn't quite sure how to do it. She thinks that because her husband is dead, we can be together. She says' – he shifted uncomfortably in his seat – 'she says she loves me.'

'If I were you,' remarked Singh, 'I'd beg

me to lock you up and throw the key away. You're in the clutches of a *very* determined woman.'

Greg Howard actually shuddered.

Bronwyn asked abruptly, 'Why did you get into a relationship with her in the first place? She must be fifteen years older than you!'

Bronwyn sounded like an angry parent and Greg responded as if she was. His voice was an apologetic whine as he said, 'It just happened. I didn't plan it.'

Singh was more brutal. 'Don't act the innocent with us, young man. You were in it for that new surfboard we found in your hotel room. I've no doubt there were a few nice meals and long beery evenings thrown in as well.'

Greg opened his mouth to deny the accusations and then closed it again. He put his face in his hands. Bronwyn noticed that he had large strong hands tanned a golden brown.

Greg said, 'All right – yes, she seemed pretty well off. She liked me. I was getting a bit tired of being broke the whole time. I didn't mean any harm.'

'There's a name for men like you,' said Singh, his bottom lip thrust out in disgust.

Greg Howard was defiant. 'Look, I was a bit foolish. But I had nothing to do with her husband's murder!'

'That might be true, of course,' agreed Singh graciously. 'But maybe you decided to make your meal ticket permanent.'

'Look, mate. I'm not that desperate.'

Bronwyn felt her sympathy for the surfer ebb away. He was nothing but a cocky twerp using an older unhappy woman and then mocking her gullibility when it was over. Despite her sudden aversion for Greg, she recognised that his protest rang true. He probably *wasn't* that desperate. Why would a good looking young man need to settle for Sarah Crouch as a meal ticket? To cover a few extra holiday expenses, certainly. But to kill her husband for the long-term benefits? It seemed unlikely.

Singh sighed. He said, 'I'm inclined to believe you.'

Greg exclaimed, 'Thanks, mate.'

'So the only question is whether Sarah Crouch was sufficiently enamoured of you to have killed her husband.'

There was a silence in the room. Bronwyn broke it. She said to Greg, 'Do you think she could have done it?'

Greg Howard shook his head doubtfully. 'I don't know. She was quite weird, I thought. Sort of quiet and brooding a lot of the time and then she'd cheer up and be a bit of a laugh. She told me her husband was too busy to spend time with her. But she had his ATM card and that was all she needed to make sure we had a good time.'

'Did she say what he was doing?'

'No, not really ... I think she suggested that he'd fallen into some bad company. It was actually a joke – she said that she and her husband had both fallen into bad company. But, you know, she preferred hers.' Greg looked at them and added helpfully, 'She meant me.'

Bronwyn glared at the surfer. He had gone from fearful to patronising very quickly.

Greg continued, 'I swear to you – I had nothing to do with her husband's death.'

'That may be the case. But I'm afraid I'm going to keep you locked up for a while,' said Singh.

'But ... but why? I've told you everything I know!'

'Yes, but I need leverage over Sarah Crouch. And...' Singh paused and Greg blurted out, 'And what?'

'I don't like you.'

The main line rang. Its strident insistent tone shattered the peaceful morning. Wayan, half asleep behind the main desk, picked it up hastily. It was a call for Sarah Crouch. He put the call through to the villa that had been the Crouch home for six months and then, wide awake now, quietly picked up an extension.

Singh had told him in no uncertain terms

that he was assisting the police in their inquiries. Wayan had no intention of annoying the fat man with the turban by ignoring his instructions. Guest privacy would have to take a back seat to important investigative work. He betrayed his youth with the grin that suffused his features like a light bulb coming on in a dark room. Playing policeman was certainly more fun than manning the front desk of a largely deserted hotel.

'Sarah, is that you?' The line crackled, distorting the masculine voice.

'Yes, who is this?' Her reply was thin and echo-less on the phone.

'It's me, Tim ... Tim Yardley.'

Sarah suppressed a sigh. She had successfully avoided Tim since telling him about Richard's death although he had been all ready to comfort the grieving widow. He was becoming a major nuisance. She really needed to do something to rid herself of his attentions. She wondered whether to tell him about Greg. She smiled at the thought of her young man. It took ten years off her age. Inspector Singh would not have recognised the beaming woman holding the phone reluctantly to one ear.

'Sarah, are you there?'

She dragged her mind away from her lover – it was an effort of will as painful as a physical separation. 'Yes, Tim. But this isn't a good time. I've been through a lot. I'm sure you understand that I need some rest and privacy.'

Tim's voice was high and excited, almost girlish. He said, 'I've done it, Sarah. I've done it!'

'What have you done?'

'I told Karri I wanted a divorce.'

There was a silence at the other end. Tim said again, 'Did you hear me? I asked Karri for a divorce. Sarah, we can be together!'

Sarah closed her eyes. The years that had fallen off with her smile returned in the lines engraved deeply around her eyes and mouth.

'Tim, we shouldn't be too hasty...'

For the first time, there was hesitation. She thought she heard a sigh, a soft round sound tinged with self-doubt.

'What do you mean, Sarah?'

'This is a difficult time. I know we talked about our future. But I need a break, some time to get over Richard's death. You know, to understand my own mind.'

There was a plaintive note in Tim's voice, like a child whose toy had been snatched away by the playground bully. He whispered, 'But you said we could be together ... you said that only Richard stood between us.'

'They've tracked the red motorcycle to an apartment in Denpasar,' said Bronwyn. She

201

had just been briefed on the phone by the Bali policeman. 'Agus followed the bike from Ubud. There was a young man on it. There was no way to be sure he was from Java – on anywhere else other than Bali – but Agus said he "seemed foreign".'

Singh grimaced. 'Have we traced the registration?'

'It's being done. We're a bit short of resources – what with the investigations into the bombings and the security arrangements for the purification ritual.'

'*What* ritual?'

Bronwyn said, 'The Balinese are having a ceremony – to ... erm ... exorcise the evil at the bomb sites – later this week.'

'At the sites? Have they finished the forensics?'

'Apparently... I think there's some politics going on. The investigation's been a success, but that's no use to the Balinese unless they can persuade the tourists to come back. Besides, it's not an act, is it? The Balinese are genuinely religious. They want to appease their gods.'

'So what do *you* think we should do next?' asked Singh, making a mental note that he was beginning to rely on the judgement of his Australian counterpart.

'What do you mean?'

'How about talking to the owner of the red bike?'

Bronwyn hesitated. 'We're not even sure these are the right guys...'

Singh paused and chewed on his lower lip hungrily. 'I tell you what – get that cop, Agus, to pick Wayan up and go and sit in a *warung* across the road. If Wayan confirms that these are the right men, we'll have a chat with them.'

'How do you know there's a *warung* across the street?' asked Bronwyn curiously, taken aback by this apparent omniscience.

'Isn't there always?'

Bronwyn nodded. He was right, of course. It was part of the Balinese way of life to stop at a small stall and have a drink or a bite to eat and chat to friends and strangers. As a result, there was a *warung* every twenty yards.

She reached for a phone. In a moment, she was explaining Singh's instructions to Sergeant Agus.

She listened to the acknowledgement at the other end, said goodbye and hung up.

'All done, boss,' she said cheerfully. 'What next?'

Singh squinted as if they were outside in the bright Balinese light rather than in a small dingy room.

Bronwyn, watching him, thought it was the first time in the investigation that he had seemed at a loss. He had been in turns cynical, angry and amused – but never uncertain. She suspected it was not a state he found himself in very often and she wondered why he felt that way now.

She said briskly, 'We're making progress!'

Singh looked even more perturbed. His brow creased in parallel lines.

Bronwyn asked, 'What's bothering you?'

'Usually, at this point in an investigation – I *know* who done it.'

'You usually solve a murder in less than two weeks? I thought you said that only happened on television.'

Singh ignored the snide tone.

'I might not have solved the crime in the sense of made an arrest. But I have a good idea of who the culprit is – it's just a question of finding enough evidence to make sure he or she swings.'

'Are you ever wrong?' asked Bronwyn, unable to hide her irritation at this certitude.

Singh grinned. 'It's been known to happen. But not often.'

His smile metamorphosed into a frown.

'We're working in a vacuum. We don't know enough about the dead man. We know he was unhappy with his wife, he wasn't keen on her expat friends and *she* had a toy boy on the side. We know he made some friends amongst the incomers – because his job as an engineer travelling the world meant he was unusually comfortable with "native" types. We know he had a fair bit of money and that he took a lot of it out in Bali – we don't know to what end. Did he buy a yacht? Did he have an expensive girlfriend? The thing that is really bothering me is that we have no sense of his history, no sense of his past. What was Richard Crouch actually like? Was he the sort of man to make enemies?'

'Well, someone killed him,' pointed out Bronwyn.

'But that's the wrong way of looking at things,' Singh said impatiently. 'To find a murderer, you almost have to ignore the fact that the victim is dead. You need to understand their lives and their relationships and the sort of people they were – who were their friends and enemies, what were their personality traits. When you know everything there is to know about someone – and then he turns up dead – well, you're in a position to know who killed him.'

Bronwyn nodded slowly. 'I see what you mean, I think.'

Her mobile phone rang and she flipped it open impatiently. She pushed the hair away from one ear and held the phone to it gingerly.

Singh could just make out an excited babbling on the line. He watched as Bronwyn's tired, crumpled face smoothed out. He waited, his growing impatience manifested in the vigour with which he drummed his foot on the stained synthetic carpet.

She snapped her phone shut and grinned broadly at the inspector. 'That was Wayan.'

Singh's calf muscle was suddenly afflicted with cramp. He leapt to his feet, trying to stretch and groaning with pain. 'Well? What did he say?'

'He listened in on a telephone conversation between Sarah Crouch and Tim Yardley...'

Eleven

'"If Richard was out of the way, we'd be together." That's what you said to the wife of one very dead man. Is there any reason I shouldn't arrest you for the murder of Richard Crouch right here and now?'

Tim Yardley sat in the same cell that had been occupied by Sarah Crouch the previous day. His comb-over had been the first thing to collapse under the pressure of a police interview. The carefully arranged strands were now hanging limply over one ear, the crown of his head as bare and smooth as an eggshell. The three legs of the cheap plastic stool were buckling under his weight, showing white where the major stresses were.

Singh wondered whether this man, who had through his own words been catapulted to the top of the suspects' list, was going to end up in a heap on the floor. Well, if that happened, he, Singh, wasn't going to help him get up. He'd slip a disc, for sure.

Yardley wiped his hands on his shorts. Moist streaks showed against the khaki. His crotch was damp as well, Singh hoped with sweat. It was early in the interview for the man to wet himself.

'Well?' demanded Singh.

'I just meant that there was nothing to stand in the way of our being together – with Richard dead. I didn't have anything to do with his *murder!*' His words were of firm denial but his tone was that of an overtired child who did not expect to be believed when he insisted that it was not him who had put the cricket ball through the window.

'Shall I tell you what I think?'

Tim recognised this as a rhetorical question. He sat sullenly, his chins folded like an accordion against his chest.

'Sarah wanted to get rid of her husband. She faked some affection for you. Told you a pack of lies. You killed Richard Crouch. She has her freedom and you're going to be hanged from the neck!'

'It … it wasn't like that at all. Sarah and I fell in love. She was lonely because Richard never paid her any attention. He was always hanging around with some scruffy locals. I've not … been happy with my wife, Karri, for a while. We found each other.'

There was a pathetic dignity about a man asserting that, in his late middle age, he had discovered true love on a tropical island.

Singh felt sorry for Yardley. He hoped that his own disenchantment with marriage would not lead him to make such a fool of himself one day. He shook his head slightly to dislodge the irrelevant line of thought.

This was not the time to feel pity for a suspect. This was the time to press home his advantage. He leaned forward aggressively. 'So you killed Crouch for your happy ending!'

'No! I swear to you – I won't pretend that I didn't want him out of the way – but I was shocked when he turned up dead. I almost felt guilty – you know, as if I had *wished* death on the poor bastard.'

Singh realised that he almost believed Tim. He seemed such an unlikely character to have summoned up the gumption to buy a gun and shoot a man in the forehead. Still, Singh knew better than most not to judge by appearances. After all, wasn't he constantly underestimated by those who assumed that a fat man in shiny white shoes couldn't possibly be a detective out of the top drawer?

The inspector said thoughtfully, 'Well, if it wasn't you, it must have been Sarah Crouch. Do you think she would have shot him herself or hired someone?'

Tim levered himself to his feet using the table between them as a support. He shouted, his face mottled red, 'Sarah is a kind and gentle woman who would never hurt anyone!'

Singh looked thoughtful, as if he was seriously contemplating adopting this view of the widow's character. He suggested unhurriedly, 'Perhaps she asked the *other* boy-friend to do it?'

The blood ebbed, leaving Tim's face waxy and pale. 'What are you talking about?'

'Come along, I'll show you!' said Singh cheerfully.

He led the man down a narrow corridor until they reached the holding cells. Greg the surfer, dressed in a pair of shorts and a vest with the Bintang logo on it, was lying on his thin cot looking bored. When Singh peered through the bars, he leapt to his feet. 'You going to let me out, mate?'

Singh shook his head. 'No, I just wanted to introduce you to someone.'

He turned to the man next to him. 'Tim, this is Greg Howard, Sarah Crouch's lover.'

Wayan and Agus the policeman sat in a *warung* sipping tea, listening to the gossip of their fellow patrons. In the not so distant past, the conversation would have been about local politics and village rivalries. The customers might have fretted about the weather and the nice crops. Now, it was all about the Bali bombings and the arrest of Amrozi.

The two men had their eyes fixed on the apartment block across the street. It was three storeys high and extremely run down. Paint was peeling away from the building in long strips, exposing the brick underneath

210

like bed sores. The structure had the stamp of shoddy third world constructions – even the concrete seemed crumbly. Clothes were drying on poles protruding from windows. Some of the panes had curtains but many were bare. Seeing undressed windows was like looking into the eyes of the blind, thought Wayan. A few windows were boarded up with plywood. There was no elevator. Instead, there was a flight of stairs leading down to street level. Wayan concentrated his gaze on the entrance over the rim of his tea cup. All he could see was the small altar on the pavement by the staircase.

He asked, stretching his legs out under the table, 'How do you know they are in there?'

'I don't,' said Agus. 'But I saw one of them come back to this block yesterday evening. On a red bike.'

'Did you see which apartment he went in?'

'No, I did not want to give myself away so I stayed out here. But it was definitely this building. I had a look later – there are only six apartments in there – so we should be able to track them down if we need to do it.'

'I don't see a bike or anything,' complained Wayan, who was not happy about being dragged away from his increasingly tenuous job to spend a hot afternoon at a roadside stall.

'They could be out,' suggested the policeman. 'We did not get here that early.'

Wayan, stung by what he thought was an accusation, said, 'That's not my fault.'

'Nobody said it was. It is a long way here from Ubud. But if they have gone out, we just have to wait for them to come back.'

'What about my job?'

'This is police business. Your employers will understand.'

Wayan's nose wrinkled in disbelief at the naïve optimism of the policeman.

'Are you sure you will recognise these men if you see them?'

Wayan looked doubtful and began to chew nervously on a fingernail. 'I am not sure. I saw them a few times. But I did not look at them so carefully.'

'I hope you do,' said the policeman. 'Otherwise this will be a real waste of time!'

They both sipped their tea in silence, listening to the rumble of traffic and the hissing of gas flames as the *warung* owner fried noodles for his customers. A few birds were singing but their valiant efforts were drowned out by manmade noises.

'What did he look like?'

'Who?' asked the Balinese policeman, leaning forward and putting two brawny arms on the formica-topped table.

Wayan scowled at him. 'The man on the red bike – who else?'

Agus glared back. 'I did not get that close. I had to follow him all the way from

212

Monkey Forest Road in Ubud. I was afraid of getting spotted.'

'You must have some idea!'

'He seemed good looking. Quite small-sized but he appeared strong. He had quite long hair.' The policeman put a hand up to his shoulder to indicate the length of his quarry's hair. 'He rode his motorbike very fast. I struggled to keep up with him and once on twice I was sure he was going to have an accident.'

'Maybe it is the same man,' said Wayan optimistically.

'Why? Does my description sound familiar?'

Wayan scratched a pimple on his nose. 'No, not really, but I remember seeing him ride his bike out of the motel compound once – he was very fast.'

The policeman did not discount this as coincidence. Instead, he beamed. 'I too think it might be the same man.'

Again the men lapsed into silence, each engrossed in his own thoughts. People came and went from the apartment block but whenever the policeman raised an inquiring eyebrow at the youth sitting sullenly opposite him, he received a firm shake of the head.

'Do you know what these men have done?' asked the policeman at one point.

'Don't you know? I thought you were the police!'

Sergeant Agus looked embarrassed. He blinked rapidly but said a little defiantly, 'I was just told to follow the red bike. I ended up here. Next thing I knew, they asked me to fetch you and see whether you could confirm the ID.'

Wayan said knowingly, 'That policeman from Singapore – he just tells people what to do. He never does anything himself!'

Agus contemplated the Sikh inspector – even in the absence of the looming presence of the fat man, he felt the hairs on the back of his neck stand up. He said, wondering why he felt the need to defend the Singapore officer, 'I am sure he is very busy also.'

Wayan said bitterly, 'Their time is precious but I can sit here all day and lose my job.'

'It is the way of the world, young man,' said the policeman in an amused tone. 'Are they drug traffickers, do you think, the owners of this famous red bike?'

Wayan shook his head, pleased to have some small advantage over the figure in authority. 'They were friendly with some Englishman who stayed at the holiday villa where I work.'

'So what?'

'So, he is dead!'

'How?'

'Shot – and his body left at the Sari Club just before the bombs.'

'Ayoh! Are these guys the murderers? Did

214

you see them do it?'

Wayan was tempted to embellish his story – force the policeman to treat him with some respect – but he decided reluctantly that it was a tactic that could backfire spectacularly.

'Not so exciting! That fat policeman just wants to ask them some questions.'

Agus hunched over in disappointment, his neck disappearing into his muscular shoulders. He had been sure that he was going to apprehend his first murderers. What a feather in his cap that would have been. He would have made a special trip to the Tanah Lot temple on Legian beach if the gods had been so bountiful.

He stared across the road. He spotted a bike cruising down the street. It was red. There were two men on it. The driver was the one he had tailed from Ubud the previous day. He had not seen the pillion rider before. The motorbike pulled up in front of the apartment block and the two men alighted. The older one glanced up and down the street but not across in their direction.

As the men disappeared into the stairwell, Wayan said, his voice an excited whisper, 'That's him. The younger one. He picked up Richard Crouch sometimes. The other one I do not recognise!'

The policeman broke into a broad smile. As they stared at the building, a light came on in one of the windows on the third floor.

He said, 'And we know which flat they are in!'

Wayan nodded. 'What now?' he asked.

'We report success!' said Agus enthusiastically.

Wayan grinned. Perhaps it had been worth the long wait after all.

'Where have you been?' demanded Singh crossly. 'I had to interview Tim Yardley on my own.'

Bronwyn ignored his question and the petulantly pursed lips of her superior officer. She asked, 'What did Yardley say? Do you think he did it?'

Singh sighed. 'It would be a great solution, clean and neat. I have no doubt that Sarah Crouch was lining him up to remove her burden of a husband. But I wasn't convinced that Yardley has what it takes to make the transition from wishful thinking to action. He's one of life's spectators, eating cheese and onion crisps, drinking Coke and watching other men get the girls and win the lottery.'

His sidekick nodded so vigorously it caused her pendulous bosom to bob up and down like a boat on a fractious ocean. Singh averted his eyes.

She said, 'When we met him the first time, I didn't cast him in the role of murderer either. He *was* acting peculiar though. Like he wasn't surprised by Richard Crouch's death.'

The inspector from Singapore muttered, 'Yes, I noticed that too. At least, now we know why – Sarah Crouch had already told him that Richard was dead.'

'That makes sense,' said Bronwyn in a pleased tone. She continued curiously, 'Did you tell him about surfer boy?'

Singh grinned maliciously. 'I introduced them to each other!'

'You did what?'

'You heard me

'That was a nasty thing to do,' said Bronwyn firmly. 'Tim Yardley must have been devastated.'

'Tim Yardley might have killed a man. You'll forgive me if I think that's more important than hurting his *feelings*.'

Bronwyn ran her tongue over her teeth. She was not sure she had the streak of cruelty that appeared to be necessary to investigate a murder.

She asked, 'What was his reaction?'

'I think Yardley is sitting on a beach with a six-pack of Bintang wondering why women are incapable of the sort of loyalty and love he has shown both his wife and Sarah Crouch.'

Singh stuck a cigarette in the corner of his mouth and fished in a pocket for his lighter. Bronwyn glared at him and nodded at the red and white 'No Smoking' sign above his head. The Sikh inspector ran his thumb over the lighter and held the blue and yellow flame to the tip of his cigarette. He inhaled deeply, causing the end to flare a deep orange, exhaled a thick cloud of grey smoke into the room and said, 'We still need more suspects.'

His deputy waved her hand in front of her face, ostentatiously fanning the smoke away. She said smartly, 'Well, I have one!'

Singh's cigarette was perched on his bottom lip. It danced as he spoke. He asked, 'Who?' His voice was sceptical that Bronwyn could have found something that he had missed.

Bronwyn decided to ignore the provocation. She said, 'I watched the CCTV tapes from the various banks and ATMs. That's why I didn't come in for Yardley's interview.'

'And...?'

'On the day before the bombs, Crouch withdrew the largest single sum at the Bank Mandiri branch in Kuta, ten thousand US dollars. This man was lurking in the background.' She slid a blurry black and white print of a man across the table. The inspector picked it up and stared at it from a distance of a few feet. He needed glasses for his long-sightedness, guessed Bronwyn.

Singh said, his brow creased with puzzlement, 'He looks familiar. I'm sure I've seen him on television.'

Bronwyn passed him the photographs she had taken of Sarah Crouch's friends after their interview with them. 'It's Julian Greenwood!'

Singh smacked a hand to his forehead. 'I didn't recognise him.'

Bronwyn grinned triumphantly.

The inspector growled, 'When you're done patting yourself on the back, perhaps you could find out if there's any reason Greenwood might have been tempted by the wads of cash in Richard Crouch's pockets?'

The flat was a mess. Nuri had not cleared up after breakfast. Ants had gathered in writhing black masses to devour the bits of crust and traces of *kaya*, a coconut jam. The chairs were disorderly and the whole front room smelt rank. Ghani felt his temper flare uncontrollably. Was this what a husband deserved after a long day?

He strode into the bedroom. Nuri was lying on her side under the covers. It was the same position he had left her in that morning. He remembered that when he had gone to bed the previous night, his wife was feigning sleep. He had watched her – huddled under the blanket, facing away from the door, eyes tightly shut, and felt a stab of exasperation. He had climbed into bed and turned to face the other way. They had lain back to back, two feet between them despite the narrowness of the bed. It was the universal image of a marriage in trouble.

Now, twenty-fours hours later, he stared at her, a petite figure on the bed. her long hair was spread across the pillow like a fan. It was a small room – with the windows and door shut and a sweating human presence in it, the atmosphere was muggy and stale.

Ghani said roughly, 'Nuri!' and when she did not respond, a little louder, 'Nuri!'

Nuri turned slowly, blinking against the light, a bare bulb hanging from a yellowing wire. Ghani had switched it on as he walked in.

She stared at him as if he were a stranger.

He asked in a gentler tone, 'Are you unwell?'

She shook her head and sat up. He noticed that the pillow on which she had been lying had a damp patch on it. Was it sweat or tears, he wondered. What in the world did his young wife have to weep over?

He had provided well for her. Her parents, although respected in the village for their unswerving faith and religious knowledge, had not been well off. He remembered his visits to the house. It had been a small wooden building with an *attap* roof. The floor was hard grey cement without even a straw mat to keep the damp out. The rooms were partitioned with plywood, flimsy erections that barely provided privacy. There had been a rusty stand fan to cool the front room and a few rattan chairs with well worn cushions covered in faded cloth. He, Ghani, had given Nuri a much more comfortable house in that Sulawesi village. Not luxurious. He could not afford it and it would not have been fitting for someone who had always led an austere, God-fearing life. But it had been a vast improvement on the home she was married from.

He treated her kindly as well. Her father had been a stern taskmaster, ruling his children with iron discipline.

Perhaps, coming from such a regimented background, the freedom he had granted Nuri had been too much. She was young. Bringing her to Bali had been a mistake. Bali was a shock even to a Moslem who was hardened to the decadence of the Westerners. How much more so for an innocent like Nuri?

He remembered her laughing with delight on the ferry from Java to see the young boys dive into the churning water to retrieve coins that passengers threw for them. She had been so filled with enthusiasm for new experiences.

Now, his wife sat on the bed looking at him with sad eyes and unbound hair, waiting for him to censure her or beat her or divorce her. It would be so easy to do any of these things. She deserved a scolding for the state of the house. He was certainly well within his rights as a husband to knock some sense into her. Divorce might be an extreme step, but he had only to utter the words and she would, in the eyes of God, be his ex-wife. For a moment, he was tempted. He wanted to wipe that blank look off her face.

He felt a hint of self-doubt. Was he too old and unattractive? He knew that he was twenty years older than her but he had been much sought-after as a husband. When he had been instructed by the spiritual elders to settle down, he had no difficulty choosing Nuri. She had caught his attention with her sheer unobtrusiveness as she slunk into the room wearing her full *hijab*, to clear a glass or serve some food to the menfolk. Her father's reputation as a scholar had reached far beyond their small village. Truly, his marrying Nuri had seemed like a match made in heaven, sanctioned by his peers, her family, his spiritual leaders and Allah.

She was still looking at him. It seemed to Ghani that she was almost willing him to do or say something hurtful, as if it would validate her opinion of him. Her eyes shocked him. Thus did he imagine the eyes of lost souls who had fallen from the grace of Allah. Never had he expected to see that expression of utter emptiness on the face of his wife. Ghani opened his mouth and raised his hand as if he was about to say something and emphasise it with a gesture. Instead, he turned slowly away from her and walked out of the room. Just before he shut the door again, his arm snaked in and switched off the light. Inside, Nuri was plunged into sudden absolute darkness. She closed her eyes and lay back on the pillow.

Ghani stood at the doorway. Abu Bakr and Yusuf had come in while he was in the room with Nuri. Ramzi was sitting on a chair at the dining table, rocking it back and forth on its back legs.

Abu Bakr asked gruffly, trying to hide his embarrassment at the marital discord, 'Is everything all right?'

Ghani nodded.

Yusuf seemed to realise something was amiss because he said, his voice quickening with anxiety, 'Is Nuri all night? Is she unwell?'

'She'll be fine if she has some rest.'

If the brothers were curious as to why Ghani was putting up with the mood swings of his wife and their sister, they had the tact not to ask. On at least, Abu Bakr had the tact not to ask and he had pulled Ramzi aside and warned him to remain silent on the subject of their sister.

Ramzi had rubbed his cheek where Nuri had slapped him the previous day and said,

'As you wish, brother. My face still hurts!'

Bronwyn exclaimed, her usually pale cheeks rosy with excitement, 'Sergeant Agus just called. Wayan confirmed the identity of at least one of the men. We've found the mysterious incomer friends of Richard Crouch!'

Singh scratched his neck with quick, repetitive actions like a flea-ridden mongrel. He asked, 'Is Nyoman outside?'

Bronwyn nodded. Nyoman had become their personal driver in Bali. He drove them everywhere and hung around outside the hotel lobby or police station when they were not on the move, smoking his *kreteks* and indulging in small talk with the other drivers. Bronwyn, worried about the wasted hours spent waiting for them, had urged him to ferry other passengers. Nyoman had declined, assuring her that it was a privilege to wait for such important clients. She had been impressed by his loyalty but the cynical inspector from Singapore had pointed out that Nyoman had a lot more to lose from their finding another chauffeur. He was not being loyal, he was being prudent.

They clambered into the back seat of the Kijang and Bronwyn recited the address to him.

Nyoman laughed. 'Tough neighbour-hood,' he said. 'Nothing to see and nothing to buy. I have no cousins there at all!'

'We're on police business,' snapped Singh. Nyoman's constant good humour grated on him – it was like fingernails on a blackboard on the clinking together of steel cutlery. It set his teeth on edge. It was the same with all the Balinese. They were always so friendly and happy. Even the pall cast by the Bali bombings did not stop them inquiring politely where one was from, whether one liked Bali, how long one was staying and a thousand other similarly innocuous questions which, when repeated every day by dozens of Balinese, really annoyed the taciturn inspector.

Nyoman turned his head to look at them in the back seat with a wide, excited grin. 'Police business? That is very exciting!'

'Not half as exciting as your driving while looking backwards,' growled the inspector.

Nyoman sniggered at what he assumed was a witty sally by the fat man but did turn his attention to the road – just in time to narrowly avoid a family of four crammed on the back of a small bike.

'So, are you going to arrest someone? Is it about the Bali bombs?'

Bronwyn said, 'No, far from it. We're just interviewing some witnesses. If we were going to arrest anyone in connection with the blasts, I think you'd see a lot more back-up!'

'Pity I have no siren,' exclaimed Nyoman, accelerating recklessly in his excitement. Singh snorted derisively and the rest of the drive was conducted in silence.

Twelve

Singh stood at the door, listening hard. He could make out the sound of lowered voices. He heard an advertising jingle – it was a television. Hopefully, it meant there was someone at home. He did not relish clambering up the three flights of stairs again. Singh rapped on the door sharply. There was a sudden silence. The television had been switched off. After a few moments, he raised his great fist and pounded on the door. Bronwyn glowered at him. He guessed she thought he was acting too much like the lumbering policeman.

Before he could annoy her further by kicking the door down without a warrant, it swung open, squeaking tiredly on its hinges. Singh held up his badge and said a trifle breathlessly, still trying to recover from the steep stairs, 'Police. We need to ask you some questions.'

The bearded man who had opened the door hesitated for a moment and then stepped aside reluctantly. The two police personnel strolled in.

Singh's first thought was that he had never seen a more unlikely lot for striking up friendships with expats. The men were unkempt and seemed tired – as if they worked long hours or the night shift. Singh guessed they must have come to Bali to work in the construction or cargo industry. It was hard work for low wages but Bali was still a magnet for men with families to support.

The men remained silent and watchful. Singh was not surprised. Crooked cops often hounded vulnerable incomers, demanding bribes for not entangling them in bureaucracy.

Bronwyn, her blue shirt showing damp perspiration patches under her armpits, had picked up the same nervous vibe. She said reassuringly in the Indonesian language, 'We just need to ask you a few questions about a friend of yours?'

Singh had no difficulty understanding her – the difference between the Indonesian and Malaysian versions of the Malay language was largely a question of accent. The inspector's face remained impassive but he was annoyed. These men were being questioned as witnesses. It was always best to keep those who had dealings with the police on edge. Reassurance was counterproductive. When was Bronwyn going to get over this need to comfort suspects? The correct tactic was to pile pressure on them until they cracked like eggshells.

He demanded abruptly, his tone belligerent, his chin thrust forward, 'Tell us who you are.'

It was the man who let them in who broke the silence. He said, 'I am Ghani from Java. These are my friends Abu Bakr, Ramzi and Yusuf.' As he introduced them, he indicated with a pointed thumb the man he was referring to and they nodded in acknowledgement. All, that is, except Ramzi. With a broad smile to indicate that he, at least, was not intimidated by the police, Ramzi walked over and shook hands with Singh vigorously. He nodded at Bronwyn in a friendly fashion and then retired to his corner of the room. Singh decided that, in contrast to the confident Ramzi, Yusuf appeared simple. He looked at them vacantly, his face expressionless and his eyes blank. Singh could almost smell the musky odour of a trapped beast from where he was standing. Yusuf must have had a really bad experience with the police, thought Singh almost sympathetically, to turn into such a bundle of nerves at the mere sight of a couple of cops.

'Are you all from Java?' This was Bronwyn, her tone light and conversational.

Ghani hesitated and then said, 'No, just me. The others are from Sulawesi.'

'You've come a long way,' remarked Singh.

'We need the work,' muttered Ghani. He

hoped the others remembered the simple story they had put together for instances like these.

'What do you do?'

'Mostly we work on the construction sites as day labourers.'

'So why are you looking for us?' It was Ramzi, unable to hide his curiosity.

Singh stared at him long and hard. He knew the type. Cocky, lots of nervous energy – men like Ramzi generally overrated their own abilities. According to Agus, the rider of the red bike had been young and square-jawed with wavy black hair. The description fitted this impatient young man in tight jeans.

His older brother – they had to be siblings, the resemblance was so marked – had the same chiselled features but his hair was short and he had a wispy beard with hints of grey in it. Abu Bakr was glaring at the younger man as if to chastise him for speaking out of turn or, more likely, restrain him from doing it again.

Singh said mildly, 'We are looking for information on Richard Crouch?'

There were genuinely blank stares all around. The inspector felt a frisson of doubt. Was this a wild goose chase?

Ghani said categorically, 'We do not know anyone by that name.'

Singh noted that he and Ghani were

almost the same height. They both had grizzled beards. There the resemblance ended. Singh had gone soft doing a job that used his brain but left his muscles to atrophy. Ghani was strong, with the powerful build of a manual labourer. He did not have the sculpted muscular build of the dilettante body builder. Ghani's physical strength was real and practical and visible in his thick neck and stocky shape.

Bronwyn asked, 'Are you sure?'

Ghani nodded firmly and his actions were echoed by all the men except Yusuf. Singh did not think that Yusuf's stillness suggested he knew Crouch. It merely indicated that he was too engrossed in his own internal dialogue to follow the line of questioning.

Singh said, pointing at Ramzi aggressively, 'But you have been identified – witnesses have seen you with him!'

All the men turned as one to glare at Ramzi – like landlocked synchronised swimmers, thought Singh.

Ghani was livid – his face was mottled and his jaw clenched. Singh wondered why he was quite so angry.

Ramzi appeared genuinely taken aback. There was nothing exaggerated about his puzzled frown.

Singh decided on the spot that if Wayan had got the identification of Richard Crouch's friends wrong he would lock him

231

up for twenty-four hours with every Balinese deadbeat he could find.

Singh asked, grasping at straws, 'You have a big red motorbike?'

Ramzi said cautiously, 'Ya.'

'And you've been to Ubud?'

'Ya.'

'And yet you deny knowing Crouch?'

Ramzi nodded in emphatic fashion.

None of them had heard the bedroom door open so when Nuri spoke, the men jumped.

She asked, her voice literally trembling with anxiety, 'Why do you ask about Richard?'

Singh and Bronwyn both turned to stare at the latest addition to the room.

The thin, exhausted-looking woman with puffy eyes and lank long hair asked again, 'Why do you ask about Richard Crouch?' This time her voice had a panicky edge.

Singh was the first to respond. He asked a question in turn, 'Did *you* know him?'

She nodded once.

Ghani intervened. He said furiously, 'What are you saying, wife? You are talking nonsense. How could you know this Richard Crouch?'

At first it did not appear that she had heard him. But then she whispered, 'What do you mean? We all know him...'

There was consternation in the room.

Ramzi barked, 'I think you have gone mad, sister.'

Ghani shouted, 'Be quiet – you don't know what you are saying!'

Abu Bakr stepped forward, trying to usher the young woman back into the bedroom. Nuri stood her ground and Singh intervened. 'Why do you say you know Crouch?'

'He was our ... friend. What has happened to him?'

Bronwyn had been looking in the folder she was carrying and now she took out an enlarged copy of Crouch's passport photo.

She walked over to Ghani and held out the picture silently. Nuri sidled towards him. She reminded Singh of a small hungry beast looking for a scrap of food amongst predators. Her husband took the photo and gazed at it curiously. Blood drained from his face like sand through an hourglass.

Singh stated categorically, 'You *do* know him.'

Ghani hesitated. His sudden pallor made him look older. The lines of worry and the single scar that radiated from the corner of his eye and disappeared into his hairline were clearly defined, as if a sculptor had gone over the lines with a sharp knife, determined to bring out the character in his subject's face. Abu Bakr and Ramzi edged closer, anxious to have a peek at the photo.

Ghani said, trying to inject a lighter tone

into his voice, 'Yes, we know him. He is a friend – we met him in Ubud.'

Bronwyn did not try and hide the puzzlement in her voice. 'But then why did you deny it?'

Ghani answered quietly, 'You asked whether we know Richard Crouch? We do not know Richard Crouch. We met this man at a mosque. He told us his name was Abdullah.'

Singh exhaled, a gusty sound, audible to all.

From the expressions on the faces of Abu Bakr and Ramzi, they were flabbergasted as well. Ramzi, especially, looked shocked. His pupils were dilated and his mouth was agape, revealing the tips of even, white teeth.

'You became friends?' Singh was anxious to understand how the relationship had developed.

He did not miss the warning glance Ghani gave the rest of the men. If Ghani wanted to be official spokesperson, Singh decided, he would let him adopt the role. But he would not hesitate to separate the men and question them independently if he did not like what he heard.

Ghani spoke slowly and clearly. The Sikh policeman suspected he wanted to make sure the others didn't contradict him. 'We met at a mosque in Denpasar. He was friendly. A really good person. Sometimes we would meet him for a meal in Ubud or he would come to Denpasar. Ramzi would pick him up on the bike.'

'Isn't it a bit odd that you should be making friends with *expats?*' asked Singh, looking around the small, dingy apartment, an incredulous expression on his face.

If Ghani knew he was being provoked, he gave no sign of it. He replied evenly, 'We are outsiders here in Bali. The Balinese do not like anyone from the rest of Indonesia. They say we take their jobs and pollute their Hindu religion. But we are just here to earn some money. When Abdullah, the one you call Crouch, was friendly – well – it was nice for us.'

The explanation sounded well rehearsed, thought Singh, but it could also be true.

He asked rudely, 'But what did *he* get out of it?'

He was trying to annoy Ghani but, as he should have guessed, it was the hot-tempered Ramzi who took offence.

Ramzi spoke through gritted teeth. 'Why do you ask such a question? Because he is *white?* Because he is a Westerner you think he is too good for us?' He turned suddenly to Bronwyn, pointing at her with an accusing finger. 'Does *she* think she is better than us too?'

Abu Bakn walked over to Ramzi and put a

235

hand on his shoulder. He said quietly but firmly, 'Brother, let Ghani do the talking. The police – it is their tactic to provoke anger.'

Ghani added, 'Abdullah is a devout Moslem. He did not find that much to amuse him in Bali.'

It was Nuri who spoke again, her body stiff and tense as she looked at the policeman from Singapore. 'Where is he? Where is Abdullah?'

Bronwyn and Singh glanced at each other. Was this the time to reveal what they knew and, if so, how much?

This case was going nowhere fast, thought Singh, and dropped his bombshell. 'Richard Crouch – Abdullah, as you know him – is dead.'

There was a sharp intake of breath from Ghani. Abu Bakr muttered something under his breath. He might have been uttering a prayer or swearing, Singh couldn't tell. Ramzi was looking down at his feet but at Singh's words he raised his head and their eyes met fleetingly. For a split second, Singh had the impression that Ramzi was keeping secrets.

None of them had been watching Nuri. It was the sudden exclamation from Yusuf that drew their attention. She had collapsed. Yusuf rushed over and tried to raise her head.

Bronwyn, ever efficient, hurried forward and knelt by the girl. She felt for a pulse and fanned Nuri's pale cheeks with her hand. Abu Bakr handed her a magazine. She smiled gratefully at him and continued to fan the girl, this time using the magazine.

Ghani was staring at Nuri in bemusement. He said, a little plaintively, 'My wife has not been well recently.'

Bronwyn said briskly – she had slipped into ward matron mode, thought Singh – 'I think she's just fainted. Perhaps I could have a wet towel?'

It was Yusuf who hurried over to the sink, eyes worried behind his glasses. He carefully rinsed out the cloth, squeezed it as hard as he could and brought it to Bronwyn. She started to wipe Nuri's face gently. Yusuf hovered over her like a mother hen, intermittently tugging at his beard.

Ramzi ignored the melee around his sister. He asked, 'How did he die?'

When there was no immediate answer, he repeated the question more urgently, 'How did Abdullah, our friend, die?'

Singh said casually, 'Oh! He was shot through the head.'

'So, what do you think?'

'About what?'

Bronwyn glowered at the man sitting next to her. It was a wasted gesture. He was

237

staring pensively out of the tinted window of their Kijang.

Nyoman asked enthusiastically from the front, 'Did you catch anyone?'

Bronwyn took out the irritation she felt for her colleague on the driver. 'Do we look like we've arrested anyone?'

Nyoman retreated into huffy silence and Bronwyn said apologetically, 'I'm sorry, Nyoman. We're all a bit tired, that's all.'

She glanced at her watch, pressing a button so that the hands were backlit. It was getting late. She waited for a few minutes but then realised that the inspector had not noticed that she was giving him the cold shoulder. She abandoned the effort to draw the policeman's attention to his own conversational shortcomings and asked, 'Do you think they had anything to do with it?'

'The murder of Richard Crouch *alias* Abdullah?' Singh's voice crackled with amusement. 'Now that was an unexpected development!'

'His being a Moslem?'

She sensed rather than saw Singh nod his head in the darkness of the quiet street.

Bronwyn said, her voice growing more confident as she saw that the inspector was equally unsure about what to make of Richard Crouch's friends, 'It does explain why an expat might have been friendly with incomers.'

'Yes,' agreed Singh. 'It's almost believable that they formed a bond based on feeling excluded.'

'*Almost* believable? Does that mean you don't believe it?'

'I never believe anything unless I have some proof of it,' said Singh smugly. 'It's the first rule of a murder investigation – everybody lies!'

'I don't think that's true,' said Bronwyn. 'People surely realise that if they have nothing to hide it's better to come clean with the police.'

Singh slapped his hand down to emphasise his disagreement and was overwhelmed by a violent paroxysm of coughing triggered by the dust he had dislodged from the car seat.

Bronwyn remarked, 'You ought to vacuum this vehicle once in a while, Nyoman.'

Nyoman muttered, 'As you wish, *Ibu*,' and then lapsed into silence, his stiff back the only clue that he was offended.

She said in exasperated tones, 'I was just joking, Nyoman!'

'Yes, *Ibu*. But I will still clean the car tomorrow.'

Singh was blowing his nose into a handkerchief. He said, 'I shan't do that again.'

When there was no response from Bronwyn, he asked, 'Do *you* think those men had anything to do with the murder?'

She shook her head doubtfully. 'I can't

think why they would have killed Richard Crouch...'

'Did you think they were hiding something?'

Bronwyn replied tentatively, 'They did act a bit defensive – but nothing unusual for an incomer, I would assume. We *did* go in and ask them whether they knew anything about a murdered Bali expat. That must have really frightened them.'

Singh said, 'Well, the half-wit looked scared enough!'

Bronwyn feigned ignorance of whom he meant – she did not approve of the inspector's terminology for Yusuf. She asked, 'Whom do you mean?'

Singh ignored the question. He continued musing, 'I'm sure that Ramzi guy knows something.'

'The hot-tempered, handsome one?'

'Hot-tempered certainly. I didn't notice that he was good looking.'

'Drop dead gorgeous.'

'All right, I'll take your word for it. But did you think he was hiding something?'

'No, not really.'

Singh snorted. 'Well, my long experience of this job tells me that something is amiss with that fellow.'

'I thought the girl was the most peculiar.' Bronwyn made the suggestion with some trepidation. Singh was clearly in a mood to shoot down anyone's ideas except his own.

'She *was* odd – how is it that she knew that his name was Richard Crouch and the rest didn't? And what was all that fainting about?'

Bronwyn said, 'She was really out of sorts, poor thing. She smelt like she hadn't bathed. Her hair was none too clean either. She was dehydrated. Her lips were dry and chapped.'

Singh added, 'And she really caught the others by surprise, even her husband, by knowing that Crouch and Abdullah were one and the same person.'

'Which means that she was better acquainted with the dead man than the rest of them...'

Singh clapped his hands together. It was a sudden, sharp sound and Bronwyn jumped. She asked crossly, 'What is it?'

'I think our good Moslem was having an affair with that young lady.'

'Don't be ridiculous!'

'Why do you dismiss it? He was unhappy with his wife. Nuri is young and, I expect, under all that grime, quite attractive. She knows more about him than is easily explained away. She acts like someone with a broken heart. It makes perfect sense!'

'But...' Bronwyn was struggling to articulate her doubts.

'But what?'

'But they seemed like such a religious bunch – they met Abdullah at a mosque – I thought Moslems really frowned on adultery.'

Singh chortled, a hearty, cheerful sound. 'My dear girl – in my experience, the lusts of the flesh trump God every single time!'

After the police left, there was a hush in the room. Nobody had the courage to break it. Nuri, who had swooned like some character from a soap opera, thought Ghani in disgust, had been carried to her room and laid on the bed. Ghani was anxious to talk to her. It was exceedingly odd that she should be the only one to know that Abdullah's original name, before he converted to Islam, was Richard Crouch. Why would he have confided such a thing? And to his wife? He had not thought that they were close. He was not aware of any private conversation between them.

He cast his mind back to Abdullah's visits to their apartment. He had come by a number of times. Nuri had been present. She had served the food and drinks in her normal quiet, even subservient, way. He had not noticed her, which meant that her behaviour had not been out of the ordinary. If she had been chatting to Abdullah about his past life, he hadn't been present at the conversation.

Abu Bakr broke the silence. His tension was visible in the sinews of his neck, which were stretched taut and painful. He asked, 'What now?'

'What do you mean?' demanded Ramzi.

Abu Bakr ignored him and said again, turning his body slightly so that the question was directed at Ghani, 'What now?'

Ghani was irritable. His leg shook furiously, up and down, up and down as he sat in the only armchair in the room. He said, 'I have no idea what you are asking me.'

Abu Bakr flushed. The red blood suffused his face, the high tide at the apex of his cheek bones. He stood his ground. 'Do we cancel our plans?'

Ramzi shouted, 'Of course not.'

This time his brother could not ignore him. Still red, but this time in anger, he whirled around on the ball of one foot. 'Who appointed you the boss, younger brother? Your job is to wait for instructions and carry them out. Leave the decision-making to your elders ... and betters!'

Ghani intervened. 'Why should we cancel our plans?' he asked. His voice was cold and brittle.

'Why? You ask why? Did we not just have the police at our door, in our flat, asking us questions about Abdullah?'

'Yes, they were here about Abdullah. *Not* about us! They know nothing about us. Why should we stop?' Ghani's voice grew steadily louder like someone turning up the volume button on a stereo. He finished near a shout. His face was crimson except for the pale rings around his eyes and his mouth.

Abu Bakr took a deep breath. In another culture, one might have suspected him of counting to ten to keep a lid on his temper. He said now, slowly and pedantically, as if he was talking to children or fools, 'Abdullah was shot. We do not know by whom and neither do the police. But they are not just asking us friendly questions, they are looking for a murderer. That is serious. They will investigate thoroughly. Look how they traced us – all because my fool of a brother likes big red bikes.'

Ramzi glared at him.

Abu Bakr reiterated, 'I always knew that bike would be trouble! I still can't believe you purchased it.'

Ghani was calm. He said, 'That is in the past now. Remember, the police know nothing. They are hunting for a murderer. We are just witnesses. We need to hold our nerve.'

'Hold our nerve?' asked Abu Bakr, his tone high-pitched with anxiety. 'We have more to do than that, Ghani. Abdullah is dead. Our *bomb-maker* is dead!'

Thirteen

Singh was lying in bed fully clothed. He was on top of the covers, his back supported by a stack of three soft pillows. He lay at a slight angle so that his footwear was sticking off the side of the bed. Although his sneakers appeared fairly clean, he had no intention of letting them rest on his bedding. Brought up to go barefoot indoors, he found it difficult enough to wear shoes in a hotel bedroom. It seemed thoroughly unhygienic to walk up and down the pale carpets in his sneakers. Only the knowledge that every previous guest had done so prevented him from going unshod. He grimaced at what his mother would have said if she had caught him with shoes on the bed. He would have felt the bamboo cane she kept for situations requiring memorable discipline.

Singh groped around the side table and found the television remote. He had been unfit before, he thought. If he spent much longer in this tiny hotel room where everything was within reach, from the fridge near his bed to the control panel built into the side table, he would get even fatter. As it was, his belly at its apex was obscuring the bottom of the television screen. Singh hitched himself up a bit higher on the pillows and flicked channels until he found a news programme.

One of the Bali bombers, Amrozi, was being interviewed. Indonesian policing methods were still in the dark ages. But Amrozi didn't look like he'd been at the receiving end of a thrashing. Despite this, he was singing like a canary. He seemed extremely pleased to be able to hold forth on television, laughing and joking and justifying his actions.

The doorbell to Singh's room rang. He dragged himself to his feet with difficulty. Bronwyn filled the entrance. She had showered and changed and looked re-energised. Her hair was damp and darker than usual, wet tendrils that looked like rat's tails dripped water onto her shoulders. Singh wished that he had bathed rather than watch Amrozi explain why mass murder was acceptable. He did not feel fresh. He decided not to take his shoes off while Bronwyn was in the room. His socks probably smelt like *belachan*, the Indonesian prawn paste that caused white tourists to gag and clutch at their noses.

Bronwyn said, 'Well, may I come in?'

Singh realised that he was still blocking the doorway while he considered the condition of his socks. He must be tired. He was not thinking straight. He moved aside to let the Australian enter.

'Your room is bigger than mine,' she remarked.

Singh glanced around the room with a jaundiced eye. He was sick of the place. He was really looking forward to getting back to Singapore. Not even the presence of his wife with a month's backlog of nagging could dull his longing to wander barefoot about his three-bedroom house. His home needed a paint job and a bit of fixing up but it was as familiar as an old blanket and just as comfortable. This hotel room was pastel and barren. Not even an attempt to incorporate Balinese features – carved teak chairs and frogs spouting water from their mouths instead of taps – could hide its essential soul-lessness.

The television was still on. Bronwyn glanced at the screen in disgust. 'I was watching a bit of that in my room,' she said.

Singh grunted. 'I have no idea why they are parading this comedian on television.'

'So that the locals can see that there was Indonesian involvement in the bombings – there's been a lot of scepticism.'

'That makes sense, I suppose,' he admitted reluctantly. He grabbed the remote and switched off the television. 'Enough of that. Let's make a plan for tomorrow.'

'What do you want to do next?'

Singh rubbed his eyes with the palms of his hands. 'Julian Greenwood first, I think. We shouldn't forget the earlier suspects just because we've had an influx of new ones. Agus called and said Greenwood owes some local gangster a fair amount – a gambling debt. He might have been tempted by all that money Crouch was pocketing at the bank.'

'And then?'

'Get the girl alone!'

'Which girl?'

'The Indonesian who was in love with Crouch.'

'The Indonesian who *might* have been in love with Crouch,' said Bronwyn. 'Do you want her arrested?'

'No, not yet. Get someone to watch the flat tomorrow. When the menfolk go to work, we'll pay another visit.'

'Even if she was having an affair with him, you don't think she killed him, do you?'

Singh shook his head. 'The news of his death came as a complete surprise to her. She wasn't faking that collapse.'

'How do you know that?'

'Oh, it's quite easy to shut one's eyes and slump to the ground – but it's not possible to turn pale on command. She was as white as a ghost.'

Bronwyn twined her fingers together and leaned her chin on them with a resigned air.

'All right, we question her. But if she didn't do it, what are we hoping to prove? We'll just upset the girl.'

'You need to get over this reluctance to distress people in the midst of a murder investigation,' said the inspector pointedly. 'Treating witnesses with kid gloves isn't going to help us find a murderer.'

Bronwyn sighed. 'It just seems cruel – that kid is suffering.'

'Richard Crouch is *dead*.'

'I guess you're right.'

'I am right! Think about it, if this girl was having an affair it opens up whole new avenues.'

'Like what?'

'It gives Sarah Crouch another motive – jealousy. That girl's husband could have done it. He looks like a tough cookie.' Singh grinned broadly, forgetting his homesickness and smelly socks. 'Bronwyn – we're making progress!'

Bronwyn looked embarrassed. 'I was wondering whether I could have some time off.'

'Time off?' Singh's eyebrows almost met in his consternation. 'Why do you want time off?'

'Just the day after tomorrow...'

'Planning a picnic? Going for a swim when we're on the verge of a breakthrough?'

'No,' said Bronwyn, laughing. 'There is

that purification ritual for the blast victims outside the Sari Club. I just feel I ought to go.'

'You honour the dead by finding their killers – not sitting around chanting and burning incense,' said Singh curtly.

Bronwyn was adamant. 'I would like to go.'

'Well, I can't really stop you. I'm not actually your superior officer. But if I crack the case and take all the credit while you're wasting your time, don't blame me.'

Ghani gazed at his foot soldiers, the foot soldiers of Allah.

There was Yusuf, nervous and doubting, sitting cross-legged on the floor. His eyes behind his big glasses flickered from side to side as if he was watching an imaginary tennis match.

Ramzi, at least, looked the part. Tall and handsome, he was leaning against a wall, arms folded in front of him. He was less on edge than the rest of them, thriving on the adrenaline of danger.

Ghani was painfully aware that Abu Bakr was his only reliable ally. He had great faith in the judgement of Abu Bakr. He had proved himself in the fighting in Mindanao and he was competent to advise young volunteers, quoting carefully chosen passages in the Quran to great effect.

And then there was his wife. Ghani had decided against letting Nuri in on their plans. He was not convinced that she would understand that the wave of attacks against Bali was a natural extension of the war against the infidels waged in Afghanistan and Iraq. It was better for all concerned that she believe that they were in Bali to set up a religious school.

Ghani felt a flash of impatience as he remembered how Nuri had fainted when she heard that Abdullah was dead. She was going to have to pull herself together or she was going to be a real burden to the team.

'So, what's the plan?' asked Ramzi, cracking his knuckles as if he anticipated a fistfight.

Ghani said heavily, 'Let us sit at the table.'

Ramzi was not showing him enough respect. It was not a foot soldier's place to stand tall while the field commander sat on a creaking rattan chair or to question him before he was ready to speak. Ghani decided to hold his peace. They were a small group. He could not afford to lose anyone now. He would rein in Ramzi when he had to – but not before.

Ghani hauled himself out of the deep chair and led the way to the dining table. He sat at the head and Abu Bakr sat down to his right. Yusuf hesitated painfully. Even the decision of which chair to take at the small

251

table was too much for him. He settled tentatively on the chair at the tail, opposite Ghani. Ramzi strode over and managed, by twirling his chair around so that he was sitting with his legs spread and his arms resting on the back, to make the act of sitting down an expression of individuality.

Ghani said, 'We are in the countdown to the next attack.'

Ramzi slammed his fist into the palm of his other hand. 'It's about time! What's the target?'

Ghani ignored him. He continued, 'We need to assemble the bomb.'

Complete silence greeted this remark. Abdullah the bomb-maker, who had disappeared without a trace after preparing the explosives for the first blasts, had turned up dead. They were going to have to manage without him.

'Abu Bakr has been instructed in bomb-making techniques at the Afghan military training camps. He will construct the bomb.'

Abu Bakr said, 'By the grace of God, I will find the strength and knowledge to do it.'

Again, it was Ramzi who interrupted. 'Where is the equipment?'

Ghani explained, 'In a safe house.'

'Why not here?' asked Yusuf curiously, his first contribution to the discussion.

Ramzi snorted. 'Because it is better that

we don't spend time with stuff that is designed to blow up!'

Yusuf retracted into his shell. It was a visible process. His back hunched, he pulled in his neck and ducked his chin – his mental retreat from the aggressive Ramzi was reflected in his physical behaviour.

Abu Bakr interrupted the fractious conversation. 'How will we deliver the bomb?'

'A closed vehicle of some sort...'

'And is young Yusuf here going to be the driver?' asked Ramzi.

Ghani said quietly, 'Yes, Yusuf has been selected by Allah for the ultimate sacrifice and the ultimate reward.'

Yusuf smiled weakly. It seemed as if he was about to speak and then changed his mind and stared down at the floor.

Abu Bakr said gently, 'Yusuf, we are happy to hear your words.'

Yusuf mumbled something that no one could make out.

'Speak up, Yusuf. No one can hear you! You need some self-confidence. At this rate even the seventy-two virgins waiting for you in heaven won't be interested!' Ramzi laughed loudly at his own joke.

Ghani said angrily, 'Enough, Ramzi. My patience is wearing thin. Allah will reward his martyrs as they deserve.' He turned to Yusuf and asked, 'What did you say, Yusuf?'

Yusuf whispered, 'I hope there are more

Americans this time than in the first bomb.'

Ghani nodded. 'We hear your request, Yusuf. We will look for such a target.'

Ramzi asked eagerly, 'What should I do? Can I look for a target too?'

Abu Bakr and Ghani looked at each other.

Ghani made up his mind. He said, 'Ramzi, use some of the ill-gotten talents of your youth – steal an unmarked white van.'

Ramzi asked, 'May I take the bike?'

'All right.'

Abu Bakr grumbled, 'I just wish that bike was not red.'

Ramzi said cheerfully, 'Nonsense, I love red bikes. Besides they don't sell them in Islamic green.'

Ghani groaned inwardly at this flippancy but did not argue.

Abu Bakr said, 'Be careful, brother. That bike which you bought has already caused us a great deal of trouble.'

Ramzi saw that there were lines of real concern on his older brother's face. He said, 'Do not worry. I will be as prudent as you would be.'

Ghani said, 'We cannot ask for more than that.'

Abu Bakr said, 'Very well, field commander. If it is your decision that we proceed, we will do so. I will construct the bomb to-morrow with Yusuf's help.'

'You see, we never needed the bomb-maker!' Ghani was exultant.

'Just as well as someone appears to have shot him in the head,' remarked Abu Bakr. 'I wonder who did it?'

Ghani was not interested. His mind was completely on the job at hand now. He said dismissively, 'We will never know.'

Ramzi was not willing to let the subject drop. 'It is curious though. Why would someone do that? Do you think it was the first cell? Perhaps he let them down somehow or they thought he was a security risk?'

'It's possible, I suppose,' said Abu Bakr doubtfully. 'But he seems to have done his job well. The bombs exploded. That is all you can ask of a bomb-maker.'

Ramzi was enjoying speculating. 'Or perhaps it was the wife...'

'There was a wife?' asked Ghani in surprise.

The others nodded.

'He brought her for cover. So that it would look like he was just another expatriate in Bali. But she was not a Moslem,' explained Abu Bakr.

Ghani said rudely, 'Oh? Then it was probably her!'

Tim Yardley was chewing on his fingernails. The television in the small villa was on. He stared at the screen. He was mesmerised by the black and white film – it was a tale of courage and loyalty, love and sacrifice. The hero was large and broad-shouldered, with a crooked grin. The woman was pretty and feisty – and devoted to her man. Was it only on television that happy endings were possible, he wondered. Or perhaps events only ended well for those who were tall and good looking with the bodies of athletes.

He had married Karri hastily. He acknowledged that to himself. He had not known her well enough – not known her at all, really – before he had begged her to be his wife. It had seemed like such a bold, grand gesture – sweeping the girl off her feet – just like in the movies.

The television cowboy was riding off into the sunset, the girl perched sidesaddle in front of him with his muscular arm around her waist. Perhaps they got home, got married and it turned out he had wed a harpy with a cruel tongue. Maybe that was why the old films hardly ever had sequels.

He had made a mistake with Karri – but he had been convinced that life was giving him a second chance. He remembered meeting Sarah for the first time. His first thought was that he liked the way she wore her hair. The sleek blonde bob was so restrained and dignified compared to his wife's wild efforts. He had admired the quiet way she spoke, her natural poise. He had felt sympathy and fellow feeling as it became obvious that all was not well in the Crouch marriage. Richard and Sarah were distant from each other, the failure of their relationship manifested in coldness rather than cruelty. He had thought Richard a fool for failing to appreciate his wife.

But he would never have thought he had a chance with her – would never have had the courage or the ego to believe that she had an interest in him – if Sarah had not dropped a hundred subtle hints. Their movie was playing in his head now, a silent reel of quiet smiles and brushing hands. Eventually, she had started confiding in him, telling him how she longed for her freedom, for a fresh start with a good man who would treat her with kindness and consideration. She would look at him from under her eyelashes when she said this, just like that woman in the film. Perhaps he should have realised that it was all just acting – men like him never got the girl. He had asked her why she did not divorce Richard. A single tear had coursed down her cheek – Richard wouldn't give her a divorce – he was determined to punish her for wanting to leave him. She was becoming afraid of him – he was behaving more and more peculiarly – unbalanced even – never in public, of course.

Tim was only too willing to believe her – she wanted an ordinary loving man, one just like him – but she also needed a hero, and perhaps he could be that man too.

He had never told her, but he had confronted Richard. It was the morning of the bombings. In many ways, for him, the blasts had just been the exclamation mark at the end of that day.

He remembered that Richard had turned and waited when he had called to him from further down the street. His expression had been courteous but mildly impatient. Tim had found it almost impossible to begin. It was only when Richard had said, 'I hope you don't mind, but I'm in a bit of a hurry,' that he blurted out, 'I want to talk about Sarah!'

Crouch had looked genuinely puzzled. 'Sarah?'

'Yes – why won't you give her a divorce? She's desperately unhappy with you!'

Crouch shook his head. 'I've no idea what my wife has been telling you – but I wouldn't rely on it too much.'

'You'll give her a divorce?'

'No.'

Richard had turned and walked away.

Tim the hero had stumbled after him, determined to say his piece, to get his concerns off his chest, to protect Sarah.

Yardley got to his feet and walked slowly to a mirror. A rheumy-eyed man, his belly pushing the elastic band of his shorts to the limit and flabby arms exposed in a cheap cotton singlet, stared back at him.

His mind flew to the image he had been avoiding all day – of the young man with the brawny tanned arms – just like the guy on television – and sunkissed hair, propping himself up on one elbow and staring intently through the prison bars with bright blue eyes.

Tim closed his hand into a fist and slammed it against the glass. Shards fell to the ground like knives. Blood from his knuckles trickled down his hand and dripped onto the broken mirror.

Ghani went in to confront his wife. He needed to know what was going on. How had she known that Richard Crouch was Abdullah?

She was lying on the bed, her back to the door – and to him.

He said roughly, 'I want to talk to you.'

There was no response from the still figure and he wondered whether she had fainted again.

He said once more, 'I want to talk to you.'

Nuri stirred but did not turn around. He waited, feeling his wrath grow within him. The small flickering flame was threatening to consume him.

He walked around to her side of the bed and stared down at the prone form. She knew he was there, he saw her eyelids flutter. But still she would not look at him, her husband.

He grabbed the covers with a clenched fist and flicked them off her.

As the thin blanket came away, Nuri opened her long-lashed eyes and gazed at him. He was shocked by the despair he saw within them but also angered.

He shouted, 'What is the matter with you?'

'Nothing.'

'How can you say there is nothing the matter? You are not doing your duties as a wife. You smell disgusting.'

'I am not feeling well, that's all. Are good Moslem wives not allowed to fall ill?'

Ghani realised with a shock that she appeared to hate him. He could not understand it. She had seemed happy, at least content, until they came to Bali.

'How did you know what Abdullah's name was?'

'He told me.'

'You spoke to each other?'

She shrugged, a careless gesture expressing complete indifference to his opinion. 'Yes.'

'When?'

'What does it matter?'

'It matters!' He spat the words at her. 'As your husband, I want to know in what circumstances you would talk to this man.'

Nuri sat up in the bed. She leaned back against the headboard and looked at Ghani. Again, he sensed her dislike. It hurt him.

She said, 'We were friends.'

'That is nonsense. There is no friendship between a man and a woman. Men are lustful creatures. They have to be kept at a distance! Are you telling me you failed to do that?'

She did not answer. Her head dropped and the long hair, usually hidden under her *hijab*, fell over her face.

Ghani remembered that she had come out of the room to see the police without covering up, not even a scarf. She had appeared before a non-Moslem male without any modesty in her clothing.

He shouted, 'What is the matter with you? Why have you forgotten your duties as a Moslem?'

Nuri said clearly and coldly, looking at him without fear, 'You are *nothing* to me.'

He hit her. With an open, calloused hand, he struck her across the face with all the force he could muster. She turned her head and jerked back as she saw the blow coming but there was no escaping his all-consuming rage. Nuri fell sideways on the bed, holding her cheek and jaw. He hit her again and, when she whimpered in pain, again. Instead of relieving his feelings, each blow seemed to make him angrier.

261

At last, when his wife was a small ball on the bed, no longer even trying to ward off the blows with her thin arms, he found it in himself to stop.

Ghani saw that there was blood. He had split her lip. If he had closed his fist, she would have lost teeth. He guessed that her body would be marked by the outpouring of his rage. Hot angry tears were welling up in her eyes and coursing down her cheeks like an overflowing monsoon drain.

Ghani stared at the wreck that was his wife and contemplated the ruin of his marriage. His heart was heavy. He had convinced himself that he was picking a wife that met his various practical criteria; a devout Moslem girl from a religious family with connections to the network so that he could cement the ties between families. But the truth was he had seen this girl, the gentle young sister of Abu Bakr and Ramzi, and married her for love, for that sense of peace and respite she gave him from his life as a soldier.

Ghani wondered why he was being tested in this way by his God. He looked at Nuri again – lying there in the bed, blood oozing from her mouth, uncaring about his power over her. She seemed to relish the physical pain as a distraction from her mental anguish.

Ghani walked out of the room. He moved

slowly, like a landlubber on the deck of a ship trying to find his sea legs.

The others were valiantly keeping themselves occupied. Yusuf was squatting against a wall, reading his Quran, his finger tracing the lines as he recited the passages to himself.

Abu Bakr washed the dishes with much clumsy clattering.

Ramzi was slumped on the couch watching the Bali investigation progress reports on television.

Ghani suspected, notwithstanding the hive of activity in the small apartment, his colleagues had been listening hard to see if they could figure out what was going on between him and Nuri.

Abu Bakr asked, wiping his hands as he finished the last plate, 'Is everything all right?'

Ghani said clearly and loudly, 'Yes, everything is fine.'

The flickering television screen showed the Bali bombers being paraded before the media. The men turned as if of one mind to watch the news.

Abu Bakr nodded at the screen. 'Those are men of courage,' he said. *'Insha Allah,* God willing, we will emulate them.'

Ghani felt a rush of cold sweet adrenaline course through his veins. He closed his eyes and enjoyed the spine-tingling sensation. It was as if Allah was pumping courage directly into his body. He felt strong and able, the time was right, the plans were made. Ghani said exultantly, 'We are almost there, men. Show courage and determination and we will strike a blow that the world will never forget.'

Fourteen

Julian Greenwood's drooping moustache quivered. He had his hands gripped tightly together. He sat very upright on a chair in the living room of the luxurious villa he shared with his wife. Singh stood over him. If it had been a social occasion, his physical proximity to Greenwood would have been inappropriate, an encroachment into his personal space. In the circumstances, having demanded to see Greenwood and intimated that he had questions about Richard Crouch that could not wait, Singh was merely intimidating.

Julian queried, and Singh noted that, under pressure, his accent was less upstairs than downstairs, 'What ... what did you want to ask me?' As he spoke, his eyes flickered to the door.

Singh did not appear to hear the question. He glanced around the room. 'Nice place you've got here,' he said approvingly, taking in the rich furnishings, sea view from the patio and fresh lilies in crystal vases that gave the room a rich heady atmosphere.

'Thank you,' said Julian and then reverted to a tense silence. He unclasped his hands and placed them on knees that were pressed together with virginal enthusiasm.

'So why don't you sell some of this stuff – I'd bet that painting is worth a lot.' Singh nodded at a complex painting of Balinese deities in rich colours.

'Why would I do that?' asked Julian.

'To pay off your gambling debts, of course. I hear you're within a few days of having your legs broken...'

Julian was not given an opportunity to deny that he had debts, gambling or otherwise.

A voice from the door said, 'He can't sell any of it because it all belongs to *me*...'

Emily Greenwood sauntered into the room, her bedroom slippers – fluffy pink rabbits with floppy ears – the reason for her quiet approach.

Singh was all smiling politeness. 'Mrs Greenwood, it's nice to see you again.'

'Likewise,' she responded and sat down on a comfortable sofa. She invited Singh to do the same with a lofty wave of her hand. He complied and found himself sinking into the plush sofa like an elephant in quicksand. He struggled for a bit to sit upright and then abandoned the battle. He suspected he looked a little like a beetle on its back, desperately trying to right itself. He made a note to himself that Emily was a smart woman. He, Singh, standing upright and angry, had thoroughly demoralised Julian. Sunk into the cushions, he was a figure of fun.

Emily asked, 'What has my dear husband done now?'

Singh put on his most formal tone. 'As you know, we are making preliminary inquiries into the murder of Richard Crouch. We have reason to suspect that your husband might have been involved.'

'Nothing he does would really surprise me – but kill Richard – why would he do that?'

Singh opened his eyes wide. There was to be no instinctive support from a loving spouse. He tried to sit up a little straighter to show his interest but it was impossible to defy gravity and he sank back down. Singh glanced at Julian, wondering whether he was going to say anything in his own defence. He seemed mesmerised by his wife, staring at her as a snake might look at a mongoose, waiting for her to go for the jugular.

'Robbery!' snapped Singh.

'Did Richard have money?' Her tone was that of the very wealthy, mild surprise that anyone else might have a few dollars tucked away.

'He was carrying ten thousand US dollars when your husband followed him out of a bank – the day before his body was recovered from the Sari Club.'

Singh thought that he had very rarely, if

ever, interviewed a murder suspect who sat silently by while his wife did the talking. Julian's lips were pursed shut as if words were as valuable to him as money.

Emily addressed her husband directly for the first time. 'That would have been a useful sum to you, Julian.'

'I didn't kill him...'

'You had motive and opportunity,' pointed out Singh. 'In my experience, that usually indicates guilt!'

'You have to believe me – I didn't kill him. I happened to be at the bank' – he looked at the other two pleadingly – 'trying to get a loan if you must know. I saw Richard – it was just a coincidence. I didn't know he was going to be there. He withdrew a large sum of money. I had no idea he was flush ... I followed him ... and asked him if I could borrow a few dollars.'

Julian fell silent, unable to complete the tale.

Singh noted that Julian was directing his excuses at both his own wife and the policeman. If anything, he seemed to fear the judgement of his spouse more than the suspicions of the police. It was an interesting departure from the normal priorities. Controlling the purse strings had given Emily a degree of influence over her husband that most women could only dream of – except for his own wife, of course. Singh was distracted momentarily by a memory of the woman who dictated his leisure hours and nagged him about his absent ones.

Emily took up the questioning with natural poise. 'What did Richard say when you asked him for money?'

Singh turned his attention back to the matter at hand.

Julian did not seem to notice that the cross-examination was now being conducted by his wife. He answered in a quiet voice, 'That he could not approve of my gambling habit – and the money was needed for a project he was working on.'

'I wouldn't have thought that Richard Crouch was such a sensible man,' remarked Emily to no one in particular.

Agus, watching the apartment, reported that the men had left. Two of them had ridden away on the red motorbike. The other two had walked down the street. They might have caught a taxi around the corner, he wasn't sure. There was no sign of any woman so he was fairly sure their quarry was still in the apartment.

Singh and Bronwyn hailed Nyoman and set out for the dingy flat. Nyoman drove quickly and quietly, still sulking from Bronwyn's suggestion the previous evening that he vacuum the back of the taxi. The two cops were relieved. Nyoman's constant prattle had started to wear them down. Singh knew it was the Balinese way to be friendly. Whether it was a natural disposition or a skill well-honed by the exigencies of the tourist trade, he was not sure. He imagined that a tourist meeting such good cheer and polite interest in the minutiae of their lives would find it very attractive. They would return to their homes talking with genuine enthusiasm of the cultured island and its gracious people.

He, Singh, felt that he'd had quite enough friendliness and nosiness. He had given up maintaining a stony silence in the face of Nyoman's curiosity. Curt, monosyllabic answers hadn't worked either. Now he just grunted.

Bronwyn was more civil than him. She had started out by answering Nyoman's questions fully. As a result, thought Singh, he, the reluctant eavesdropper, knew far more about Bronwyn than he needed for the purposes of a functioning working relationship. He really did not want to know that she had decided against a third child because her marriage was on the rocks or that she disliked her younger son's girlfriend. He was pleased to note that Bronwyn was resorting to shorter and shorter responses to Nyoman's incessant chatter. Even she had her limits.

Singh stared at the traffic beyond the window. It was the morning rush hour Bali style, with motorbikes and four-wheel drives competing for road position with beat-up minivans and cars with 'go faster' stripes.

Bronwyn interrupted his train of thought. 'Holiday cancellations are falling in Bali...'

'How come?'

'Apparently the speed with which the police have arrested the bombers has reassured tourists.'

The progress in the investigation had been fantastic, thought Singh. Many commentators were describing the terrorist organisation as having been crippled. Some were insistent that the Bali bombings had been a one-off. The terrorists had got lucky. It suggested to Singh that a fresh complacency was developing.

Singh muttered, 'I hope they're not going to play down the danger.'

As a policeman, he knew how easy it was to launch an attack like the Bali bombings. As long as there were young men, and perhaps women, indoctrinated from an early age into *jihadi* philosophy at one of the *madrasahs* and *pesanterens*, there was no difficulty in procuring the materials and making a bomb. He had read in the newspapers that the potassium chlorate used to make the Bali bomb had been purchased from a chemical shop in Surabaya, ostensibly to be used as fertiliser. It was not even necessary to risk buying explosives on the

271

black market or from a crooked army officer.

He wondered again at his role investigating a solitary murder when all around him were dealing with the aftermath of mass murder. He sighed. He could only do his best. He didn't have the skills to pursue terrorists. Catching terrorists was about forensic analysis and infiltrating networks. It was about security operations at airports and at docks. There was nothing personal in the hunt because a terrorist's anger was non-specific. He did not care whom he killed. The usual means of tracking down a killer by examining the life of his victim was of no use. That, Singh thought, was his speciality – to let the dead speak. But the dead in the Bali bombings did not know and had nothing to say about their killers.

Singh looked at the woman next to him. Her lips were pressed together in a thin line and the wrinkles around her mouth were deeply engraved. She appeared older.

He asked, 'What's the matter?'

'Nothing in particular,' she replied. 'I just have this overwhelming sense of worry, I don't know why.'

'Probably something you ate,' suggested Singh and was rewarded by an angry glare and then a sudden open-throated laugh.

'You're right, of course. I'm being silly.' She shook herself, like a dog caught in a rain shower, trying to physically dislodge her sense of foreboding.

'We're here,' said Nyoman coldly.

Singh and Bronwyn exchanged a glance and then a smile. It was a moment of fellow feeling. Bronwyn was a good sort, the inspector decided. Just a little bit large and opinionated for him to feel entirely at ease.

Bronwyn opened the door and asked, as she levered herself out, 'So do we have any tactics or are we just going to wing it?'

Did he detect a note of sarcasm, wondered Singh. He replied coolly, 'We will develop a strategy on the ground based on an ongoing analysis of the witness and her attitude to questioning.'

'So we're going to wing it then,' said Bronwyn and shut the car door smartly.

'I'm sorry, Sarah.'

The woman sitting on a large multi-coloured towel on the beach did not look like she'd heard the muttered apology.

She was staring out to sea. Storm clouds were gathering on the horizon. It made a peculiar contrast, the extreme blue over their heads versus the thick accumulating blackness in the distance. The wind was blowing in from the ocean so the storm would be upon them relatively soon. She thought it was apposite, if a little theatrical, that the weather should be reflecting her life – it reminded her of the low-budget tactics that a third-rate movie might use to set the mood.

She remembered that the whole time she had been looking for Richard, the weather had been sublime. She had to give Richard some credit, she thought. He had shown more loyalty and commitment to their marriage than she had done. After all, it was he who had suggested coming to Bali to try and repair the damage that his burgeoning religiosity had caused in their relationship. She, on the other hand, had been swept up in her grand romance with the young Australian surfer and not spared a thought for her husband.

She looked at the surfer lying on the sand in his board-shorts, propping himself up with an elbow to look at her, the fine sand peppering the golden hair on his chest. His surfboard was lying on the beach a little further down.

She had agreed to meet him on the beach at his request. She had brought a champagne breakfast that she had packed with her own hands, imagining a romantic morning that would ease the knots in her shoulders and mark the beginning of her new life with Greg. She had sensed his withdrawal when she tried to embrace him. He had not wrapped his arms around her as he had done so many times in the past. He had let her hug him until she had stepped back and asked, 'What's the matter, Greg? Is anything wrong?'

He had refused to meet her eyes, gazing over her shoulder, out to sea, anywhere except at her. Finally, he had flung himself down on the sand like some character from a daytime soap and said, 'It's over.'

'What do you mean?' Sarah was amazed she could articulate words – she felt painfully out of breath, as if she had run a mile on the soft sand.

'Look, mate – this was great, you and me. I really admire you. But – you know – with the trouble with the police and stuff – well, I want out.'

'Out?'

'Yes.' This time he looked at her. 'I'm ending our relationship.' And then, as if she was incapable of understanding his simple words, he continued, 'I don't want to see you any more.'

When she remained silent he had uttered the meaningless, facetious words, 'I'm sorry, Sarah.'

Sarah glanced at his surfboard again. If she had thought there was any hope of changing his mind, the sight of that sleek board with its wave motif would have destroyed it. This man whom she loved with the heady passion of a teenager had brought his surfboard along so that he could hit the waves the minute he had dealt with the unpleasantness of evicting her from his life. In his eyes, she did not even amount to a holiday romance, just a meal ticket – come to think of it, a surf ticket as well. She was quite sure she had paid for the shiny new equipment.

She wondered for a moment why she was not yelling, demanding that he change his mind, begging him to love her, persuading him somehow to stay in her life. The sheer enormity of her naivety was acting like insulation from the shock and the pain. She knew she would feel it soon but this brief moment of respite was a blessing. She stared at the storm clouds again. They were much closer. Greg probably wouldn't get in much surfing. She got to her feet slowly, feeling like an old woman. She picked up her towel and wrapped it modestly around her thin body. She walked up the beach, narrow feet sinking into the coarse sand. She did not look back. Sarah Crouch knew that her future was now in her past.

Abu Bakr asked, 'Yusuf are you ready to go?'

'Where?'

'The bomb factory, of course. Where do you think?'

Abu Bakr was immediately sorry for snapping at Yusuf. He said in a kinder tone,

'Come on – let's go.'

Yusuf followed him obediently to the door. Abu Bakr wondered whether he should send him back for a shower; the man reeked of dried sweat and fear. He saw that Yusuf's fingernails were filthy and his clothes were food-stained. He frowned. He had seen it before with young men under his command. Sometimes, if the certain knowledge of death became a burden too great to carry, young soldiers started to abandon the ordinary routine of life. Cleanliness, he had noticed, was always the first to go. It was a mistake, he sometimes explained to his men. In a complex, changing world with unknown threats and dangerous missions, routine was the last thing that should be allowed to lapse. That was what kept the fear at bay – the distraction of the ordinary. He would have to give Yusuf the lecture. He didn't have too long to hang on but Abu Bakr didn't want the wheels coming off before then.

The bomb factory was a secluded bungalow set well back from the road with high stone walls all around. It was not far from the main drag through Sanur with its usual Balinese mix of five-star hotels, tacky tourist shops, cheap backpacker motels and roadside stalls. Abu Bakr and Yusuf caught a taxi to the street but stopped a few hundred yards from the main door. This was no time to show potential witnesses an incriminating destination.

Abu Bakr opened the door slowly and cautiously. The house smelt musty. No one had been in for a while. The doors and windows were fastened tight. There was a thin layer of dust on every surface.

Yusuf followed him in and asked in a whisper, 'Where is the ... you know, the bomb things?'

Abu Bakr walked slowly across the hall, unfurnished and with bare walls and floor, towards an arched entrance that led to the rest of the house.

If he was given to *haram* analogies, thought Abu Bakr, he would have said that he hit the jackpot. He stood aside so that Yusuf could peer in.

Yusuf asked, his mouth opening and closing like that of a goldfish in a bowl, his voice crackling with tension, 'What is all that?'

Abu Bakr understood Yusuf's bemusement. There was an assortment of boxes, wires, cigarette cases and empty plastic filing cabinets in a neat heap in the middle of the room.

He took a penknife out of his pocket and slit open one of the cardboard boxes. There were small drums of fuel oil packed neatly within. He looked in another box. Coiled wires, timers, crocodile clips and a couple of brand new mobile phones were arranged within.

He said to Yusuf, 'This is all we need to make a bomb!'

Yusuf said rather wistfully, 'I hope we find a good target. I don't really want to kill Moslems or anyone except the Americans.'

Abu Bakr eyed him cautiously. 'You must remember, Yusuf – Moslems who are not committed to *jihad* as it is written in the Holy Book are also infidels.'

'What are you doing now?' asked Yusuf, trying to change the subject.

Abu Bakr was rolling out a cable, leaving it snaking across the floor in his wake. 'This wire will be attached to the bomb. I will add some sort of trigger to the wire for detonation,' he explained.

Yusuf fell silent. He knew whose job it was to pull the trigger. He realised that he was not looking forward to it. It was one thing to reap a deserved reward in heaven. But he had to blow himself to smithereens first and that did not sound like it was going to be very pleasant.

Besides, he would miss Nuri.

They told Nyoman to wait and crossed the road. It was the usual mad dash across a dusty street, narrowly avoiding motorbikes and stray dogs. Singh was panting by the time he reached the other side. He leaned against the grimy wall and put a hand on his heart. He could feel it hammering against his chest. His was not a physique that allowed for sudden sprints.

Bronwyn asked, a look of concern on her face, 'Are you all right?'

He nodded but couldn't speak for a moment.

She waited while he caught his breath and then said pointedly, 'You need to get in better shape. Not much use avoiding the traffic if you're just going to have a heart attack on the opposite side.'

Singh scowled and marched into the apartment block purposefully. He looked at the steep flight of stairs and turned to Bronwyn, a rueful expression on his face. 'You might be right.'

He started up slowly, holding the banister for support.

The block of flats was even more decrepit in the day than at night. The paint on the walls was stained and peeling. There were small piles of rubbish, plastic bags and plastic bottles mostly, tucked away in the corners. A gecko lay dead on a step, its corpse covered in small black ants. The stairwell smelt of mould, death and piss. That stink and the climb combined were making Singh light-headed.

He wheezed, 'She'd better be in.'

Bronwyn said reassuringly, 'I'm sure she is. Sergeant Agus said only the men had left. He was quite clear about that.'

Singh decided not to expend precious energy on a sceptical response. He concentrated on the last flight of stairs. Perspiration stung his eyes. He blinked rapidly, trying to soothe the smarting with tears. He wondered why he had found it easier the previous night. The difference between the cool night air and the sweltering heat of day in the claustrophobic confines of the stairwell, he supposed.

Bronwyn, who had followed meekly behind him for two flights but then overtaken him, was waiting outside the door. Singh noticed that there was no peephole. That was good. Nuri would not be able to refuse to see them without opening the door first. And once the door was ajar, Singh thought to himself smugly, he was a past master at inserting a big, sneaker-clad foot into the crack and preventing any hasty door slamming.

Bronwyn raised a hand to knock and looked inquiringly at the inspector. He nodded assent. It was time to confront the young woman about her relationship with the Englishman whose body parts were at the mortuary with the remains of those whose deaths had involved less personal animosity on the part of the killer.

Bronwyn rapped on the door. Singh approved of her style. It was a mildly authoritative knock. It was the request for entry of a meter reader or a census taker rather than a policewoman. It might entice a young woman alone to open the door. But there was no response. Singh, concentrating hard, could not hear any sound from within the apartment. Bronwyn knocked again, more firmly this time. This knock conveyed bureaucratic urgency. The inspector placed a large hairy ear to the door and shut his eyes to the world. He still could not hear anything within.

Singh took matters into his own hands. It was time to be threatening. He raised a heavy fist and thumped loudly on the wood, shouting, 'Police! Open this door!' When this did not elicit a response, he hammered and shouted again. Singh continued to do this intermittently for a few minutes and then, with one last frustrated thump, gave it up as a lost cause.

He started hunting in his pockets.

Bronwyn asked, 'What are you doing?'

'Looking for something to pick the lock with...'

'You can't do that!'

'Watch me,' said Singh with his usual robust disregard for police protocol.

Bronwyn put her mouth close to the door and yelled, 'Nuri! We know you're in there. We just want to ask you some questions about Richard Crouch. There's nothing to be afraid of – you're not in any trouble.'

Singh spoke in an undertone but the sarcasm was still audible. He said, 'It's OK to lie to a witness but not OK to break into a house where you suspect the commission of an offence?'

Bronwyn whispered back, 'We do not suspect her of anything.'

'I do!'

Their argument was interrupted by the sound of a bolt being drawn.

The door opened a fraction and the small, heart-shaped face of the Indonesian girl peered out. She stared at them fearfully and then made up her mind. The door was pulled open and she stepped aside to let them in.

Nuri ushered them into the small living room and gestured for them to sit down. She slipped into a room and reappeared a few moments later with a scarf tied loosely around her hair.

The cut on her lip was visible to both police personnel – a red gash, the clotted blood forming a jagged line across top and bottom lip. There was bruising around her jaw as well, the delicate skin was tinted red and orange.

Singh asked, holding his own jaw to indicate what he was talking about, 'What happened?'

Nuri was not interested in discussing her injuries. She said in a painful whisper, her mouth moving awkwardly, 'What happened to Abdullah?'

'He was killed – shot by someone – through the head.' Singh's brutal delivery of the facts had an impact. She drew in, wrapped her arms around her knees and bowed her head for a moment. When she looked up again, the bruising was stark against the pallor of her skin and her eyes were filled with tears. But she did not break down.

Singh had rarely seen such a conscious physical effort to rein in emotion. He acknowledged to himself that the girl was tough. She was labouring under an immense burden but still able to function – albeit only to achieve her limited goals – which right now appeared to be information.

Nuri asked, 'Who did it? Who killed him?'

Singh said bluntly, 'That's what we're trying to find out.'

She appeared to think for a while, trying to decide what to do or ask. Singh let her contemplate her next step. This was not a witness to badger or bully. Not yet anyway.

She said, her voice clear and firm, 'You must find out who did this to him.'

Singh cracked his knuckles and she flinched slightly. The assault that had left her cradling her jaw had also made her nervy. He asked, 'Can you help us?'

'What can I do? I do not know who killed him.'

'Tell us everything you knew about him. We have very little background – it makes it difficult to hunt the murderer because we do not know who Richard Crouch's enemies were.'

'I did not know him very well...'

Singh leaned forward, compressing his large belly against the broad platform of his thighs. He said, sounding asthmatic, 'You knew him better than the others – your husband and your brothers. They didn't even know that his name was Richard Crouch.'

Nuri changed the subject abruptly. She turned to Bronwyn and asked, 'Do you have that picture?'

Bronwyn was perplexed. Her face creased into a questioning expression and Nuri replied to the implied query, 'That picture you showed us yesterday – of Abdullah.'

Bronwyn reached into the folder and brought out the blown-up passport photo. The smiling young man with watery blue eyes stared back at her and she remembered that all she had ever seen of him was a singed piece of skull with a bullet hole in it.

Nuri snatched the picture from her hand almost before Bronwyn had an opportunity to hold it out to her. She asked, 'Can I keep this?'

Singh asked, 'Why do you want it?'

Her eyes were still locked on the picture with a schoolgirl's intensity over the poster of a rock star. She responded in a whisper, 'I have nothing else.'

Singh stood up and ambled over to the window. He drew the curtain gingerly – it was soiled – and gazed out. The street below was busy. Across the road, a *warung* was doing brisk business in imported soft drinks and local delicacies. It was probably the stall from which Wayan and Agus had staked out the apartment. In the midst of tragedy and loss, Singh thought, life went on exactly as normal for everyone else. Grief was such a personal emotion. It could not be shared. He knew that the young Indonesian woman with the delicate skin and soft brown eyes was grieving. And he was sure he knew the cause.

From the window, without turning around, he asked in a gruff voice that nevertheless had a thread of sympathy running through it, 'You were in love with him?'

Bronwyn glanced at her fellow policeman sharply but he was still gazing out of the window. She turned to Nuri, watching her face as she wrestled for an answer.

When it came, it was blunt and to the point. 'Yes,' she said, 'I loved Richard.'

Bronwyn said gently, 'Tell us about it.'

Fifteen

The streets were almost deserted. Puffs of pink-tinged cloud, like cotton candy at a fairground, filled the sky. Usually, the merry-makers would be out, getting started on what would be a long evening of drinking and dancing. Today and every day since the bombs, there were only a few morose shopkeepers, perched on stools beside their carved long-tailed wooden cats and dusty bamboo wind chimes. The crowds that had thronged the streets were gone.

Ghani kicked the ground impatiently as he walked, sending a stone skidding into a nearby drain. He stopped and rubbed the back of his neck. The tension was taking its toll. He could feel his muscles bunched under the skin. The operation had not gone smoothly so far.

Ghani scratched his beard, which was itching in the evening humidity. He admitted to himself that he was afraid. It didn't bother him much. He had learnt to channel fear and make it work to his own advantage. Fear enhanced his concentration. It sharpened his eyesight and hearing. To walk down a street with fear sitting

287

on his shoulder was almost to have a companion, a second pair of eyes.

It had been the same in Afghanistan. He was forty-five years old and had already been for three tours of duty. Each time he stepped onto the parched earth of western Afghanistan, he felt as if he was coming home. His delight in the smell of red earth and gunpowder did not make him careless. Ghani was a *jihadist*. He would be delighted to lay down his life for the cause and be hailed in this life and the hereafter as a martyr – but he had an obligation to Allah to make sure that he did not throw his life away cheaply.

Ghani scowled. It was all a moot point if he could not identify an appropriate target.

He ambled idly towards a flyer pinned to a lamp post. He read it with growing interest. Ghani glanced at his digital Casio watch and then up and down the street. His heart was racing with excitement, its echo pounding in his ears, as he contemplated the enormity of his idea. His facial scars glowed pale in the half light as the rest of his face was suffused in hot blood. He tried to think coherently. It was a struggle. The plan had leapt into his head so fully formed that it was hard to analyse it objectively, to check for flaws and risks. Could it work? There were enormous difficulties. There was bound to be agg-ressive security. But in deserted Bali, the place would be full to the brim with potential victims.

Ghani hurried to the mosque he frequented in Bali. It was a small rundown building. The gold paint on the single onion dome had faded to a pale yellow. The decrepit condition of the building annoyed Ghani. There was not much money for mosques in Hindu Bali, he thought angrily – only for the hundreds of temples that littered the landscape. Ghani took off his sandals and washed his hands, feet and face under a tap on the outside wall of the mosque. It was a ritual purification and he felt cleansed, both inside and out. He walked respectfully into the mosque, found the arrow indicating the direction of Mecca, knelt down and touched his forehead to the ground.

It was time to give thanks to Allah for showing him the target.

Nuri spoke and the police listened without interrupting. Her voice was low but steady, her tone even – almost monotonous – as if she was reading out a shopping list. Neither Singh nor Bronwyn had any difficulty identifying the passion beneath the surface. They recognised that Nuri could only communicate her story by distancing herself from it. She was trying to separate the narrator from the protagonist in the sorry tale she was unfolding.

'I met Richard when Ramzi brought him here,' she said quietly in Indonesian. 'I didn't know who he was. It seemed strange to me that my brothers had Western acquaintances but it was not my place to ask.'

Nuri re-tied the scarf around her head, pulling the knot tight. She continued, 'I was curious about him. Partly, I suppose, because I was bored with the routine here. I did not go out much. My husband, Ghani, said that Bali was a very wicked place. The few times I went out, I could see that he was right. There was so much that was *haram*.' She pressed her hands to her cheeks like a Victorian maiden.

'I did not speak to Richard – it would have been frowned upon by my husband and brothers. But I looked at him – he was so tall and pale and his eyes were blue – like the sky above my village on a bright day. I knew he was Moslem because they called him Abdullah. I was glad of that. He was foreign and different but he was also a brother.'

She knotted her fingers together and fell silent. Singh wondered whether he would have to drag her back to the present. He was reluctant to do so. It would remind her to whom she was speaking – and undermine the honesty of her disclosures. At present, they were getting the complete story without exaggeration or omission. It was a policeman's dream. He shifted in his chair, undecided what to do and fidgeting in his uncertainty. The slight movement caught her attention and she opened her mouth to speak again.

'I served him food and drink when he came to visit. Sometimes, when I glanced at him, I would find him looking at me. It was like we had a connection – our eyes were drawn to each other at the same time ... and when our eyes met, I felt as if we had spoken about important things.'

She half-smiled. 'Isn't that strange?'

Singh was reminded how young this girl was. In her early twenties. Married to an older man. She would have found the sudden physical attraction to Abdullah puzzling. In fact, Singh would wager that she hadn't even realised it was a physical attraction. Nuri was young and romantic. She probably thought they were mingling souls. He mentally sighed, a breath of thought clearing the cobwebs in his mind. The tragedy and appeal of youth were all wrapped up in this slight figure before him, hair escaping from under her scarf, swollen lip and visibly broken heart.

Nuri continued. 'Often when he came, I was sent to wait in the room.'

Catching a glimpse of Bronwyn's startled look, she said simply, 'The men had important matters to discuss. It was better for womenfolk not to be involved.'

Bronwyn, the feminist, nodded a fake understanding, anxious not to distract the girl from her story.

'In the room, I would sit and think of Richard and wonder what it would be like if, when we looked at each other, he smiled. Once or twice, I would hear him laugh. I saw him smile at my brothers a few times and I was so envious!'

Her voice had lightened, revealing delight and anticipation. Singh knew she was not just retelling the past but reliving it as well. A naïve fool presenting her husband to them as a suspect.

'Ghani let me go out more often. I am not sure why. Probably because he and the others were too busy to do the shopping for *halal* food. Maybe he could see that I was growing impatient being in the apartment all the time. I guess he trusted me not to be influenced by the ungodly things I witnessed.'

She shrugged her narrow shoulders. Singh could not tell if she was dismissing her husband's faith in her or his earlier doubts.

'One day when I was out, I bumped into Abdullah on the street.' She grinned. Her sudden burst of youthful exuberance filled the room like a sunburst. 'I think,' she added in a confiding tone, 'that maybe he followed me or waited for me? But at the time I thought it was a coincidence! We started to talk. He smiled at me like I was hoping he would. It was as if' – Nuri patted herself over the heart – 'when he smiled, there was a thread from my heart to his and it got tight and painful but also very special.'

She gazed at them challengingly, as if daring them to disbelieve the bond she had felt with Crouch. Neither cop said anything. Singh felt old. This girl, walking them through her journey towards tragedy, was taking a toll on him. He found himself envying the intensity of her feelings. He was not sure he had ever felt that strongly about anyone, certainly not his wife. Was there someone out there waiting for him whose smile would tighten a bond with his soul? Singh almost laughed out loud. The image of himself as the hero in some sort of grand romance was too comical for the cynic in him. But he could not shake the sliver of envy that had pierced his heart.

'After that, we saw each other a lot. I did not ask him why he was always waiting for me. We only walked along and talked. He helped me with the shopping – he would carry the bags. When we were in the apartment with the others, we did not speak or tell the others we had met. I knew it was a secret and what I was doing was wrong – but it *felt* right and I didn't care anyway.'

Her defiance was threadbare but determined. Her audience was sympathetic – she did not suffer the criticism, express or implied, that she feared.

'He was very unhappy in his marriage. His wife was an infidel who did not understand why he had converted to Islam.'

Singh was shocked to hear such strong, intolerant language from such a sweet-faced young thing. He reminded himself that he was dealing with a girl from a small village in Sulawesi. Even so, he, the least tactful person on the Singapore police force, found her language distasteful. He supposed it was because she was not being sarcastic or ironic or even intentionally offensive. The language of 'them' and 'us', of exclusion and membership, came naturally to her. It was part of her everyday vocabulary to speak of non-Moslems as infidels, to reduce them to dimensions less than human.

Unaware of Singh's discomfiture, the girl carried on her narrative. 'Finally, one day he asked me to come away with him. He said he had a job to do – but after it was complete, I should join him. He would take me as his second wife. He did not want to divorce his first wife – he said he had a responsibility towards her.'

She fell silent again and Bronwyn asked quietly, 'When was this?'

Nuri stared at her in genuine surprise. She had almost forgotten there were others in the room, so lost had she been in her memories. She said, 'That is easy to remember because of the Bali bombs – it was the day before that.'

'Did you agree to go away with him?'

'Of course! I loved him. We belonged together. We were so happy that afternoon. We walked on the beach. He held my hand. We did not kiss or ... anything – he said there was time enough when we were married. I regret that. It would have been wrong. But he is dead and I will never have the chance to be with him now.'

It was Singh's turn to ask a question. Was that the last time you saw him?'

Her eyes were awash with tears. 'Sort of – Ramzi saw us on the beach. He wanted to know what I was doing – he saw we were holding hands, you see. He was very angry.'

She closed her eyes. Singh could sense her fear of the hotheaded young man he had met briefly the previous night.

Nuri continued, 'Richard said that he had no time to explain, it was already evening and there was something important he had to do.'

The girl's smooth forehead wrinkled with puzzlement. 'Ramzi grabbed me and dragged me away. I had bruises up and down my arm the next day. Abdullah shouted to me not to worry, to go with Ramzi, he would sort it out later. Ramzi made me come back to the apartment with him. I asked him if he was going to tell Ghani. I was afraid of his reaction. I mean, it would have been all right if he had just divorced me – that was what Abdullah and I were planning anyway...' She trailed off and put her hand absent-mindedly on her bruised jaw.

Bronwyn noticed the gesture and asked, 'You were afraid he would harm you? Beat you?'

'I suppose so,' she said doubtfully. 'He had not done it before but he was a soldier so I was a little afraid. Actually, I was probably more afraid of Ramzi.'

'He was a soldier – I thought he worked in construction as a day labourer?' Singh was confused and annoyed about it. He didn't like getting his facts wrong.

Nuri did not meet his eyes but she said adamantly, 'He was a soldier before.'

'What happened when you got home?'

'Did Ramzi tell Ghani?'

The questions were being fired at her from all directions. Nuri adopted an instinctively defensive posture, her arms across her chest. 'We walked home. Ramzi told me he would deal with me later. I don't think he told Ghani...'

She sat up straight in her chair, squaring her skinny shoulders. 'I waited for Richard to come for me and take me away. I couldn't understand why he didn't. I even wondered if perhaps he had been toying with me, just having a bit of fun. It bruised my soul. I was still waiting when you came in yesterday and told us he was dead.'

The dam broke. The young girl who had found a tenuous romantic love and lost it to violence put her head down on the arm of the chair and sobbed – great big, shoulder-shaking, muffled sounds.

Bronwyn fidgeted uncomfortably in her seat, distressed by the grief but uncertain how to assuage it.

Singh, on the other hand, was a happy man. He stood up, portly and satisfied, and beckoned imperiously for Bronwyn to come with him.

She gestured silently at the girl. Her question was implied but easily understood. How can we leave her like this?

Singh was indifferent. He felt sorry for the girl but she was young, she would recover. He, Singh, had only one concern – who had killed Richard Crouch? The list of suspects was lengthening, not narrowing, but Singh didn't mind, he didn't mind in the least. A picture was forming – of the dead man and his life – and that was the only certain way to find a murderer.

Sixteen

'Why are we leaving in such a hurry?'

'Got everything we need,' answered Singh, huffing and puffing although they were going downstairs this time.

'And what is everything?'

'More suspects!'

'The husband?'

'Yes – and the brother.'

'Surely not ... I know he was annoyed about finding her with the boyfriend – but murder?'

'I wouldn't usually think a brother a likely suspect,' admitted Singh. 'But you heard some of the language she used. These chaps are pretty committed Moslems – family dishonour by a sister would be taken seriously.'

'You might have a point,' agreed Bronwyn. They reached the street and made the mad dash across. 'I haven't actually heard anyone referred to as an "infidel" in conversation before...'

'I can't stand nutters of any stripe,' complained Singh, conveniently forgetting his earlier sympathy for the girl.

Nyoman drew up in the Kijang. Bronwyn hopped in and Singh clambered aboard more slowly, carefully navigating his belly through the door, which could not be opened fully as Nyoman had drawn up next to a row of parked cars.

Inside, car doors slammed shut, air-conditioning a welcome relief from the stuffy flat and the hot dusty street, Bronwyn was upbeat. 'My money's on the husband.'

'Ghani?' asked Singh thoughtfully. 'You may be right – according to Nuri he was in the military before. He would know how to handle a firearm.' He fell silent, nibbling on a fingernail.

'What's up?' asked Bronwyn.

'He seemed genuinely surprised when we told him Crouch was dead – and really puzzled that his wife had inside information on the man.'

'Could have been acting!'

'Could have been acting ... but that sort of man, repressed, middle-aged, with limited imagination, ex-soldier – I just don't see him being that convincing an actor.'

'All right,' said Bronwyn with undiluted good humour. 'The brother then.'

Singh scowled at his partner. 'Why are you in such a good mood anyway?' he asked, not trying to hide his aggravation.

Bronwyn laughed and patted the Sikh policeman on the shoulder – a gesture of camaraderie that surprised him and moved him a little. 'I don't know. For some reason,

I'm having fun. A murder investigation is fascinating work!'

They sat in uninterrupted companionable silence for a while.

Singh pondered the fact that he had grown quite fond of this woman. She was still annoying. But he was willing to concede that she had strengths as well. She was patient, competent and hardworking. Her ability to remain good tempered in the face of his snappy temper and abrupt manner was quite a talent. In his working career to date, such characters had been exceedingly rare.

'What now, boss?'

Singh did not object to the title. He was not her boss in any strict sense but he was more experienced than her and had taken the lead in the investigation. She had shown no resentment over his assuming command. Instead, she carried out his various instructions cheerfully, including tasks that another police officer might have refused or sulked about having to do.

Singh considered telling Bronwyn that she was doing a good job. He guessed that, for all her surface indifference, she was insecure about her future as a policewoman. She had only found a temporary refuge from her perceived insubordination. Her ill-timed comments were sure to dog her career in Australia. If he told her she was performing well it was bound to make her feel better.

The inspector leaned back against the car seat and locked his fingers as they rested on his belly. He decided against saying anything complimentary. He didn't want anyone who worked for him to get cocky.

Bronwyn asked again, injecting an impatient note into her voice, 'What now, boss?'

He answered slowly, thinking his way through the labyrinth of suspects and clues. 'Well, there are a few things we need to do – question the husband and brother, ask Sarah Crouch why she omitted to mention that her husband was Moslem *and* had a bit on the side...'

Bronwyn nodded. 'What do you want to do first?'

'Not sure – go back this evening and talk to the brother and husband? Save Sarah Crouch for tomorrow?'

'Could do – don't forget I plan to go for this remembrance ceremony thing they're having at the Sari Club.'

Singh flared his nostrils in ill-disguised irritation. 'I forgot about that. All right, I'll see Sarah on my own. Have someone go up to Ubud first thing in the morning and bring her to the police station.'

'She won't want to come,' warned Bronwyn.

'Not my problem,' said Singh brusquely.

'If she makes trouble, tell them to arrest her.'

'For what?'

'I don't really care. Murder, obstructing the police in the course of their inquiries, perjury...'

'You don't have *reasonable* grounds to suspect her of any of those things.'

'My dear girl,' he said, watching her nose wrinkle in disgust at the term of patronising endearment, 'we're in Indonesia right now. There are very few advantages to trying to solve a murder outside one's own juris- diction. One doesn't know the society, the people, the culture – anything that might help a policeman understand a crime. But – when the jurisdiction is, how should I put it, not quite as concerned about due process as we might expect, we need to use that to our advantage and catch ourselves a murderer! So, tell one of your Balinese flunkeys that I want to see Sarah Crouch tomorrow morning. I really don't care how they make it happen.'

He settled back comfortably in the seat having delivered himself of his little diatribe and then sat bolt upright again. 'In fact,' he added, 'I really don't want to climb those filthy stairs and hang around that stinking apartment any more. Get someone to wait outside till those men get home and then bring them to me!'

'Yessir!' said Bronwyn smartly.

Singh swivelled his great head and gazed at her suspiciously. Was she being sarcastic?

She looked at him demurely and then began to laugh.

It was infectious. Singh found himself guffawing as well. He deserved to be mocked, he supposed, issuing orders like some parade ground sergeant.

Ramzi was on the red motorbike. He had ordered a fresh set of number plates from a small vehicle repair shop. He drove around Denpasar and Kuta, looking for a vehicle to steal. Ghani's instructions had been clear. Ramzi was to identify a van and make sure it was indistinguishable in every way. He was to steal the vehicle, swap the number plates and drive around for a while to make sure that he was not followed. Ghani had stressed the importance of prudence. This was the endgame.

Ramzi's back ached from hunching over the bike and his eyes smarted from the dust. He revved the bike in irritation. He could hardly believe that the bomb-maker had been found with a bullet in his head. It was so unlikely. Ghani had dealt with the invasion of the police competently. His explanation for their interaction with Richard Crouch, pre-prepared, he assumed, had been plausible. The police – what an odd combination they had been, the short fat man in the turban and the large white woman – had not appeared to suspect anything out of the ordinary.

Unfortunately, his sister had not done their cause any favours by first acknowledging that she, and they, knew Crouch and then by fainting so dramatically when news of his death was announced. Ramzi realised that he would have to be careful of the turbaned policeman. The man looked like a fool and Ramzi's instinct was to dismiss him as one. But the way he had dropped his bombshell about Abdullah – crude and shocking – had produced results. Ramzi felt a stab of anger. They were within twenty-four hours of carrying out a successful attack. It would be devastating if his sister's lack of control was the reason for their failure. He gritted his teeth and was tempted to accelerate, to leave his rage behind in a burst of speed. But it was a sure way of attracting attention. He needed to focus on finding a van. This was not the moment to be dwelling on Nuri's iniquities.

Ramzi decided to head out of town. A third of the way towards Ubud he spotted a small white van parked by a boarded-up shop. He stopped to have a look and saw a notice that the outlet was closed for a few days. Ramzi peered through the glass front, his hands cupped around his eyes to block the glare – it was an art gallery. He walked around the premises. The place was deserted. Balinese families often lived in buildings attached to their shops. But not this artist. There was no residential dwelling protruding out the back.

Ramzi walked back to the vehicle. It was small, but there was enough space for the bomb. It had no windows in the back. The mudguards were caked with dirt. There were a few nicks and scratches along the sides – nothing extraordinary in a place like Bali where every road trip was an adventure.

Ramzi opened his bag, took out a wire coat hanger and quickly twisted it into a hook. He used a pair of small pliers to rip the rubber lining off the window. He slid the coat hanger into the door directly under the lock. In a few seconds he had found the lever and yanked on it. The doorlock popped open. He put away his tools and climbed into the driver seat. Ramzi checked the glove compartment and sun visor for spare keys. There were none to be found. It did not bother him. He had not expected to get that lucky. He removed the panels around the ignition switch. He traced the two wires he needed, both red, removed the rubber cover and hotwired them. The ignition lights came on. He found the starter wires, stripped the ends and touched them together. The engine coughed into life. Ramzi grinned broadly. He hopped out, opened the back, dragged the motorbike in and shut the van door gently. He unscrewed the number plates, replaced them with the ones he had purchased and chucked the old plates into the bushes. Back in the driver's seat, he shifted into first gear and drove out to the main road.

Ghani was under arrest, hands cuffed in front of him. He was frog-marched to a waiting police car. They bundled him in firmly, but without rough treatment. Ghani hoped that meant he was not suspected of anything serious. If they knew he was part of a *jihadi* cell, they would not have been able to resist giving him a bit of treatment.

The police had been waiting for him, two of them, in uniform, outside the door. He had not set foot inside the apartment. He had no idea what the situation was within. Where was Nuri? Had they searched the flat, found anything incriminating like their small cache of weapons? He tried to think, tried to stay calm. Most likely his detention had something to do with the bomb-maker's killing. He could swear on the Quran he had nothing to do with that. But if they decided to keep him overnight, the game was up.

Ghani stole a glance at the stolid policemen on either side of him. They were large men. He was tightly wedged between them, his arms sticky from the forced human contact.

He screwed up the courage to ask, 'What is this about?'

There was no answer.

Ghani asked again, 'Why have you arrested me? I have done nothing.'

One of the policemen hunched his shoulders, deciding, Ghani hoped, that there was no harm in talking to him. 'No idea,' he explained. 'They don't tell us anything. Just to arrest you when you came back.'

'And the other one,' added the second policeman.

Typical Balinese, thought Ghani dismissively. They looked the part of professional policemen, well built and clean shaven with neatly pressed uniforms. But they could not resist the temptation to gossip.

He asked in a friendly tone, 'What other one?'

'Your friend,' explained the bigger of the two policemen. 'Long hair, no beard, good looking.'

They wanted Ramzi too. That did not bode well. Why would they want to see Ramzi? He could not have had anything to do with the murder of Abdullah.

'Do you know where he is?' asked the policeman to Ghani's right.

Ghani shook his head adamantly. He had received a text message that Ramzi had stolen a van and was on his way to the safe house. He did not plan on sharing that piece of information.

The same policeman murmured in an apologetic tone, 'The colleagues we left to wait for him are hungry, you see. But they cannot leave their post till he turns up.'

The police car drew up at the Denpasar police headquarters. The policemen escorted Ghani into the building. They led him to a small room with a table and two chairs. One of them unlocked the handcuffs. Ghani rubbed his wrists, which, chafed by the restraints, were red. He felt a heavy hand on his shoulder. He was ushered to a chair and told to sit down. The two policemen walked out, one of them with a friendly wave. Ghani heard the sound of the bolt. He was locked in. He sucked in a deep breath of stale air. He was terrified. He could feel his heart thumping in his chest – it felt like a wild animal trying to escape a cage. His hands were clammy. He wiped them on his trousers. What if they knew something? He would have failed his leaders and his God. He needed to be cool and composed and helpful to the police – an innocent man unexpectedly entangled in a police investigation.

The door opened and the fat policeman in the turban and his female sidekick walked in. Ghani could have wept with relief. It *was* about Abdullah, the bomb-maker. Singh waddled over and sat down on the only other chair in the room. He faced Ghani across the small, scuffed table – two swarthy, bearded, stocky men with matching expressions of determination on their faces. Bronwyn leaned against the wall with her hands on her hips.

Singh asked, with a superficial and highly unconvincing smile on his face, 'Is there anything you would like to tell us about Abdullah's death?'

'I told you everything I know already.'

Singh sensed that Ghani was relieved by his opening gambit. That was odd. What in the world had he been expecting that an implied accusation of murder should be welcome?

He said, 'Plead guilty, tell the judge your mitigating circumstances – I bet he won't even send you to jail.'

Ghani's expression, which had been un-convincingly puzzled, now seemed more like the genuine article. He muttered, 'I don't understand.'

Singh said, 'We don't *blame* you for killing Richard Crouch. Frankly, in your position I'd probably have done the same. But it would be much easier for everyone if you just confessed.'

'But I did not kill him.' The protest rang true. Was he that good an actor, wondered Singh.

'But he was sleeping with your wife...'

Ghani's face drained of blood. His hands, which were laid flat on the table in front of him, bunched into fists. He sat there for a moment trying to regain control of his temper. It was a losing battle. He stood up and leaned forward, hands splayed, eyes popping like golf balls in the mud. He shouted, 'Why do you speak such lies to me?'

Singh was leaning back in his chair. He had not moved a muscle. Bronwyn was standing bolt upright, rocking slightly on the balls of her feet, ready to enter the fray if Ghani attacked the senior policeman. Singh hoped she knew a martial art.

The inspector from Singapore took his courage in his hands and said nonchalantly, 'You didn't know – about your wife and Crouch?'

Ghani slammed his fist on the table. Singh noticed for the first time that he had a long thin scar running up his forearm. It looked like a knife wound. Ghani shouted, 'It's not true!'

It was Singh's turn to stand up. He leaned forward and eyeballed Ghani. 'Look, I'm not making this up. She told us herself.'

'What do you mean? Who told you?'

'Nuri,' and he added helpfully, 'your wife. We went to see her this afternoon. She told us that she and Crouch were planning to run away together. From the condition of her face, it looks like you don't mind trying to resolve your marital problems with violence.'

Ghani collapsed back into the chair and put his hands over his face, his elbows resting on his knees.

Singh sat back down. He picked his nails, flicking any real or imagined dirt onto the floor. Singh was indifferent to the raging internal conflict of the man in front of him. He had decided reluctantly that he was not the killer of Richard Crouch. His shock at the affair between his wife and the dead man had been like another person in the room, so tangible was the emotion. This man was no longer a credible suspect. If he had not known about Nuri's infatuation with Crouch, he had no motive. At most he was a witness – perhaps he would be able to give them some insights into Ramzi's character.

Again, Singh wondered why Ghani was afraid – if it was not of an accusation of murder.

Ghani sat up. His eyes were red-rimmed but dry. He straightened his spine and pulled back his shoulders.

Singh was reminded that he was a soldier.

Ghani said calmly, 'I had nothing to do with the death of Abdullah. I thought he was a friend. If what you say is true – I will question my wife – I do not regret his death.'

Singh said in a friendly tone, 'I believe you.'

'Does that mean I can go?'

'After you tell us if Ramzi killed Abdullah.'

'Ramzi? Why would Ramzi kill him?'

'Same reason. *He* knew about the affair. He might have been trying to protect the family honour.'

'He knew? You are saying Ramzi knew about my wife ... and that man?'

'That's exactly what I'm saying,' said Singh, steepling his fingers and looking at the other man over the apex.

The policeman from Singapore suspected that Ghani had rarely been told that his broad face was a mirror to his emotions. Under the weight of the revelations that Singh was flinging at him, it was possible to read his thoughts from the expressions flitting across it. There was shock that Ramzi might have known about Nuri and not told him, a brief flurry of disbelief and finally a sinking sensation that if Ramzi had known, it was not impossible that he had killed Richard Crouch.

Singh was sure that Ghani had no real knowledge of Ramzi's guilt. His fear that Ramzi was involved was based entirely on his intimate knowledge of the young man's character. In their short encounter, Singh had put the young man down as a contrary young fool with a misplaced self-confidence. Looking at Ghani's worried face, he knew that his assessment was correct.

Singh stood up, held open the door to the interview room and said abruptly, 'You can go now.'

The prisoner who, a short while earlier, would have made a dash for freedom if he had been given half a chance, walked slow and stooped towards the exit. He stole a sidelong glance at the policeman as he walked past, fearful of the comic figure who knew so many secrets.

Bronwyn tossed a few words after him. 'We don't want any more attacks on your wife. Not unless you want to spend a lot of time in a Bali prison. And I promise you – I will make it happen.'

Ghani had paused in mid-step as she spoke – now he continued on without looking back.

Singh closed the door and leaned on it, looking across at his colleague. 'What did you think of that?'

'It was a bit mean of you to suggest that Nuri was actually *sleeping* with Crouch.'

Singh grunted. 'It would've been too dull to describe the love-struck shopping expeditions.'

She asked, 'Do you think he killed Richard Crouch?'

Singh rubbed his forehead with thumb and forefinger. 'No such luck.'

Bronwyn whipped out her mobile phone and made a quick call. 'The brother hasn't come back to the flat yet,' she explained, holding the phone away from her ear for a moment. 'Do you want someone on Ghani's tail?'

'Nah, waste of manpower – he didn't do it. We need to look elsewhere for the killer of our philandering Moslem.'

Bronwyn laughed. 'It is a bit of a contradiction, isn't it?'

'I told you that lusts of the flesh always trump God!'

'It seems that you're right. Do you think he'll hurt Nuri? Should we send her some protection?'

'He heard your warning.'

Singh scratched his beard. He was troubled. He didn't know why. He felt he was missing something. And he had no idea what it could be. It was disturbing because the investigation was going well. He was down to two suspects. Sarah, the wife, and Ramzi, the brother of the girlfriend. He didn't really suspect either Tim Yardley or Julian Greenwood, despite their solid motives. Neither of them had the temperament to shoot a man in the head. He remembered Greenwood skulking nervously in the presence of his wife. He could imagine him attacking her in a fit of rage, but not Richard Crouch. Greenwood was a man to flee his troubles, not to confront them with violence. Besides, according to Agus, he still owed money to the gangster who was threatening retribution. Presumably if he had followed Crouch out of the bank and killed him, he would have had the sense to empty the dead man's wallet and pay off his debts.

As for Yardley, a clever, manipulative woman like Sarah Crouch might have persuaded him to murder a rival – she *did* remind him of Macbeth's wife. But he suspected it would have taken longer than the few months they had known each other and would have involved a method slightly less bloody. Probably, Sarah would have had to guide him every step of the way and he had found no evidence of any careful planning between the pair.

Richard's death had come as a shock to Nuri so she was out of the running. Ghani had not appeared to know about his wife's infidelity of the heart, if not of the body, so his motive was tenuous at best. For all sorts of practical reasons like access to weaponry and temperament he would have put his money on Ramzi being the killer. But he was not yet absolutely certain. He needed to see Sarah and Ramzi again. He was confident that once he confronted both of them with what he knew, it would become obvious who had murdered Richard Crouch.

Bronwyn was sitting quietly across from him writing up the notes from their interview with Ghani. Her pen scurried across the page in orderly rows, like planting or ploughing, he thought. He wondered why he was indulging in agricultural metaphors – he who had lived in a city his whole life.

It might be the news Bronwyn had broken to him about Wayan. He had lost his job at the villas where Sarah and Richard Crouch had stayed. Occupancy was almost zero – only Sarah's enforced, extended stay kept the place open. But there was no money for a full complement of employees in this post-bomb Bali landscape. The young man who was regularly prevented by the police from doing his job was the first casualty in the pursuit of a trimmed down workforce. He had come to see Bronwyn that evening, almost in tears, hoping she would help him keep his job or find a new one. Singh had forbidden her from leaning on the hotel. There was no point, he explained. The police might have contributed to the promptness of Wayan's dismissal but the underlying reason was the absence of tourists. In those circumstances, there was no point bullying the owners.

Bronwyn's expression had been rebellious.

Singh had asked, 'You don't agree with me?'

'It *is* partly our fault.'

'Yes,' said Singh patiently, 'but mostly the bombers'.'

'It just seems so unfair...'

Singh could not tell if she was referring to Wayan's predicament or that of Bali more generally.

He answered, 'It isn't fair – but there are worse hard luck stories than Wayan's. There are families the length and breadth of this island that have lost not only their livelihoods but family members.'

'I know, but you should have seen his hands.' Bronwyn's voice caught in her throat with sympathy.

'His hands?'

'Yes, they were all cut and bruised. He's gone back to working on his father's paddy field. His hands aren't used to the hard labour. He was a mess and in quite a lot of pain too.'

'He'll get used to it.'

'That's what his father told him. That he just had to keep at it, his hands would toughen up.'

Bronwyn was annoyed at the advice but Singh thought it was sensible and practical. A young man like Wayan would soon get used to his new life.

Indeed, it was not Wayan who interested

him but Ramzi. He asked, his tone staccato and impatient, 'No sign of Ramzi?'

The pen did not stop moving but Bronwyn said evenly, 'No more sign than about five minutes ago when you last asked me...'

'Shouldn't you call again and make sure that the cops haven't wandered off for dinner or something?'

Bronwyn was firm. 'No – they know that the scary policeman from Singapore will have their badges if they screw up.'

Singh grinned, baring his small brown smoker's teeth. 'Really? Excellent!'

'What about Sarah Crouch?'

'Agus will get her for you in the morning.'

When he got to the safe house, Ramzi was already there.

Ghani walked straight up to his brother-in-law. The young man grinned at him. 'I got the van, boss. Just as you asked.'

Ghani hit him. With all the power his squat strong body possessed channelled through one angry clenched fist, Ghani struck Ramzi on the chin. The young man rocked back on his heels in shock, tried to recover his balance, failed and fell heavily against the explosives-filled plastic cabinet nearest to him.

Abu Bakr screamed, 'Be careful! You'll set it off.'

Everyone froze. It was as if someone had

pressed pause on the video player in the midst of an action film. Ramzi lay motionless on the ground, his back to the cabinet. Ghani, who had taken a few angry steps forward, anxious to continue his assault, stopped – his fists still raised. Yusuf dropped his Quran, which he had been reading feverishly, and stared at the others in open-mouthed confusion.

The silence and the stillness lasted for thirty seconds. It felt like an eternity to the men in the room.

Abu Bakr said, in a voice several octaves higher than usual, 'Ramzi, move away – slowly.'

Ramzi did as he was asked. Still on the ground, he inched away from the device.

Ghani allowed his hands to fall to his sides. He was still panting. The look in his eyes suggested that Ramzi should opt for maximum prudence.

Abu Bakr asked, his voice back to normal, 'What's the matter? What has Ramzi done?'

Ramzi was irritated that his brother had assumed that Ghani's anger was justified. He said peevishly, holding his jaw, 'I haven't done anything.' He stopped, winced in pain and spat a tooth into his hand. 'Now see what *you've* done,' he continued in an aggrieved tone.

Abu Bakr ignored his younger brother and asked, more insistently this time, 'Ghani –

why are you so angry? Ramzi has performed well. He has brought us a van.'

Ghani spoke through gritted teeth. 'Did you kill him?'

It was Abu Bakr who asked the question that Ramzi should have done. 'Kill whom? Who do you think he has killed?' Ghani said, 'He knows. Look at his face! He knows.'

They all stared at Ramzi.

Ramzi did not know it but his face was the spitting image of his sister, Nuri, when she had been speaking to the police earlier in the day. He had the same swollen jaw, split lip and expression that combined guilt and defiance.

Abu Bakr asked in a voice barely above a whisper, 'Brother, what have you done?'

Ramzi stared down at his feet. Their relationship had suffered a terrible strain in the last few weeks but his brother was still the only one who could get through to him, make him revisit his actions with a critical eye. He muttered something inaudible.

Ghani spat on the floor. 'He killed the bomb-maker. That's what he did – he killed Abdullah and led the police right to our front door.'

Ramzi said, his voice thick and slurred because of his mouth injuries, 'I didn't mean to do that – lead the police to us, I mean.'

'But you killed the bomb-maker.' It was a

320

statement, not a question by Abu Bakr. He continued sarcastically, 'Was there any reason or did you just want your elder brother to construct an improvised explosive device without proper training?'

Ramzi stole a quick glance at Ghani. He found the truth too difficult to explain to Nuri's husband.

Ghani said bitterly, 'You are afraid to tell me that my wife was having an affair with this Richard Crouch? That fat policeman with the pointy turban was not so worried about my feelings.'

In the corner, Yusuf yelped like a stray dog that had been kicked by a passing stranger. None of the others noticed.

Ramzi said pleadingly, 'They were going to run away together. She told me herself. I wasn't going to kill him. I just took the gun with me as persuasion.'

'What happened?' asked Abu Bakr.

'I went to see him.'

'Where?' Ghani's question had the abruptness and clarity of a gunshot.

'The safe house of the first cell.'

'But how did you know where it was?'

Ramzi muttered sheepishly, 'I knew one of the boys in the first cell, Iqbal. We were at school together. I know we were not supposed to communicate but we exchanged texts a few times – we were just so excited to be involved, I guess. When I needed to find

Abdullah, I just asked him where they were. It was a house in Denpasar.'

Ramzi knew that he had broken every rule in the book. He was struggling to maintain his usual sang froid. Killing the bomb-maker probably wasn't as bad in the eyes of the others as communicating with the first cell.

Ghani said in an even tone, 'Go on.'

Ramzi looked at him doubtfully. The quiet voice of the field commander was belied by the hands clenched into fists by his sides. Ramzi touched his jaw gently. He didn't want to be on the receiving end of another blow. 'There's not much to tell. I confronted Crouch. He refused to leave Nuri. I was very angry. He was desecrating the family honour. I showed him the gun. He still refused – he said that he loved Nuri and planned to marry her. I lost my temper and pulled the trigger.'

Ramzi shrugged to show that killing a man had not been difficult – omitting to mention that Iqbal had found him throwing up in the bushes. The sight of Richard Crouch lying on the grass with a smoking, bleeding hole in his forehead had been too much for the young *jihadi*.

'What did you do with the body?'

Ramzi ran his fingers through his hair and then yanked until his eyes watered. He needed a stab of pain to sharpen his senses

322

– the sensation in his jaw had dulled to a low throbbing ache. 'That's what I don't understand,' he said plaintively. 'Only Iqbal was there. The rest were out. It was his job to load the van with the bomb. I helped him and then we put the body in the van too. One of the others took the vehicle bomb to the Sari Club and detonated it. I can't imagine how the police found enough of the bomb-maker to discover he was shot ... you can understand that, right? I thought we were safe.'

As the others stared at him in disbelief he reiterated, 'Don't you see, the body was in the vehicle bomb. It must have been blown to bits.'

Abu Bakr said wryly, 'Well, when Ghani murders you for jeopardising the mission, we know what to do with your body.'

Seventeen

Yusuf knew that Ghani would have him flayed if he found out that he had snuck out of the safe house after telling the others he was having an early night to prepare for his role the following day. He was risking the success of the plan for personal reasons. It would be unforgivable in the view of the others – perhaps even in the eyes of Allah. He hoped his martyrdom the following day would be sufficiently exculpatory. But he found that he could not – just could not – leave Nuri without saying goodbye.

She was at the apartment in Denpasar – on her own. She must be wondering – worrying – where they had all gone. Or perhaps she was still mired in the terrible sorrow he had sensed in her these last few weeks – a sorrow which had sharpened into an anguish so intense when the police had broken the news of Abdullah's death that Yusuf had feared for her sanity. He vaguely understood that she had fallen in love with the bomb-maker. He knew in his head that it was a terrible betrayal of her husband. But he could not find it in himself to condemn her. After all, sometimes the heart was difficult to control.

He, Yusuf, had found a way out of his troubles. He was lucky that it was a method that also reflected the greater glory of God. But what of Nuri? She had not been given the option of martyrdom as a cure for a broken heart.

A small part of Yusuf was envious of the affection that Abdullah had inspired in Nuri. But it was not his predominant emotion. Mostly, he felt wretched that this girl whom he had adored for so long was suffering and that he could do nothing to alleviate her pain. He, Yusuf, had never stood a chance with her. He understood that instinctively and completely. There was no way a creature like Nuri would ever feel anything stronger than pity for a man like him. He had been content to be her friend – he had wished her nothing but happiness.

Yusuf tugged on his beard and remembered that Ramzi had mocked him for doing so. He shoved his hands into his pockets. It was a shame, he thought bitterly, that Ramzi had not been selected for a martyr's role. Yusuf blinked rapidly, trying to dismiss such thoughts from his head. He reminded himself that it was a privilege to lay down his life. The *imam* at his mosque in Sulawesi and Abu Bakr had both explained that the scriptures valued *jihad* above all else. To wish such a fate upon Ramzi as a punishment was to wilfully misunderstand everything he had been taught.

Yusuf let himself into the apartment. There was a fetid damp smell that he had not noticed previously. The place was in darkness, only the dim glow of distant street lamps created shadows and silhouettes. Yusuf felt his heart turn over – it caused him a physical pain – perhaps she was not there. Perhaps Nuri was not there and he had come all this way for nothing. He flicked on the light switch.

Nuri was curled up in a corner of the moth-eaten sofa. She stared directly at him, but he had the sense that she was almost looking through him, past him. Yusuf thought sadly that it was the dead man, Abdullah the bomb-maker, who loomed large in her mind's eye.

He said tentatively, 'Nuri?' and when she did not respond, a little louder, 'Nuri!' Yusuf's hand went to his beard again. He whispered, 'Nuri, I have come to say good-bye.'

Ghani and Abu Bakr stood on the porch of the safe house. Abu Bakr was smoking a cigarette. He was not a heavy smoker but after a day spent handling high explosives followed by the revelation that his younger brother had killed the bomb-maker, he felt he deserved one.

Ghani asked, "What is the status of the

explosive devices?'

Abu Bakr sucked on the end and exhaled a white cloud of smoke through his nostrils. The heavy scent of cloves mixed with night jasmine from the garden. It was a heady, romantic scent – coupled with the clear skies and twinkling stars, it made for a beautiful night on the Island of the Gods. Neither man noticed. They were both concentrating hard on the mission. There was hardly any time left to get everything in place. Ghani felt the pressure as a physical force bearing down on him. He dared not fail.

'The big bomb is ready to be loaded into the van. The aluminium nitrate and diesel fuel are mixed and I have packed it with shrapnel – mostly nails that Yusuf bought at a hardware shop in Sanur,' said Abu Bakr calmly.

'Detonation?'

'The primary explosive is PETN. I've wired it to be triggered by mobile phone, and added a manual switch as well.'

Ghani's brow lightened somewhat. 'That sounds good.' He continued, 'And the backpack?'

'There was half a kilogram of C4 in the stuff shipped over from Java. I was going to use it as the detonator ... after you asked for a portable device, I used the plastic explosives for that.'

Ghani nodded in agreement. 'Good move. It will be lighter and much harder to detect. Same trigger?'

'Yes – a manual switch and a mobile phone detonator.'

'That should be all right,' said Ghani. He looked at the other man, debating whether to raise his doubts. At last he asked, 'Yusuf?'

Abu Bakr understood the question. He sighed. 'I'm not sure. He is acting very peculiar. Not speaking much. Jumping at shadows. That's the main reason I wired the devices with alternative triggering mechanisms.'

'In case he chickens out?'

'In case he chickens out, yes.'

Ghani kicked a stone into the shrubbery in disgust. 'We're supposed to be God's warriors – instead, we seem to be a bunch of cowards and idiots.'

Abu Bakr did not disagree with the harsh characterisation of Yusuf and Ramzi. He said reassuringly, 'We are almost there, Ghani. Tomorrow we will strike a blow that this island will not forget for a thousand years.'

'I don't believe you!'

Yusuf blinked rapidly. He said, 'It is true, Nuri. God has selected me to be a martyr.' When she did not respond, he continued, his tone tentative, desperately seeking some acknowledgement of his sacrifice but too afraid to ask for it directly. 'I could not leave you without saying goodbye.'

Nuri's stomach was clenched as if she was preparing for a body blow. Her hands were trembling. She had been such a fool – believing everything she had been told by Ghani about their visit to Bali. It had seemed so plausible that they were there to set up a religious school. She knew that Ghani was devoted to the cause of oppressed Moslems everywhere. He had spent years fighting in Afghanistan. But she had not even suspected that he had turned his attention to Bali.

She asked, her voice a whisper, 'My brothers?'

Yusuf said, 'We are all in this together...'

Nuri's face, already pale and drawn, blanched white. Her thin fingers gripped the arms of the chair like a nervous passenger on a turbulent flight.

The bespectacled young man leaned forward and spoke hurriedly. 'But don't worry, I am the only martyr. Your brothers are not in any danger.'

Her first exhalation of relief was immediately replaced with fear – not in danger – how could he even say that?

'But why did nobody tell me? Why was I brought along?'

Yusuf's face was blank. Nuri felt a

hysterical desire to laugh. She bit it off with difficulty. Her husband might not have seen fit to share his plans with her, but she doubted that Yusuf would have been privy to much information either. She supposed her role was a combination of comfort, convenience and cover. No one would suspect the menfolk of being terrorists if they had a dutiful wife and sister in tow.

Terrorists – it was the first time she had used that word to describe her family's activities, even in her own mind. She had shied away from the thought – focusing on the facts, the bizarre, shocking facts that had been recited nervously by Yusuf, his eyes fixed on her face, seeking to read her reaction from her expressions.

She remembered that her own father had clapped and cheered on September 11th. She could remember him crowing and cackling, 'The infidels have suffered a blow they will never forget!'

Ghani had insisted that the victims of the Bali bombings deserved to be punished. 'Allah be praised,' he had said and she had not disagreed – after all, she too had been shocked by the unruly, unholy decadence of Bali.

Yusuf interrupted her reverie. 'Nuri?'

She looked at him. His hands were clasped together. He seemed to be praying for forgiveness, for understanding, or maybe just

330

for a bit of attention.

Nuri whispered, 'When?'

'Tomorrow...'

They both sat in silence, trying to absorb the enormity of his statement.

It was Yusuf who spoke first. He said, his voice barely audible, 'I know that your heart lies with Abdullah – and I understand that. But I just wanted you to know that I have always been here for you. I am sorry that I have to leave you now – when you are so troubled in your heart.'

It was the longest speech Nuri had even heard from him. But she had stopped concentrating from the moment Abdullah's name had crossed his lips. Images were flooding through her mind. Abdullah's visits to the apartment. The numerous discussions amongst the menfolk when she had been told to wait in the bedroom – and the quiet single-minded devoutness of her would-be lover that had appealed to her even as she had been triumphant that she was his only weakness.

She breathed, 'Abdullah?'

Yusuf's expression was puzzled, vacant.

She said again, 'Abdullah? He was involved in this ... this plan?'

Yusuf nodded briskly, pleased to have understood her question, vaguely aware that he had a greater hope of her respect if he was a fellow conspirator of her lost love.

'He was the bomb-maker. He made the device for the first blasts. He was supposed to construct one for us too...' Yusuf trailed off uncertainly.

Nuri guessed that he did not want to remind her of Abdullah's death – as if her heart and mind were not screaming that fact at her every instant of every day.

'Fortunately, Abu Bakr has the skills to continue his work,' added Yusuf hastily.

Nuri remembered how Abdullah had told her he had something important to do on the evening prior to the Bali bombings, something that could not wait. She understood now why he had left her with Ramzi, insisted that he had to go, promised that he would come back for her.

Nuri wrapped her arms around her knees and rocked back and forth, back and forth.

She focused her gaze on Yusuf, still looking at her with longing in his eyes. Her lost love's legacy was in his hands.

Eighteen

It was an exquisite morning, thought Singh. The sun was already bright although it was still early. The air had the lingering cool of night time. Birds and flowers were both abundant, riotous colour amidst verdant green. Singh wished suddenly he knew more about birds. What, for instance, was the bright yellow one with the strange elliptical trajectory? He recognised the mynahs and sparrows – they were common in Singapore as well. But there was a little red bird darting in and out of a hibiscus bush, the same shade as its lush flowers, that he had never seen before. That was what he was missing, Singh decided, a healthy hobby. Definitely, he would take up bird-watching when he was back in Singapore.

Nyoman was waiting and Singh lumbered over.

'*Ibu* Bronwyn not coming today, sir?'

'No – she's going to that remembrance service on Jalan Legian.'

Nyoman nodded wisely. 'Yes, I drove near-by there just now – already the road is full of people going to the site. There is a lot of traffic and security and priests – it is a big mess!'

'We're going to the police station in Denpasar,' said Singh. 'So we should be able to avoid the crush. I want to have a chat with Sarah Crouch.'

His mobile phone rang. He answered it and uttered a curt 'hello'.

'In a good mood as always, I see,' said Bronwyn. 'You need to drink less coffee. It makes you irritable.'

'What makes me irritable is young women who don't get to the point.'

'Young? Why thank you, Inspector. No one's called me that in a while.'

'Only compared to me,' grumbled Singh. 'It was not a compliment.'

Bronwyn's abrasive laugh came through the airwaves and Singh held the phone away from his ear. It was like scraping out his ears with sandpaper, listening to her sometimes.

'I just called to let you know that I'll be at the Sari Club. Are you sure you don't want to come with me? I think it will be a really good way to honour the dead of Bali.'

For a moment, Singh was tempted. Perhaps an event to mark the horror visited on this beautiful island deserved to be respected, even by him. Singh, the atheist, was not a great fan of religious ritual. On the rare occasions his wife dragged him for a Hindu wedding or a funeral in Singapore, he would stand outside the temple and smoke cigarettes with like-minded men while the women, dressed richly or simply as the occasion demanded, would take front-row seats to the spectacle. And it was always a sight to behold. Priests in white cotton sarongs, coconuts smashed into the ground, incense burning, ululating in Sanskrit, holy oil and water, fires burning – Singh found the whole complex religiosity tiresome – but it was an entertaining sight for the uninitiated.

He said, more gruffly than he felt, 'Someone needs to get on with solving this murder.' And then feeling a little bit guilty for his rudeness, he continued, 'But one of us should be there – so I am glad you're going.'

Singh scratched his beard and wondered if he was growing soft. He scowled. He was not the type to develop a liking for sidekicks. They were there to fetch and carry for him and sometimes to pick up the pieces after him. That was all.

Nyoman stopped the car and Singh got out. He headed for the now familiar interview room. Sarah was waiting within. She was dressed smartly, her hair neat and freshly cut. Light make-up added freshness and colour to her usual death mask. It was so much easier to tell when women were moving on, thought Singh. They took pride in their appearance. It was a signal that they had recovered from bereavement. Men looked exactly the same before and after.

No clues could be derived from week-old stubble or an un-ironed shirt that could not be discounted as typical male behaviour rather than grief.

Sarah said, 'I'm planning to leave Bali soon. I'd appreciate it if you would return my passport.'

'Running away with surfer boy?'

She ignored the question and asked irritably, 'Why have you dragged me down here?'

'I'm curious to know why you didn't tell me that Richard was Moslem.'

Sarah's hands twisted the handkerchief she was holding. She said sheepishly, 'It was all a bit embarrassing, that's all. I've never told *anyone* – especially after the bombings. He got religion and was a right pain about it.'

'What do you mean?'

'He was always reading the Quran, even when we were out at restaurants and things.' Her shame at this behaviour was apparent in her reddened cheeks. 'He would pray five times a day. It was ridiculous ... he'd get out of bed to pray at dawn!'

Sarah was indignant and garrulous, remembering her husband's religious beliefs. 'He wanted me to convert – to become a Moslem. I said nothing doing – I wasn't going to make myself a laughing stock. It made him really angry.' The recollection of enraging her husband caused a small smile to play about the corners of her mouth.

'How did he find Allah, anyway? Was it recent?'

'He met some people in London. They took him to some services – is that what you call it? – at the mosque near our home in Finsbury Park. I told you he was looking for answers after his parents died in that car crash. Later, his job took him to Afghanistan and Indonesia and he really got stuck into this Moslem malarkey.'

She shuddered. 'Can you believe there was a point where he stopped shaving and started wearing that long green dress, it looks like a hospital gown, that some of them wear? I told him that was too much – I would leave him if he didn't dress like a normal man.'

'And he agreed?'

'To be frank, he didn't seem to care, except to say that he wouldn't give me a divorce. When he planned this move to Bali he started dressing normally again.'

Singh eyed the woman in front of him. She was a real poster child for religious intolerance. On the other hand, it must have been quite challenging to be married to someone who unexpectedly took up religion – most women only had to put up with golf.

Something was puzzling Singh. He asked, 'I know you've said that this Bali trip was supposed to be an effort to save your marriage – but it sounds like it was far too late for that. So why wouldn't he grant you a divorce?'

Distracted by her memories, Sarah was being more honest than usual. 'He was convinced that he could turn me into a good Moslem wife, that it was his duty to save me. I was still quite surprised when he proposed moving to Bali to see if it helped our marriage.'

'It didn't work,' remarked Singh.

'No, it didn't,' agreed the widow.

'So you found yourself a surfer dude and he found himself a pretty pliant Moslem woman.'

'What are you talking about?'

'Didn't you know?' asked Singh, the method actor. 'Richard, or Abdullah, as she called him, was planning to marry this lovely Indonesian girl from Sulawesi. He met her here in Bali. According to her, it was love at first sight.'

'I don't believe you!'

'I spoke to the girl myself. It was all romantic conversation and seaside walks.'

'The bastard!'

Singh noted with interest that Sarah was actually trembling with rage. He had always assumed it was a figure of speech. There was a thin white line around her lips. Her teeth were clenched so tight it was driving the blood away from her mouth. An angry vein

338

throbbed in her neck like a snake rustling through the undergrowth.

Singh did his best to make matters worse. He said in a conversational tone, 'He planned to marry her – take her as a second wife. Moslems are allowed to do that, you know. It's not bigamy.'

'Over my dead body he would have married a second wife!'

'Actually, the dead body belongs to your philandering husband,' pointed out Singh.

Sarah glared at him. 'He deserved to die.'

'Did you kill him?'

'Of course not!' She added with a flash of honesty, 'If I'd known about this woman, I would have been tempted.'

'Why are you so angry? You had a bit on the side too!'

'Well, that's over – Greg Howard said his goodbyes a few days ago.'

Her tone was brittle but matter-of-fact. Singh found that he had the capacity to feel sorry for this woman. He was spending too much time with Bronwyn, he decided. He was in danger of developing a sympathetic nature.

Sarah continued, 'And he still didn't want a divorce! Maybe he thought I would be chuffed if he brought home a second wife?' She snorted in disgust.

Singh indulged in his watching Buddha routine, leaning back in his chair with interlocked fingers resting on his beer gut. He thought that the widow was building up a very decent head of steam.

As he expected, Sarah was not loath to continue. 'It's the bloody hypocrisy, isn't it? Acting so holy the whole damn time ... talking about the suffering of his Moslem brothers in Palestine. Telling me that he'd worked with the Taliban in Afghanistan – I have no idea what he could have done. They need soldiers, right? Fat lot of good a chemical engineer would have been. But the first bit of skirt that shows him any interest, and its goodbye Mr Holy Moslem.'

Singh's own sympathy for Crouch was waning slightly. 'It's a bit ironic that he should have ended up blown to bits by a terrorist bomb then, isn't it?' he remarked.

Sarah nodded, her fine hair falling across her face like a curtain. 'It *is* ironic – I remember thinking at the time he would have been pleased about the attack by those mad *mullah* types.'

Julian Greenwood waited until his wife had left for one of her regular spa treatments. He knew she would spend hours with a couple of Balinese women kneading her plump flesh as if it was home-made dough. He grabbed a chair and quickly took down the painting that the inspector from Singapore had suggested he sell for cash. He wrapped it in old newspaper and sealed it carefully with packing tape. Julian hurried down the driveway with the package under his arm, oblivious to the carefully tended flower beds and neatly pruned bushes along the way. He hailed a Bluebird taxi and instructed the driver in rapid-fire Indonesian to take him to an art gallery in Seminyak. He tried to shut his mind, not to think about what he was doing. He stared out of the grimy windows, watching Bali in all its glowing primary colours race by him, the work of art belted into the seat next to him.

Half an hour later he had sold the painting. The price was well below its value but enough to pay off his creditors with a bit left over. The gallery owner had looked at him with narrowed eyes – a perspiring white man trying to unload a valuable painting in a hurry for substantially less than it was worth. But he had agreed – as Julian had known he would. Times were too tough after the Bali bombings for any entrepreneur to place unconfirmed suspicions above a handsome profit. There were very few people in the position of his wife who did not have to allow the constant pursuit of a few dollars to affect their behaviour or honesty.

He caught the same taxi to the bar on the outskirts of Kuta where he expected to find his nemesis playing pool under the fluorescent lights. He handed over the money silently and was rewarded with a broad grin and a handshake.

'Good, good! I would not have liked to make an example of you.'

Julian did not acknowledge the comment. He was in a hurry. His wife would be home eventually. She would notice the gap over the mantelpiece immediately. It was as obvious as a six-year-old missing his two front teeth. He did not doubt that Emily would guess what he had done and take steps to recover her property – her art and him, both bought and paid for and kept around the house as decorative pieces.

Outside, on the dusty street, he hopped onto a bus – he had to conserve his remaining cash and obscure his trail. He squeezed into a rickety seat next to an old woman with a chicken in a woven basket on her lap. It reminded him of the cockfighting so when she grinned at him broadly with *sireh*-stained red teeth sprouting like poisonous mushrooms from her gums, he smiled back.

He would take the crowded ferry to Lombok and then another one to Java. His wife would not be able to trace him. He was free of her and free of his debts. Julian knew he was never coming back to Bali.

Back at the villa in Ubud, Sarah Crouch was hastily flinging clothes into a suitcase. She was seething, her blonde hair in disarray, as she remembered what Singh had told her. Richard had been having an affair. He, who was too bloody holy to grant her a divorce, had a bit on the side. She was pleased he was dead. She had been glad before, but that had been for practical reasons – she wanted her freedom and his cash. But now she was glad he was dead at a visceral level. Sarah ground her small white teeth together audibly.

There was a tentative knock on the door. She scowled. She was leaving that day. She didn't need her bed made for the last time. The last thing she wanted was an army of Balinese workers, armed with mops and buckets and fresh towels, crawling around the villa like worker ants.

There was another knock at the door, still hesitant but a bit louder.

She flung the door open, yelling, 'No need to clean today!'

It was Tim Yardley. The expression on his face was that of a lost puppy – droopy eyes, downturned mouth and limp jowls.

Sarah suppressed a sigh. She said, 'Now is not a great time, Tim.'

He gazed past her into the room, noting the open suitcases and heaps of clothes and other belongings.

'Are you leaving?' His tone was conversational.

She looked at him suspiciously. Was it possible he was going to be grown up about her departure? She answered in a more friendly tone, 'Yes, Bali holds too many painful memories for me now. I hope you can understand that.'

'I understand painful memories – I understand pain very well indeed.'

So much for grown up, thought Sarah. She wondered again whether Tim had actually killed Richard. She doubted it. She had planted the seed but had never had much expectation of it sprouting. She glanced at him in disgust. This was not fertile soil.

Tim stepped into the hall. She tried to block his entrance but he used his size to good effect. She found herself physically sidelined, bounced out of the way by his bulk. She conceded the ground so as not to engage in an undignified scuffle. He smelt unwashed – layers of grime darkened his neck.

Where are you going?' he asked.

'Back to London...'

'Is that young fella coming with you?'

Sarah stood stock still, only her pale-blue eyes swivelled around to look at him. 'What do you mean?'

'That surfer ... the policeman from Singapore told me he was your lover.'

Sarah decided to promote Singh to a joint first spot with her dead husband on the 'people she most despised' list.

She said, 'I'd prefer not talk about it, Tim.'

He folded his arms. She noticed that they were hairless but speckled with freckles and moles. She remembered Greg's strong arms with their fine sprinkling of golden hair. The pang of loss was like a blow to the stomach. She felt winded. She said again, her voice much weaker, 'I'd really prefer not to talk about Greg.'

Tim seemed to swell with anger. His face turned crimson as his heart pumped blood with an intensity it had not achieved in years. 'You don't want to talk about it? I was humiliated by a turbaned cop in a Bali police station because you've been playing me for a *fool* – but you don't want to talk about it?' Each word was spat out like a loose tooth after a fight.

Sarah took two small steps backwards. She was suddenly afraid of the enraged creature looming large in her villa.

He continued, 'You wanted me to *murder* Richard. I see it all now.'

'Did you do it?' The question slipped out. She had not meant to ask, did not really want to know.

He shook his head slowly, the comb-over succumbing to gravity and falling down his cheek. 'No ... I'm afraid I still owe you a body.'

Bronwyn wondered what was appropriate wear for a remembrance ceremony.

She put on a long-sleeved white shirt and a pair of tan trousers that fitted snugly around her posterior. She craned her neck and noticed that her panty line demarcated two large mounds of flesh. Too many beers and curries with the good inspector, she thought regretfully as she struggled to do up her zip. She managed at last, scarlet-faced from the effort. Once the murder investigation was over she was going to eat nothing but green salads for a month. She grabbed a large, wide-brimmed hat on her way out. The purification rites were out of doors and it was turning into a scorching day. Some sort of head protection was essential.

She hailed a taxi and asked to be taken to Jalan Legian. The driver shook his head dubiously. 'Can try, *Ibu*. But very busy.'

'All right then – just get me as close as possible. I can walk after that.'

She was dropped at one end of the street and handed the driver a generous wad of Indonesian *rupiah*. It would take him a while to fight his way through the hordes of people descending on the blast sites. Pulling her hat more firmly down on her head, Bronwyn marched purposefully towards the temporary structures she could see ahead.

It was a mixed crowd who were making their way forward. There were thousands of native Balinese dressed in their temple best. Intricately patterned *sarongs* were worn with smart shirts and silk headdresses by the men. The women were also in *sarongs* but their blouses were in the *kebaya* design, fitting snugly with embroidery and lace to decorate the cloth. Both men and women wore long sashes around their waists and many of the women carried offerings of fruit on their head, casually balancing the load while sauntering down the uneven road without losing so much as a banana. There were many Westerners as well. Bronwyn wondered whether they were residents of Bali, tourists or families of those killed in the attacks. Probably all the above, she thought. The elderly couple walking ahead of her – the woman had tear stains on her cheeks and was leaning on her husband's arm – they might have lost a son or daughter in the bombs. But the group of young men in surfer shorts and T-shirts, tanned to a darker brown than the native Balinese, had to be tourists who had stayed on.

She walked through a gauntlet of Balinese security personnel. They gave her a cursory glance but demanded to look into the backpack of the young man behind her. She noticed for the first time that there were men in the uniform of the Bali police mingling with the crowds. She'd bet that there were plainclothes policemen too –

probably personnel from the AFP as well.

Bronwyn remembered the news programme which had optimistically suggested that Bali was already on the road to recovery. Bronwyn looked around at the silent crowds. She was not convinced. It was early days. People in Bali were still coming to terms with what had happened to them.

She made her way to the temporary scaffolding that had been put up around the entrance to the Sari Club. Bamboo canopies on metal poles provided some shade from the sun. There were signs stating that the seats were reserved for VIPs and family members of those killed. Despite the hordes of people, there were still workers in their orange reflective jerseys tightening bolts and erecting final bits of the structure.

Bronwyn sat down tentatively on a pile of rubble. It was a desperately uncomfortable seat but gave her a good view of the proceedings. She resigned herself to waiting and wondering what the inspector from Singapore was doing.

Her phone rang, its shrill tone causing her to jump although it was the most common sound of the modern era.

Bronwyn reached for it, going through her routine of flipping it open while tucking her hair behind her ear.

There was an excited tinny babbling at the other end.

She covered her mouth with her hand to muffle her exclamation of shock. Her eyes widened with horror.

She muttered, 'Oh my God!'

She listened for a bit, hung up and sat silently on the pile of debris, oblivious to the throngs of people.

At last, taking a deep breath, she rang the inspector from Singapore.

Singh barked, 'What is it?'

She could barely speak the words.

The inspector asked sharply, 'Bronwyn, is that you? What's the matter?'

'Tim Yardley is dead.'

'What?' The man who professed to know all the answers was gobsmacked. 'How?'

'Sergeant Agus just called me – Yardley walked fully clothed into the sea and never looked back. By the time anyone realised what he was up to – it was too late.'

There was a silence at the other end of the phone.

'Do you think it means he killed Richard Crouch?' asked Bronwyn.

'And couldn't live with what he'd done? No, I think he just gave up on life – the poor bastard. Sarah Crouch might not have killed her husband – but she definitely drove Yardley to his death...'

'But there's nothing we can do about it?'

'Nothing at all.'

Yusuf was within the security perimeter. Ghani's plan had worked like clockwork. He had made his way to the site in the early hours of the morning wearing the orange worker's jacket that Ghani had stolen from the site the previous day. Security had waved him in as he tried to explain he was there to put the final touches on the grandstand. 'You and everyone else,' chortled a sleepy guard. When Yusuf got closer he saw what the sentry meant. There were dozens of men working through the night to get the place ready.

He found a spot on the second floor of a deserted building down the road from the Sari Club, took off his knapsack with the cake of plastic explosives within, and lay down on the hard ground to rest. If anyone found him they would conclude he was a worker skiving on the job.

Somehow he slept despite the discomfort and his terrible nerves. He woke up with a bright shaft of sunlight shining on his face. Yusuf wiped his glasses on his T-shirt and put them on. He wished he had thought to pack some water. His mouth felt like he'd been chewing on old socks.

He took off the orange jacket, rolled it into a small bundle and hid it under a piece of fallen masonry. Then he picked up the knapsack with nervous fingers and slipped it on his back. It was light but he felt the weight of destiny on his shoulders. He wondered whether he dared say his prayers. Ghani had said there was no need. Allah would forgive him this one transgression. If he was caught praying, head down and bowed towards Mecca, he would immediately raise suspicions. Ghani had also insisted that he leave his Quran behind. The field commander pointed out that a passing guard might not recognise a cake of C4, especially since Abu Bakr had sewn the wiring for the detonator into the lining of the bag, but he would certainly know a well-thumbed Quran. It would raise the alarm. The key was to minimise risk, Ghani explained, his tone slow and patient. It had annoyed Yusuf. They all treated him like an idiot or a small child. He was not that stupid. He just struggled to put his thoughts into words sometimes.

He had asked if Nuri would be brought to the safe house. Ghani had snorted, 'She's on her own.'

Yusuf tried to protest but was told to go and prepare himself for his martyrdom – Nuri was not his concern. As usual, he felt overwhelmed by the stronger personalities around him. He had done as he was instructed, cursing himself for his own weakness. But now as he prepared to walk amongst the crowds with his knapsack, he found his thoughts turning to Nuri again.

He hoped she was going to be all right. He was grateful that Allah had given him the opportunity to say goodbye, to explain why he was leaving her.

Yusuf walked out into the street and blinked against the bright morning light. The sky was a clear cloudless blue. Even the bombed-out buildings glowed in the sunshine. It was a truly beautiful day. It felt good to be alive. Yusuf savoured the moment as he walked towards the target.

Nineteen

Bronwyn decided that her posterior had never felt worse. She had been sitting on the pile of rubble for over an hour. She was certain she could distinguish every stone through the seat of her pants. The trousers themselves were constricting her waist. The sun was beating down but at least her hat provided some protection from sunstroke. Her white shirt clung to her like a second skin.

The guest of honour had finally turned up. An entourage of officials and lackeys ushered him towards the raised dais.

Bronwyn watched the families. They were numbed to the presence of the dignitaries. Most of them were just staring at the crater in front of the Sari Club – unable to believe that their loved ones had been stolen from them in such a random act of violence.

The official ceremonies were beginning. It was not so much a memorial for the dead as an exorcism. Jalan Legian had been sprinkled with red and yellow petals. The air was thick with incense. The *gamelan*, native drums and wind instruments, was played loudly by a group of musicians sitting cross-legged on mats on the bitumen road.

There were hundreds of chanting Hindu priests lining the thoroughfare. They were dressed in white linen *sarongs*. Their upper bodies were completely bare, exposing flabby torsos with a sprinkling of dark hair. Patterns were traced on exposed flesh in ash and red pigment. Senior clerics in white and gold robes were sprinkling holy water around the area. Goats, chickens and buffaloes were being sacrificed, their blood splattering on the ground. Many of the priests had gone into trances and were convulsing with the effort to purify the blast sites.

Although the chanting and the ritual sacrifice gave the ceremony a sombre air, Bronwyn sensed that most of those present, the families of the dead excepted, were now in an upbeat mood. This was the moment, they seemed to believe, when Bali would put the past behind it. They were convinced that the biggest purification ritual ever staged would successfully cleanse their island of evil influences.

Bronwyn watched in wonder as young girls in saffron robes danced intricate patterns on the dusty road and storytellers told ancient tales of good triumphing over evil.

She tried to imagine what the inspector from Singapore would have thought of the spectacle, then smothered a smile. She could have used the company, but was glad she had not been able to persuade him to attend.

Singh's mobile rang and he answered it reluctantly. It was one of the two policemen watching the flat. Ramzi had not come back, but the other brother, Abu Bakr, had returned. What should they do? Singh pondered the question. He said, 'Bring him in – and the girl too.'

He terminated the call. The others might be able to tell him where their brother was hiding. It was odd that none of them except Yusuf had returned to the flat the previous evening. Bali was not the sort of place where construction projects went on all day and night like in Singapore. Here it was tools down as evening approached.

He wished Bronwyn was with him. He realised that he was accustomed to bouncing ideas off the Australian. Her suggestions, usually dismissed out of hand by him, had the effect of keeping him thinking. He realised why Hercule Poirot often had that daft Englishman in tow. A sounding board was imperative in a murder investigation. Not that there was much left of this investigation. If Sarah Crouch had killed her husband in a fit of rage over his demure Indonesian woman or more cynically for a financially secure future with surfer boy, he would probably never find out for certain. Singh thought it unlikely. She had wished her husband dead. She had most likely hinted to Tim Yardley that it would solve their difficulties. She had certainly played a large part in driving Yardley to take his own life. But Singh was almost certain that Sarah was too inherently cautious to have taken active steps to kill her husband.

His other key suspect, Ramzi, was nowhere to be found. He had notified the airports and ferry terminals but Singh was fairly certain that a determined young man could find his way through Bali's porous borders.

Singh wandered towards the canteen and ordered himself a cup of strong black coffee. He needed fortification by caffeine. He drained it in one gulp and stared at the dregs at the bottom. Perhaps he should have ordered a cup of tea, thought Singh. He could have read the tea leaves and confirmed that young Ramzi had killed Crouch. He seemed to have run out of policing options to reach a solution. Singh wondered again at Richard Crouch's choice of companions. Even for a Moslem convert looking for friendship amongst those who professed the same religion, they were an unattractive bunch. Singh realised that he was making the elementary error of attributing positive attributes to Richard Crouch because he felt sorry for him as the victim of a brutal murder. Murder victims were just as likely to be unpleasant human beings as anyone else. After all, Sarah Crouch had remarked that Richard would have been delighted with the work of the mad *mullah* types who destroyed the Sari Club. His new friends seemed to have equally extremist views.

Inspector Singh's legs buckled at the knees. He sat down suddenly. A sharp stab of pain in his chest made him nauseous. He shook his head, trying to physically dislodge the thought that had twisted his stomach into knots. Singh recalled how Ghani had seemed relieved that he was being questioned about the death of Abdullah – he had wondered at the time what could be worse than an accusation of murder. Singh turned pale under his dark skin – he knew the answer now.

Ramzi's jaw was throbbing from where Ghani had hit him. He supposed he deserved it. He had compromised the operation by linking up with the first cell. And it had been reckless to kill the bomb-maker. Not that anyone regretted Abdullah's passing. No one, that is, except his foolish young sister.

He was very conscious of his jaw. He stood out in the crowd because of the rainbow bruising and the swollen lip. Ramzi joined the throngs headed towards Jalan Legian. He was stopped and searched, patted down by one of the policemen – his status as a young man who appeared to have been in a fight ensured that. As he was only carrying his wallet and a mobile phone, they let him pass.

He weaved his way through the crowd until he was close to the blast sites. He looked around, trying to spot Yusuf. There was no immediate sign of him but that was no reason to panic. Yusuf was a slight, anonymous-looking character, easily over-looked. Besides, he didn't actually need to see Yusuf to carry out his orders. He knew exactly what to do. If at twelve noon, Yusuf did not detonate the bomb in his backpack, he would set it off using his mobile phone. Ramzi grinned and then winced as the action hurt his mouth. The only reason he needed to locate Yusuf was to ensure that he was not standing too close to him when the bomb detonated. He, Ramzi, was not inclined to be an accidental martyr.

Singh hurried down the corridor, his thumping heart punctuating every panicky step. Abu Bakr and Nuri were in a holding cell. The policeman at the door fumbled with the keys and Singh screamed at him to hurry. The Balinese dropped the keys in shock. Singh took a deep breath. He needed to stay calm, stay professional. But this was not a situation he had confronted before. He was a slow, methodical thinker. Not some sort of action man. He solved murders, sometimes long after the fact.

He didn't try and prevent them.

The policeman managed to open the door. Singh pushed past him and entered the cell. Abu Bakr was sitting next to his sister on a wooden bench against a graffiti-covered wall. They both turned to look at him as he stormed in.

Abu Bakr asked, 'Why have you brought us here?'

Singh did not answer the question. He demanded roughly, 'Where are the others?'

'What do you mean?'

'Where is your brother? Where is Ghani and that other man – the one with the spectacles?' Singh's voice was fraying with panic.

Abu Bakr would not meet his eyes. He said, 'I don't know. At work, I suppose.'

'Why didn't any of you come back to the flat last night?'

Abu Bakr crossed his arms but did not answer.

'Why did you come back to the flat this morning?'

It was Nuri who piped up. 'He came to fetch me. We are going back to Sulawesi. My husband has left me but Abu Bakr did not want to abandon me in Bali.' She put a hand on his arm. 'He's a good brother.'

Singh spotted a weakness. He said roughly, 'Ramzi killed Richard Crouch.'

Her face contorted in shock.

Singh drove the point home. 'You dishonoured the family. And it got your boyfriend killed. It was your fault.'

Nuri's shoulders started to shake.

Abu Bakr shouted angrily, 'Stop it! You cannot know that. Nuri, he is just trying to upset you. Pay no attention to him.'

Nuri was not listening to her brother. Tears welled up in her eyes. She brushed them away with an impatient hand. She asked, 'Is it true? Was it Ramzi?'

'You know it was.'

She nodded slowly – it had to be Ramzi. Her voice was hoarse and hurt when she said, 'I want him punished – I want him punished for what he did to Abdullah.'

'Then you must tell me where he is.'

Nuri looked at the stout policeman. He was chewing on his pink bottom lip so aggressively she thought he might draw blood. His foot – in a white shoe, she had noticed him wear it before – was tapping a silent impatient rhythm on the cement floor of their cell. She realised in that instant, as she looked into his dark stricken eyes underneath a frowning brow, that the inspector from Singapore suspected what Ghani,

360

Ramzi and Yusuf had planned.

She understood the policeman's thought processes – he had guessed, but he could not believe his own conclusions. She had felt the same way when Yusuf had come to say goodbye and told her what he was going to do. Singh was staring at her – his expression was almost pleading now – begging to be told that his suspicions were absurd, misplaced, a product of a vivid imagination.

Nuri remembered how she had gazed into the cracked mirror in the bedroom of the flat soon after Abdullah had disappeared. She had appeared cleft in two – now she realised that the fissure ran even deeper than she had perceived. At the time, she had recognised it as a reflection of the state of her heart. Now she realised she was torn in two – to tell this policeman what she knew, and destroy the legacy of Abdullah, the man that she had loved – or to keep silent and allow Ramzi to get away with murder ... again.

Nuri licked her parched lips. She could feel the ridges of skin and taste the saltiness of blood. She closed her eyes. The devastation she had seen on Jalan Legian played across her memory like a silent film. She tried to understand, tried to believe that Abdullah was right – that those people at the Sari Club had deserved to die. They were infidels, the enemies of Islam just like

361

the inspector standing before her – an un-
believer despite his turban. And yet, this
policeman had toiled hard to find the
murderer of Abdullah. He, a non-Moslem,
had worked tirelessly to find justice for the
man she loved.

'I just can't believe that anyone would do
this in Allah's name.' Unbidden, the words
that had been spoken by the elderly Javanese
woman she had met at the bombsite, popped
into her mind. She almost expected to see
her, eyes filled with unshed tears, gazing
blindly down the narrow street, praying that
her brother was safe – knowing deep down
that he had been a victim of the violence.

Nuri straightened her thin shoulders. She
said, 'They are on Jalan Legian.'

Abu Bakr shouted, 'Be quiet, sister. Don't
tell them anything!'

She did not appear to notice the inter-
ruption. She continued, 'It is a Hindu
ceremony to remember the victims of the
Bali blasts.'

Ghani was parked a few blocks down the
road from Jalan Legian. He was in two
minds whether to leave the engine running
or not. It was such a hot day that he had a
genuine fear that the explosives might
detonate. He needed the air-conditioning to
feel more secure. On the other hand, the last
thing he needed was to run out of petrol.

Ramzi had stolen the van the previous day. They didn't even know if the gauges on the thing worked properly. It was not a pleasant sensation to sit on top of 500kgs of explosives wondering whether he was about to become part of a massive fireball. Not that he minded dying. In fact, there was very little likelihood of him surviving the day. He knew that and was reconciled. It was all about the task at hand. He needed to use his vehicle bomb to cause maximum devastation to the thousands of infidels gathered to carry out their sacrilegious activities.

Ghani wondered whether Yusuf would fail them. It was quite possible. But he had Ramzi on the scene as well. Unknown to young Yusuf, his designated suicide bomber, there were alternatives if he had a change of heart.

Yusuf was sitting on the ground, part of a large group of people watching the rituals unfold. His knapsack bomb was on his back. He was pouring with sweat, his T-shirt soaked through. He shivered every time a gust of wind weaved its way through the people to him. Droplets of sweat fell off his hair and dripped onto his glasses. Wiping them with his T-shirt, he had smeared the plastic lenses. The world as he saw it was covered in a grimy smudged layer. Yusuf could, however, see enough to know that the people around him were Balinese. They were infidels undoubtedly, indulging in their unholy rituals. But they were not the real enemy. He had been determined to kill Americans. That was what the martyrs of September 11th had done and they were revered for it among *jihadists*.

Even the killing of Australians in the first bomb had bothered him but Ghani had explained, and Abu Bakr had seconded him, that the Australians were assisting the Americans in their war against Moslems. Yusuf peered around him. He could see some Westerners, of course. They were mingling with the locals, their attention on the priests and the dancers and the story-tellers. On the grandstand with its bamboo canopy, there were even more whites, the families of those already killed. It struck Yusuf for the first time that it was unfair to target these people. They had already lost loved ones. Surely they had learnt their lesson and understood not to wage war on Moslems? He wiped his glasses again and looked at his watch. Ten minutes to twelve. He stood up. It was time to wander a little closer.

Bronwyn spotted Yusuf as he stood up. She stared at him, trying to decide if it was really the quiet young man from the flat – the one who had been so concerned when Nuri fainted. Really, that young girl was quite something. Married to one man, in love with another and with a third, this rather pathetic young man with the oversized glasses and wispy beard, besotted with her.

Should she go up to Yusuf, she wondered. He might know where Ramzi was. It seemed a bit crass to accost him in the midst of a remembrance ceremony. But if she waited, there was every chance she would lose him as the multitudes swarmed away at the end. Truth be told, she was a little bored of this extended purification ritual. How long could one watch a bunch of priests chanting and wailing anyway? She imagined the inspector's face if she was to discover the location of his prime suspect. He would be pleased – but also annoyed that he had not been the one to track him down. Bronwyn felt that she knew the cranky policeman from Singapore well enough to predict his responses accurately.

Bronwyn decided on the spot that, when she got back to Sydney, she would ask to be moved to a murder squad. If she implied that it might buy her silence, she might even get her request. She would still call a few reporters and explain how she'd been sidelined for telling the truth – once she had her new position they wouldn't dare shunt her aside again. It was a devious plan. Inspector Singh would be proud.

Yusuf had made his way to the grandstand. Bronwyn made up her mind. She would corner him and ask him about Ramzi's whereabouts. If necessary, she would take him into custody. It would give her an excuse to abandon the ceremony.

She got to her feet, feeling her trousers stick to her thighs and groin. It really was too humid for words. Bronwyn made her way through the crowds, muttering apologies as she stumbled over outstretched legs.

Yusuf was not looking in her direction. He was staring at the chanting priests. He took a few tentative steps forward, stopped and glanced at his watch again.

Bronwyn's phone rang. She looked around to see if anyone had noticed. It was too embarrassing that she had forgotten to switch it off. Still, it was not like it had rung in church. The whole place was awash with noise – music, storytelling, the chanting of priests, the squealing of animals, the murmured prayers in the crowd. She fished the mobile out of her handbag. It was the inspector. She wondered whether to answer it. He knew where she was. He wouldn't be calling unless it was important. On the other hand, knowing the crotchety old bastard, he wouldn't give a damn about interrupting a religious ceremony to give her some trivial instructions. The phone stopped ringing but started again almost immediately. It was

Singh once more – she would have to answer.

Nyoman was speeding Inspector Singh towards Jalan Legian. Singh had rushed out of the police station, shouting instructions to the duty manager. An attack on the purification ritual was imminent. They needed to notify security. He was on his way to the Sari Club. He might be able to do something. Do something? Singh had no idea what he was suggesting. What could he do? His mind, usually so reliable in thinking through problems, was an unruly tool at that moment. His thoughts were flitting all over the place. Singh remembered Bronwyn. She was there – at the ceremony. He grabbed his mobile phone and punched numbers, his stubby fingers clumsy in panic.

'Why doesn't she answer?' he yelled in anger and frustration.

'What's the matter, *Pak?*' Nyoman was looking at him in the rearview mirror.

'Another bomb – same place – Sari Club,' said Singh, redialling Bronwyn's number.

Nyoman turned as white as a sheet. 'At the ceremony?'

Singh nodded.

Bronwyn picked up the phone and said briskly, 'Can't you even get through a day without me?'

Singh was almost incoherent with panic.

He shouted, 'They're terrorists. They're planning an attack where you are!'

Bronwyn pressed the phone to her ear and cupped a hand over her other ear to try and hear better. A prayer ritual was reaching some sort of climax. The cacophony was tangible against her eardrums.

She said, 'I didn't catch that, I'm afraid. Can you repeat what you said?' She spotted Yusuf again and continued, 'You'll never guess who I just saw. I'm on my way to have a word with him...'

Singh's blood turned to ice in his veins. He shouted, 'Who? Who is it?'

There was a lull in proceedings and Bronwyn heard him. 'Yusuf,' she said. 'You know, that skinny one with glasses from the flat.'

'Does he have a backpack?'

Bronwyn glanced over at Yusuf. 'Yes, why do you ask?'

'It's a bomb.'

'What?'

'You heard me – it's a bomb. Get security to take him out. The others are around as well. Look out for them.'

He could hear Bronwyn spluttering incoherent questions but he ignored them and hung up. Nyoman had brought the van to a standstill behind the barriers blockading Jalan Legian.

'I can't go further. What now, boss?'

Singh stared up and down the street. There was nothing to be seen.

He said to Nyoman, 'I'm going in. If you see a white van – it's a vehicle bomb. Call me.'

The fat policeman clambered out of the Kijang, waved his identification at the guards and hurried down the street towards the Sari Club.

Bronwyn looked around for security. There were a few Balinese policemen standing at regular intervals. If she approached them, what could they do? Any attempt by uni-formed policemen to get close to Yusuf would provoke him to detonate his bomb. She noticed for the first time the women and young children in the crowd. Bronwyn felt sick to the stomach – she had to stop him.

She decided surprise was the best form of attack.

She walked briskly up to Yusuf and said, 'Yusuf, how nice to see you here. We're looking for your friend, Ramzi. Do you know where he is?'

Yusuf stared at her blankly. Her words did not seem to have registered. Bronwyn noted the strong odour and the smudged glasses. Yusuf was petrified. She could smell the fear on him, the musky stench of a wild beast caught in a forest trap.

She said in her friendliest tone, one part of her mind admiring her ability to sound so nonchalant, 'Yusuf, we're looking for Ramzi.'

Yusuf's hands, limp by his sides, twitched. Bronwyn braced herself to leap at him. She was twice his size, she thought grimly. She might be able to keep his hands away from the detonator until backup arrived.

Yusuf asked in a dazed voice, 'You are police, right?'

'Yes, I am.'

'I don't want to do it.'

Bronwyn froze. She asked carefully, 'What don't you want to do?' All the time she watched his hands.

Yusuf waved his arms in a wide arc. He whispered, 'Kill all these people.'

Bronwyn wished she had been trained for a situation like this. Yusuf could be talked down, persuaded not to go ahead – she was sure of it. But Bronwyn was not convinced she had the skills to nudge him towards that end.

She said, 'You don't have to do it – you can change your mind.'

'They're not Americans, you see.'

This was not the time to be arguing for the universal sanctity of human life, thought Bronwyn grimly.

She made a show of looking around. 'It's mostly Balinese,' she said.

He looked at her sharply. 'They are

infidels too.'

Bronwyn nodded immediately. 'Of course! But not so wicked as the Americans.'

Yusuf nodded. 'Exactly! That is what I was telling the others...' He trailed off tugging at his beard.

'I think you should reconsider,' said Bronwyn in a firm tone. 'Why don't you just pass me the bag and we can discuss the best thing to do?'

Yusuf glanced at his watch. It was five minutes past twelve. He said in a plaintive voice, 'I was supposed to set it off at twelve.'

Well then, it's too late anyway.'

She held out her hand for the bag. Yusuf slipped it off his back and held it out to her. Bronwyn felt tears of relief welling up in her eyes.

A hundred yards away, Ramzi decided that Yusuf had blown his big chance to do the right thing by his God. Matters would have to be taken out of his hands. He dialled a number on his phone.

Twenty

Bronwyn and Yusuf both heard the phone ring in the rucksack. Yusuf was perplexed. Bronwyn guessed immediately. The terrorists had doubted Yusuf's commitment. And they had planned accordingly. Clever bastards, she thought as she grabbed the bag from the unresisting Yusuf, took two big strides and flung herself into the bomb crater in front of the Sari Club, the rucksack hugged close to her body.

Singh heard the blast and his heart seemed to stop. Bronwyn hadn't managed to prevent Yusuf exploding his device. Immediately, all other sounds were drowned out by shrill screams. Singh could see hordes of people racing towards him, running away from the explosion in a blind panic. Singh had a horrible feeling of déjà vu. Wasn't this what had happened at Paddy's Bar? Many of the eventual victims had run towards the Sari Club, towards the second, bigger bomb.

The first wave of terrified screaming people was only a few hundred yards away from him.

Singh turned around slowly. He was three

hundred yards away from the police barrier. Nyoman was parked next to the kerb. As he looked down the narrow road, Singh saw a white van pull out of a side street.

Ghani heard it. The sound of a distant explosion. Hundreds of people would soon be racing down Jalan Legian towards him. He drove slowly out to the main street, then turned the van to face the police barrier. This was the moment of truth.

Singh knew at once that the white van was the vehicle bomb. There was no doubt in his mind. He started running back towards the barrier, the crush of people almost upon him. He was shouting, gesticulating to the security at the barrier but they were staring at him in bewilderment – and staring beyond him at the crowds rushing forward.

One of the policemen began to move the barriers, pulling at them to create more space for the people to get through. Singh screamed at him to stop. He was going to give the van direct access to the crowds.

Ghani, driving forward slowly, couldn't believe his luck. The security guards were moving the barriers. He would be able to drive right through and detonate his vehicle bomb in the midst of the infidels. His earlier plan had been to abandon the vehicle, dash for cover and explode the bomb remotely. But now Allah was showing him a way to enhance His glory and Ghani's too. He thought of Nuri for a moment. She was the reason that a field commander was prepared to become a martyr. He gathered speed.

Singh was right in the middle of the unfolding tragedy and he couldn't stop it. The white van was hurtling down the street. The police had suddenly become aware of the vehicle as its speed manifested its hostile intentions. They started to drag the heavy barriers back. Singh could see they would be too late. In any event, if the van could not get to the people, the people were on their way to the van – little realising that they were fleeing a past danger and heading for a catastrophe.

All he could do was witness this disaster. He was impotent to prevent it. Singh realised in that split second that he probably wouldn't survive the blast either. He discovered, almost to his surprise, that he did not want to die.

One of the policemen pulled a gun and started shooting. The white vehicle weaved from side to side, trying to present a more difficult target. The crowd would soon be breaking like waves around the policeman from Singapore. They were so intent on running away they had not yet noticed what lay ahead of them.

He wished he had thought to try and turn them back. It would probably have been impossible, like stopping a runaway train. But he could have tried.

Singh turned back to watch the van.

He saw Nyoman manoeuvre the Kijang onto the road. What was he doing? Making a dash to get away, suspected Singh. He wished him luck. Where Nyoman had been parked was a ringside seat to a mushroom cloud. Nyoman was accelerating.

Singh realised that he was not trying to escape. He was heading straight for the white van. A few hundred yards still separated the vehicle bomb and the fleeing crowds. If Nyoman could intercept the van, hundreds of lives might be saved. But not his own. He was still too close.

Ghani had seen the danger from the determined Kijang driver. He tried to swerve. Nyoman had been waiting for the attempt and locked his wheel in an effort to spin the Kijang into the path of the speeding vehicle bomb.

Once again, Ghani wrenched the wheel to avoid the unexpected obstacle to his plan. He was screaming in frustration. Howling soundless rage at his opponent. He was too late. He rammed into the tail end of the Kijang. The van spun off sideways, running

375

on two wheels, the other two spinning in the air. The Kijang turned a neat three hundred and sixty degrees and came to a stop with a crash against the barriers.

Ghani desperately tried to control his two-wheeled van. He hit a kerb and the impact collapsed the van back on four wheels. Ghani felt the tyres burst but he didn't care. He was triumphant. The enemy in the Kijang was beaten.

And then he saw the shop wall in front of him. He spun the wheel frantically. He slammed on the brakes to the sound of screeching tyres and the smell of burning rubber. It was too late. The van hit the wall hard. Ghani flew head first through the windscreen. His head exploded against the concrete.

Singh hit the deck. The minute the vehicle bomb hit the Kijang, he lay face down in the dirt, waiting for the inevitable explosion. He knew he was too close to escape, but that didn't mean he had to stand up and greet death like a friend. If she wanted him she could drag him from the road while he hung on for dear, dear life. He didn't see, but he heard the screeching tyres and the crunching metal as the van hit the wall. Still, he didn't move. Seconds passed. There was no explosion. He raised his head. The throngs fleeing Yusuf's bomb had stopped running. Singh stood up. The van was resting against a wall, the front end folded like an accordion. Unbelievably, the impact had not detonated the bomb. The primary explosive used in the detonator was stable. Impact had not been sufficient to start a chain reaction. Trying to escape Nyoman in the Kijang, Ghani had not manually detonated the bomb. There was still enormous danger, most immediately if the smoking van caught fire.

Singh turned and ran towards the crowd. 'Bomb!' he shouted. 'Bomb in the van!'

He was not sure whether they heard him or had merely drawn inspiration from his flight. The panic-stricken people turned as one and set off back in the direction they had come. Singh chased after them, a short comic figure, panting and puffing as he ran – determined to get himself and these people out of range of the white van filled with explosives.

Behind him he could hear sirens. Reinforcements had arrived.

Epilogue

Bronwyn Taylor was dead. By jumping into the crater and covering the bomb with her body, she had protected everyone from the force of the explosion. No one else had been killed by Yusuf's knapsack bomb, not even Yusuf. When Inspector Singh heard what had happened – Chief Atkinson had come in person to tell him – he closed his eyes for a long moment. He could almost wish that he had agreed with Atkinson all those weeks ago when he had suggested that Richard Crouch's murder was best ignored. He knew Bronwyn, who had disagreed then, would have disagreed still. He did not doubt that, even if forewarned of her fate, she would have chosen to save other lives rather than her own.

Singh looked up at Atkinson and said, his gruff tone an unconvincing effort to hide his sorrow, 'Typical of her! Why didn't she shove the little runt into the crater instead of trying to be a hero?'

Nyoman had survived with minor injuries. His seatbelt had kept him in place as the Kijang had spun against the barriers. Singh realised it was the first time Nyoman had ever bothered with his seatbelt. He must have decided, in light of what he intended to do, that it was a prudent step. It had saved his life. He was being feted all over Indonesia as the brave citizen who had saved the people at the purification ritual from certain death. It gave the press something to write about other than the failure of the ceremony itself to drive the demons from Bali's shores. He did not, however, begrudge Nyoman his moment in the limelight. Nyoman had saved many lives – including his own.

Ramzi was picked up trying to get on a ferry to Java. His rainbow chin was a feature not even the Balinese police could miss. Like Amrozi before him, Ramzi was delighted to talk. He boasted of his role in detonating the backpack bomb using his mobile phone. The solitary regret he expressed was that he had only killed one Australian policewoman.

Singh was most interested in his confession to killing Crouch. Ramzi was proud of his defence of the family honour. He was particularly smug at his cleverness in hiding the body in the vehicle bomb that had left the crater in front of the Sari Club.

Ramzi asked Singh with genuine curiosity, 'How did you know he was murdered?'

'A piece of his skull this big' – Singh indicated the palm of his hand – 'with a bullet hole in it.'

Ramzi laughed out loud and slapped the

table in his amusement. 'You police are really clever, aren't you?'

Singh did not respond. He walked out of the interview room, leaving Ramzi to the AFP and the Bali police. He hoped that the prosecution would seek the death penalty for the bastard – and for the others as well. He spared a brief thought for Nuri. He wondered whether she would be charged as an accessory or released. He had put in a good word for her – explained that if she had not told what she knew, they would not have been able to prevent the attack. Singh found himself hoping that life would give Nuri a second chance at happiness.

Singh was due back in Singapore in twenty-four hours. His job in Bali was done. He had solved a murder and uncovered a terrorist plot – more by luck than judgement. Much was being made of the sterling contribution to the anti-terrorism efforts of ASEAN nations, especially Singapore, whose personnel had been so critical in thwarting the second attack. His superiors would be pleased. They might leave him alone for a few months.

There was one more thing he had to do.

He caught a taxi and instructed the driver to take him to the harbour in Legian. He got out and waved to a middle-aged, balding man with two teenage boys standing on either side of him. It was Bronwyn's ex-husband with her two sons, two grief-stricken young men trying to come to terms with their mother being a hero – and dead. The man held an urn. At Singh's urging, the ex-husband had agreed that she be cremated as soon as the DNA identification was complete. Singh did not think her sons needed to know quite how little of Bronwyn had remained after taking the full force of the explosion. Dr Barton had rushed the results. It was the least he could do, he said, very aware that he had set in motion the chain of events that had led to the death of the Australian policewoman.

The four of them did not speak much.

It was time to scatter the ashes at sea and the family had asked Singh to come along – they thought Bronwyn would have liked that. Singh was not sure about this but he agreed at once. He knew Bronwyn would have wanted him to do whatever her family asked of him. They climbed into a fishing boat. The fisherman powered the small vessel out of the harbour until they reached the choppy, open seas. The sun was setting. Singh could see the Tanah Lot temple, one of the most holy sites in Bali, glowing in the evening light. A sea eagle hovered high, screeching in the wind. The two boys raised the urn awkwardly between them and leaned over the side of the boat. Singh and their father watched silently as they tipped the ashes into the water. Immediately, the fine grey ash was caught by eddies and currents and spread out across the water's surface. The younger boy had tears running down his cheeks but his grief was silent. The older son stoically watched the ashes disappear from sight as the sun disappeared over the horizon. He said, 'Mum would have liked that.'

Singh could almost picture Bronwyn Taylor's dimpled smile.

He nodded his agreement – she would most certainly have liked that.

The publishers hope that this book has given you enjoyable reading. Large Print Books are especially designed to be as easy to see and hold as possible. If you wish a complete list of our books please ask at your local library or write directly to:

Magna Large Print Books
Magna House, Long Preston,
Skipton, North Yorkshire.
BD23 4ND

This Large Print Book, for people
who cannot read normal print,
is published under the auspices of

THE ULVERSCROFT FOUNDATION

... we hope you have enjoyed this book.
Please think for a moment about those
who have worse eyesight than you ...
and are unable to even read or enjoy
Large Print without great difficulty.

You can help them by sending a
donation, large or small, to:

**The Ulverscroft Foundation,
1, The Green, Bradgate Road,
Anstey, Leicestershire, LE7 7FU,
England.**
or request a copy of our brochure for
more details.

The Foundation will use all donations
to assist those people who are visually
impaired and need special attention
with medical research, diagnosis
and treatment.

Thank you very much for your help.